THE FALLEN

3

END OF DAYS

THOMAS E. SNIEGOSKI

Simon Pulse

NEW YORK   LONDON   TORONTO   SYDNEY

This book is a work of fiction. Any references to historical events,
real people, or real locales are used fictitiously. Other names, characters, places,
and incidents are the product of the author's imagination, and any resemblance
to actual events or locales or persons, living or dead, is entirely coincidental.

SIMON PULSE

An imprint of Simon & Schuster Children's Publishing Division

1230 Avenue of the Americas, New York, NY 10020

First Simon Pulse paperback edition September 2011

Copyright © 2011 by Thomas E. Sniegoski

All rights reserved, including the right of reproduction in whole or in part in any form.

SIMON PULSE and colophon are registered trademarks of Simon & Schuster, Inc.

For information about special discounts for bulk purchases, please contact
Simon & Schuster Special Sales at 1-866-506-1949 or business@simonandschuster.com.

The Simon & Schuster Speakers Bureau can bring authors to your live event. For more
information or to book an event contact the Simon & Schuster Speakers Bureau at
1-866-248-3049 or visit our website at www.simonspeakers.com.

Designed by Mike Rosamilia

The text of this book was set in Adobe Garamond.

Manufactured in the United States of America

4 6 8 10 9 7 5

Library of Congress Cataloging-in-Publication Data

Sniegoski, Tom.

End of days / Thomas E. Sniegoski.

p. cm. — (The fallen ; 3)

Summary: Half angel and half human, Aaron commands the Fallen in their quest
to protect humanity, drawing confidence from the girl he loves as he struggles
to make peace with his legacy as Lucifer's son.

ISBN 978-1-4424-2349-7 (pbk)

[1. Angels—Fiction. 2. Good and evil—Fiction. 3. Love—Fiction.

4. Supernatural—Fiction.] I. Title.

PZ7.S68033En 2011

[Fic]—dc23

2011016979

ISBN 978-1-4424-2350-3 (eBook)

For John and Chandra Febonio — Congratulations.
September 10, 2011

Thanks to my wife, LeeAnne, for without her love and hard work, this book would never have been completed. And thanks to Kirby for reminding me that it has been a very long time since there's been a puppy in this house.

Thanks are also due to Christopher Golden, Annette Pollert, Liesa Abrams, James Mignogna, Dave Kraus, Mom and Dad Sniegoski, Mom and Dad Fogg, Pete Donaldson, Pam Daley, Timothy Cole, and the Evolution Revolution down at Cole's Comics in Lynn.

And a very extra-special set of thanks to Erek Vaehne and Bella Pilyavskaya for helping me get this one just right.

PROLOGUE

SIX MONTHS AGO

Leonard Michaels had secretly hoped it would never come to this.

He stood, perfectly still, in the kitchen of the Florida house where he had lived for the last twenty or so years. Though his kind did not sleep, per se, he had been roused from a meditative state by the most disturbing of sensations.

His leader was dead.

Verchiel was no more.

He understood what this meant. After all this waiting, it was time for him to act.

Opening the refrigerator, Leonard removed a pitcher of water and poured himself a glass. His hand trembled as he brought the drink to his desert-dry mouth, and gulped the contents down.

Verchiel's death forced him to remember what he truly

was, what he hadn't been for so very, very long. It had been so easy to lose himself in the masquerade of pretending to be what he wasn't.

Pretending to be human.

He wasn't really Leonard Michaels, retired housepainter, but something far more wondrous . . . far more dangerous.

He was Geburah, an angel of the heavenly host Powers, and Verchiel had been their master and commander. It was he who defined their purpose upon the earth. As angels of the Powers, they had one simple objective: keep the world of man clean of evil. If it would offend He who was the Creator of all—the Lord God Almighty—then they were to destroy it.

And the Powers performed this chore with the utmost efficiency, until an evil threatened not only earth but the Shining City of Heaven itself.

He poured himself another glass of water, recalling the monstrous threat.

Nephilim.

The evil had been spawned by those who had fallen during the Great War between the armies of Lucifer Morningstar and the legions of Heaven. Those who had fled the Great War escaped to the world of man, and had mingled with the females of the species, creating children—*monsters*—the likes of which the Almighty could never have possibly loved.

Nephilim.

They grew to be Verchiel's obsession, and thusly the Powers'.

The Nephilim were a terrible plague upon the world, but the Powers met the challenge with venomous fervor, and the half-breed monsters were hunted down and exterminated one by one.

But their numbers were many.

The recollection of their screams and cries for mercy echoed through Geburah's thoughts. He recalled the savagery of the Powers' acts in the name of Heaven. There had been no other way. Their purpose had been to cleanse the world of evil, and the Nephilim had been the foulest of them all.

"Leonard?" asked a woman's voice from the darkness.

For a moment Geburah had forgotten his humanity.

His wife stood in the doorway.

"Are you all right?" the old woman asked him, her eyes squinting in the harsh kitchen light.

"I'm fine," he said, lying to the woman who had been his companion for a very long time.

He wasn't all right. . . . Nothing would be right again.

Now that Verchiel was dead.

"Bad dreams?" his wife asked, coming to put her arms around him. Before the death of his leader, he would have met this sign of affection with great warmth, reveling in the love it exhibited, but now . . .

"Yes, Lillian," he said with little emotion, placing his empty glass on the granite countertop. "Bad dreams." He kissed her lightly, sending her back to bed and telling her he would join her soon.

That, too, was a lie. For with Verchiel gone, it was time for his mission to begin.

The Nephilim were a cunning foe, some able to survive the Powers' attempts at extermination. There had even been rumors of an angelic prophecy that a Nephilim had been chosen by the Creator Himself as some sort of savior to bring forgiveness to those that had fallen during the war with the Morningstar, and allow them to return to Heaven.

The idea was blasphemous to them—some sort of Nephilim trick—and it made the Powers hate the accursed half-breeds all the more.

Verchiel had known that his, and his followers', most holy mission would be fraught with peril and the potential for defeat, and he could not bear the thought of failure. If he and his Powers were to somehow meet with death, their purpose thwarted, there would be another way to achieve victory.

Geburah was a part of that alternative plan, along with five others who'd been carefully selected by Verchiel himself.

That meeting came flooding back to him, what he and the others had agreed upon if Verchiel and the remaining Powers were to meet their end.

And it filled him with fear.

Geburah considered running, going into his room, pulling his wife from their bed, and disappearing into the night, hiding from what he was to do now that Verchiel had failed.

But the thought was fleeting, dissipating like smoke in the wind as he whipped his head around, realizing that he was no longer alone in the kitchen.

The tall figure stood by the door, having silently come in from the night outside. It took him a moment, but Geburah recognized him as one of his own.

The angel had come for him.

"Hello, Suria," Geburah greeted him. "Can I get you anything . . . a drink of water perhaps?"

Suria stared at him strangely, with a slight tilt of his head.

"I require nothing," the angel said flatly.

Geburah nodded, turning his gaze toward the hallway, imagining his wife asleep in their bedroom upstairs.

He wanted so much to be back there, to feel her warmth as he held her in his arms, *to feel her humanity.*

"Verchiel is dead," Suria stated.

Geburah looked away from the kitchen entrance, the pull of the bedroom already beginning to fade as the mask that he wore started to slip as duty called.

"Yes," he said. "I felt it as well."

Suria stared at him, eyes black and cold.

"We now have a mission to perform," the angel spoke.

Geburah was well aware of what he needed to do but found himself fighting it, struggling with the identity he'd kept hidden away these years past.

"Can I be honest with you, Suria?" Geburah said with a

nervous smile. "I'd hoped—prayed, actually—that I'd never be called to duty—that I could continue to live like this."

He looked around the kitchen, the memories of the years with Lillian cascading through his thoughts.

"Like a human?" Suria asked, his response tinged with disgust.

Angels believed themselves so superior, so above humanity. Geburah had no idea where Suria . . . where the others of their kind had been, as they waited . . . how they passed the time. Was he the only one of them to live amongst humanity? To pretend to be human?

"Like a human," Geburah repeated with a sigh, knowing there was little choice for him. He had a duty to perform.

He owed it to Verchiel . . . to this world . . . and to Heaven itself.

"Foolish, isn't it?" Geburah asked.

Suria continued to stare at Geburah, but his gaze had become harder . . . cautious. Geburah knew that if Suria believed their mission was about to be somehow compromised—that he wasn't about to take control of their mission—Suria wouldn't hesitate to strike him down, and assume command.

Again there was the foolish thought of escape, but then he saw, with more acuity than mere human eyes, movement outside the open kitchen window. Through the curtains fluttering in the warm, nighttime breeze, he saw that the others of his band had arrived and were waiting outside.

Waiting for the one who would now lead them.

"Are you . . . well, Geburah?" Suria prodded.

"I'm fine," Geburah answered with a sigh, then released his angelic nature.

The truth of what he was . . . what he had always been . . . charged forward like a wild beast, and Geburah gasped as the divine power of Heaven flooded through him after so very long.

Leonard Michaels no longer stood in the kitchen of the Florida home. Leonard Michaels no longer existed. In fact, he had never truly existed at all.

In his place stood an angel—a soldier—the new leader of the heavenly host Powers.

Geburah spread his wings, reveling in the sensation. Sparks of divine fire leaped from the tips of his feathers, igniting the structure around him, but he did not care, for that part of him existed no longer. Burned away to reveal the true nature that had lain dormant within.

"Leonard?" a scared voice cried out over the shriek of fire alarms from someplace nearby. "Leonard, what's going on?"

Geburah looked toward the doorway, the entrance to the kitchen now engulfed with orange fire, a pang of something vaguely familiar pulling at him, gnawing at him from inside, but it soon passed.

He turned his attention back to Suria.

"It's nothing," Geburah said as the fire hungrily spread. He calmly walked through the burning kitchen to the back door, and to the angelic soldiers that waited for him outside.

"Nothing at all."

The last vestiges of the humanity that he had built burned at his back.

TWO MONTHS AGO

If only they could see what I've seen with these old, dead eyes, Tobias Foster mused in response to a child's curious question to her mother as to what was wrong with the old man on the corner's eyes as they passed him on the busy Baltimore street.

He was going to answer the little girl, tell her that there was nothing wrong with the two milky orbs resting inside his skull, that he just saw things a little bit differently than most folks. Where mostly everybody saw the here and now, he saw glimpses of the future, and he'd just *seen* something that both distracted and disturbed him.

The brass horn in his grasp grew warm, reading Tobias's change in mood. The instrument started to pulse, as if it were alive.

"That's all right," he whispered softly as he held the horn closer, feeling its heat through his clothes.

"Hey, old man, play us something."

Tobias turned his head to fix his blind eyes upon the person standing on the street before him.

"What would you like to hear?" he asked, knowing that a song was probably the best thing for the horn at the moment.

"I don't know," the man said, the smell of alcohol wafting off his breath. "Play something nice."

The horn needed a soothing song now. Something to calm it down.

Tobias brought the horn up, nearly scorching his lips on the mouthpiece, and began to blow. The horn fought at first, resisting his attempt to coax music from it, but it soon relented and the sweet sounds of something bluesy that he'd thought up on the fly drifted from the horn.

That's it, the old man thought as he played, feeling the metal grow colder in his grasp. Even after all these years with the instrument, he still forgot how reactive it was.

The horn's previous holder had told him as much all those years ago when giving him the instrument; you'd think Tobias would've known not to let his emotions get the better of him, but what he had just seen . . . it was enough to ruin any man's day.

He heard the sound of change clinking against the other donations that had been tossed onto the bandanna he'd set out in front of him.

"Thank you kindly," he said as he took the horn from his lips, sensing the drunken man who wanted to hear something nice heading on his way satisfied.

The horn was copasetic again, forcing him to think about the vision he had seen moments ago without the emotional reaction.

Since he took the horn into his possession, Tobias's ability to see had been taken away, but it was replaced with something he believed to be of greater value. Tobias had been given the gift of precognition, particularly as it pertained to him, and the safety of the horn.

The safety of the world, really.

And what he had just glimpsed from behind his cataract-covered eyes would soon endanger all those things.

The old man sighed as he bent down, feeling around to retrieve the change and the few bills that passersby had given to him as he played.

It isn't bad enough that the Powers nearly released Hell on earth in their attempt to wipe out the Nephilim, he thought as he shoved the money and handkerchief deep inside his pants pocket. *Now they're at it again. And are hell-bent on dragging me into their latest folly.*

That's what he had seen in a disturbing flash: angels of the Powers host hunting for him. They were in the city, following the instrument's scent. Tobias had always been a wanderer, even before assuming responsibility for the instrument. Since taking on the horn, he'd just had a lot more time to do it.

The instrument had prolonged his life.

He really didn't remember how long he'd been on this planet. When anyone asked how old he was, he simply replied, "Very." He had seen a lot during his wandering: kings had fallen, wars had been fought, and slaves had been given their freedom. He was sure he'd witnessed many other important events, but, at the moment, he couldn't recall them.

Tobias had other, far more disturbing things on his mind.

The Powers were coming for him . . . for the horn, and he was afraid he wasn't strong enough to fight them.

Why can't they just leave it be? the old man thought as he shuffled past the busy National Aquarium, a chilling wind blowing off the harbor, foreshadowing cold times to come.

That was the problem with angels, they were so damn stubborn, always thinking they were right. Just because they were one of the first creatures created by God, they thought their opinions had greater value than everybody else's.

As much as he hated to admit it, Tobias knew it was time his wandering ended, but first he had to find someone very special.

Someone who didn't mind not dying for a very long time, and who was strong enough to take on the responsibility of the horn, and all that came with it.

CHAPTER ONE

The cold milk made Aaron's teeth ache as he spooned cereal into his mouth, careful not to dribble anything onto the front of his shirt.

He glanced across the kitchen table at his little brother, Stevie. The boy, who was supposed to be eating frozen waffles, was rolling a Thomas the Tank Engine train back and forth in front of his untouched plate.

Aaron was about to tell the boy to eat when his mother entered the kitchen, a smile on her face that reminded Aaron how lucky he was to have her as his mom.

Lori Stanley was actually Aaron's foster mother, but her smile, and the way he felt about her, made that fact inconsequential. As far as he was concerned, Lori Stanley was as close to a real mother as he would ever know.

"How's it going here?" she asked cheerfully.

Stevie didn't respond, engrossed in the repetitive movement of his train.

"We're good," Aaron said through a mouthful of sugary cereal. He needed to finish up or he'd be late for school.

A few more quick bites and he was done. He grabbed his bowl and stood to take it to the sink.

"It was nice, wasn't it?" Lori asked as he crossed the kitchen. She stood beside Stevie's chair. The boy didn't notice, but that was just how Stevie was, lost in his world of autism.

"What was?" Aaron asked, absently placing his bowl in the sink and turning back toward his mother. He wondered if he'd need his jacket. The calendar said it was spring, but it was still cold.

"This," Lori said, her eyes becoming sad as she gestured around the kitchen.

"Yeah, I guess," Aaron answered carefully. "Are you all right?"

His mother shook her head, slowly at first, but gradually with more passion. "No," she said, her voice cracking. "No, I am not all right."

And suddenly Aaron knew exactly what was wrong.

His mother was dead. So was Stevie.

This life was dead.

Lori looked at him, her eyes awash with tears. "Do you miss it?" she asked, stroking the little boy's hair as he continued to play with his train.

Aaron found himself crying as well. "Yes," he whispered,

wanting to go to her, to have her take him into her arms and tell him that everything was going to be fine. But something stopped him . . . something denied him that comfort.

"It got bad so fast," Lori said. Wisps of smoke began to waft from her body.

"Lori!" Aaron cried as the smoke became darker, thicker, and tongues of flame appeared atop her head like a fiery crown.

"Mom!"

He tried to move but couldn't, some unknown force preventing him from going to her aid. Fire completely engulfed her now, and smoke obscured the kitchen, but Aaron couldn't look away.

"So fast," the blackened skeleton said once more. Sizzling fat ran from its empty eye sockets in a mockery of tears. Her burning fingers still patted Stevie's hair.

"It's going to get worse," the little boy said unexpectedly, lifting his attention from the train to fix it upon Aaron, his gaze suddenly very much aware. "A lot worse."

Then Stevie started to play with his train again.

As he, too, began to burn.

Aaron Corbet awoke with a start, and stifled a scream before it could fully escape his lips.

He blinked repeatedly, his eyes somehow watering from the smoke of the blaze that had consumed his mother and brother.

"Aaron?" asked a voice in the semidarkness of the bedroom.

He turned his head slightly on the pillow, expecting to see his girlfriend, Vilma, but instead he looked into the worried eyes of his dog, Gabriel, who lay on the mattress beside him.

"Bad dream again?" the yellow Labrador asked in the gravelly dog voice that Aaron had no difficulty understanding.

"Yeah," Aaron said, reaching over to rub the dog's golden-brown ears. "But I'm all right now," he lied.

He was about to ask the dog where Vilma was, but as the murkiness of sleep began to recede, he remembered that she had gone back to Lynn, Massachusetts, to visit her aunt and uncle.

Aaron wished that she were here with him now; he could have used her arms around him, the warmth of her body pressed against his. Her very presence was enough to chase away any nightmare's lingering effects.

While he loved Gabriel, a Labrador retriever was no replacement for a hot girlfriend.

"Getting up now?" Gabriel asked, sitting up, his thick muscular tail thumping against the bed. *"Breakfast?"*

"Not yet." Aaron reached up and gave the dog's blocky head a final pat, then turned over on his side, pulling the blanket around his ears. "It's still early. Let's see if we can grab a few more hours of shut-eye."

Gabriel sighed with disappointment but didn't argue, settling down almost immediately. Aaron listened to the dog's breathing grow slow and heavy as Gabriel drifted off once more.

But sleep eluded him.

He tried to clear his mind, to focus on his dog's steady snore, but all he could see when he closed his eyes was the vision of his mother and brother in flames, their ominous warning echoing in his ears.

"It got bad so fast."

"It's going to get worse."

"A lot worse."

Vilma Santiago opened her eyes to the early morning, thinking that things were the way they used to be, that nothing had changed at all.

That the past few months had been only a bad dream.

But, really, it was her old life that seemed like a dream.

She lay on an air mattress on the floor of her cousin's bedroom and gazed up at the ceiling, at the cracks in the plaster that had always been the first things she saw when she awakened, when this used to be her room. She remembered all the times she'd lain there, early in the morning, before the rest of the house began to stir, wondering what the day would have in store for her.

School, homework, chores, making sure her younger

cousins weren't getting into any trouble. She'd never really thought about that life as she'd lived it, believing it all so predictable, so boring and inconsequential.

If only it could be that way again.

Vilma quietly rose from her bed, careful not to wake the little raven-haired girl who slept soundly in the bed next to her, wrapped in the Disney Princess bedding she'd received the day before for her seventh birthday. She picked up her clothes and shoes, and tiptoed to the bedroom door. Vilma hated to leave yet again without saying good-bye to the little girl, but the last thing she wanted, or needed, was a scene.

Her abrupt departure from the household six months ago had created enough problems, although Vilma didn't see what choice she'd had. Her life had changed so dramatically since she'd become involved with Aaron. Since she'd learned what she really was.

Vilma stepped out into the hallway, quietly pulling the door closed behind her. She stood for a moment, breathing in the comforting aroma of freshly brewed coffee, then bent down to place her sneakers on the floor and pull on her jeans.

"Would you like a cup of coffee?" asked a voice from behind her.

Vilma zipped her pants and turned to find her aunt Edna standing at the end of the hallway, in the doorway to the kitchen, her bathrobe wrapped tightly around her.

"Yes, please," Vilma said, keeping her voice low. She

grabbed her sneakers and followed her aunt into the kitchen, into the full smell of the morning brew.

"How did you sleep?" Edna asked as she poured coffee from the full carafe into a mug.

"Fine," Vilma answered. Between the birthday party and the stress of being back home, she had been so tired that she probably could have slept soundly almost anywhere.

Vilma pulled out a chair and sat at the kitchen table as Edna set the steaming mug down in front of her.

"Thank you," Vilma said, pulling the coffee closer, feeling its soothing warmth in the palms of her hands.

Edna retrieved a carton of cream from the refrigerator and grabbed a square metal canister filled with sugar packets from the counter. She placed both on the table, pushing them toward Vilma, then turned back to the stove to fill another mug with coffee. Silently, she sat down across from her niece, blowing on the scalding liquid before taking a short, careful sip.

Vilma added two sugar packets and a generous amount of cream to her cup, then took her first drink as well, closing her eyes and reveling at the strong brew. Coffee always tasted better in this house. It was as if the environment added a special ingredient that couldn't be found anywhere else.

Maybe it was love. There had never been a day that Vilma had not felt wanted or cared for here. After her mother's death, her aunt and uncle had brought her home with them from Brazil and had treated her as one of their own.

"Can I make you something? Some eggs or toast?" Edna asked, interrupting Vilma's thoughts.

"No, this is good." Vilma smiled, cupping the hot mug.

"It's not a bother," her aunt reassured her.

"I know, but I'm fine with just the coffee. Thanks." She smiled again as she lifted the mug to her lips for another sip.

They continued to sit in silence, each wrapped in her own thoughts. Vilma knew the questions were coming, and she dreaded them. They'd been kept at bay yesterday with the excitement of Nicole's party, but there was nothing to hold them back now—the questions about where she had gone and what she was doing with her life. If only there were easy answers. If only Vilma could tell her aunt the truth. But Edna would never understand—couldn't understand.

Vilma's life had changed dramatically. Her understanding of the world and how it worked had been totally flipped upside down and sideways.

Normal didn't exist anymore, at least not for Vilma.

"Are you leaving today?" Edna asked in a seemingly casual tone.

Here it comes.

"Yeah. I have to get back."

"To him?" The disapproval was obvious in her aunt's voice. "To that Aaron boy?"

Vilma set her mug on the table. "Please," she begged, "why can't we just enjoy each other's company without—"

"You leave us in the middle of the night, I don't hear from you for weeks. How should I act, Vilma?"

Vilma could understand how it must seem to the woman, but the truth was so much worse. How was she to tell the woman who had been like a mother to her that she wasn't even human, that she was the offspring of an angel and a mortal woman? And how could Vilma tell her aunt that there were forces out there . . . angels . . . Powers . . . that wished to see Vilma and other Nephilim like her dead?

The answer was simple: she didn't. It was better, safer, to keep her family in the dark.

"I know how this must seem, but you have to trust me," Vilma told her, looking away into her coffee mug, not wanting to see the disappointment in her aunt's eyes.

"Your uncle thinks that I should force you to tell me what you are doing," Edna said, gripping her coffee mug so tightly that her knuckles had gone white. "Tell us where you are living, and with whom." She released the mug, bringing it halfway to her lips before stopping. "He believes you owe us that at least. We're your family, Vilma. We should know these things."

Vilma knew this conversation was going nowhere good.

"I'm sorry," she said, bending down to pull on her sneakers. "I'm sorry that I'm disappointing you, but you really need to trust me on this."

"How can you expect us to trust you when we know

nothing about your life now?" Edna retorted. "You're practically a child. And that boy didn't even finish high school! What do you know about the world—*really* know about the world?"

If only you *really knew about the world,* Vilma thought. Really *knew about the world.* She stood and leaned in to give her aunt a quick kiss on the cheek.

"It's better that you don't know," she said quietly.

"If you're in trouble—," her aunt began, eager to help in any way she could.

"I'm not in trouble, but I really need to be going," Vilma interrupted. She retrieved her fleece jacket from the back of the cellar door, where she'd hung it the day before, and slipped it on.

"When will you be back? Will you at least call to let us know if—"

"I'll be in touch," Vilma said quickly, anxious to leave before things truly got out of hand. She loved her aunt but knew that tears would be coming soon.

She opened the back door, wondering if there would ever come a day when she could share the reality of her new life with her aunt and uncle. She desperately wanted to tell them everything, but it was too dangerous.

Aaron had lost his own foster family to the forces surrounding the revelation of what he was; Vilma was not going to risk the lives of her family.

"Vilma," her aunt called out.

She turned to look at the woman standing there in her bathrobe, eyes damp with tears.

"We love you very much; if there's anything we can do to . . ."

There was nothing Vilma wanted more at that moment than to bare her soul to her aunt. "I love you too, Aunt Edna. Tell Uncle Frank that I love him, Nicole and Michael, too," she said instead, then stepped out the door, closing it firmly behind her before she, too, started to cry.

It was early, and Belvidere Place was eerily quiet, most of the inhabitants of the short dead-end street still fast asleep.

Vilma walked to the far corner of the backyard, where prying eyes, if there were any, would not be able to see what she was about to do.

She glanced back toward the house to be sure her aunt wasn't watching from a kitchen window, then closed her eyes and took a deep breath, allowing the power that resided inside her—a power that she had suppressed while with her family— to flow up, and out of her body.

A pair of large feathered wings grew from the flesh of her back, passing like smoke through her clothing without causing so much as a tear. Flexing the powerful muscles in her shoulder blades, she fanned the air, stirring a small cloud of dust and dirt. It felt good to stretch after her wings had been furled for so long—a thought that would have been totally alien to her six months ago.

It was time to return to the place that had become her home since she'd accepted what she was and the purpose she served on the planet.

Vilma thought of the abandoned school in the western part of the state, seeing all its details in her mind's eye as if she were looking at it through a window.

That was where Aaron would be waiting for her.

That was where she wanted to be.

And with that thought, she folded her wings about herself, their feathered embrace holding her tightly.

And from where she once stood, she was gone.

As if she'd never been there at all.

CHAPTER TWO

TWO MONTHS AGO

With a rush of air and a fluttering of wings, the last of the Powers appeared on the quiet street, the only witness to their arrival a stray cat on the hunt for something to eat.

The cat stopped suddenly, eyeing the six figures standing in a group in the center of Main Street. They were dressed in dark suits and wore long coats that fluttered in the early morning breeze. She flattened herself against the ground with a low, whining growl, the need to hunt suddenly replaced by the need for caution. There was danger before her, emanating from these strangers in waves. They, too, were on the hunt, she sensed, and she did not care to be their prey.

In a flash the cat darted down the alley between the post office and a greasy-spoon diner, and was gone.

Geburah followed the sudden movement, his preternatural

senses on alert. The cat was not what he sought, so its presence was forgotten nearly as quickly as it had registered.

The Powers' leader signaled to one of the other five with a barely perceptible nod. Anfial, the tracker of their angelic pack, stepped forward to sniff the air, his dark eyes closing as he processed the billions of particulates that filled the filthy air. God's favored world was sick, dying from a cancer that only Geburah and his surviving brethren had the courage to face. Soon it would be released from its misery.

But first, the hunt.

"There," Anfial said, nostrils flaring as he turned toward the diner.

Their prey, and the means for accomplishing their holy objective was inside.

Tobias sat on a stool inside Ronny's Diner and Grub, his blind eyes turned toward the door. Waiting.

Seeing the impending future.

"How's that coffee, old-timer?" Ronny asked from behind the counter.

Tobias barely heard the question. He'd come to the small rural town in West Virginia in an effort to evade his pursuers. It was just the latest in a series of stops he'd made since leaving Baltimore, and the traveling was beginning to get to him. He was slowing down when he should have kept moving. Stopping at this all-night diner in the predawn hours had been a big mistake, but he had been tired and hungry.

He should have been smarter.

"The coffee's fine, Ron, thanks," Tobias said without moving. "But I'm afraid I've caused you a bit of trouble."

Ronny laughed. "What are you talking about? It's no trouble at all. Listen, I've got some leftover apple pie if—"

"Forget the pie," Tobias interrupted rather sharply. "You need to get out of here, through the back door, as fast as you can before—"

The bell over the door jangled merrily, announcing new customers.

"Morning," Ronny said cheerfully to the six men who strolled in. "Sit anywhere you like. I'll get you menus and some coffee in a sec."

Tobias reached across the counter and grabbed Ronny's arm in a steely grip. "Get out," he rasped. "They're gonna kill you and think nothin' of it."

Startled, Ronny pulled his arm away. "I don't know what you're talking about, old man, but maybe it's time you hit the road."

The six men approached the counter and formed a semicircle around the old black man.

"We've been looking for you, human," Geburah said, ignoring the man behind the counter.

Tobias could sense Ronny's confusion. He wished the owner of the diner had listened to his warning.

"You fellas know each other?" Ronny asked.

"Let's just say that we're aware of each other's activities," Tobias said. The angels' presence was making his skin tingle as though a mild electrical current was passing through his body.

"It has always fascinated us that the Archangel Gabriel would bestow such a sacred task upon lowly humans."

Tobias felt for his cup, brought it up to his mouth, and drained the last of his coffee noisily.

"Probably 'cause he realized the likes of you couldn't be trusted," he replied. "Probably 'cause he knew that at the first sign of trouble, you'd be blowing the horn to bring the curtain down. Let's be honest, your kind never really did care much for humanity."

The leader of the remaining six Powers stepped closer, bending down to speak directly into the blind man's ear.

"You're right," he whispered. His breath smelled of spice and decay. "We've always believed that the Lord of Lords could have done better . . . actually *did* do better."

Tobias laughed. "What?" he asked incredulously. "You think the angelic hosts are the best He could do?" He laughed some more, shaking his head. "Most of humanity ain't no prize, but I can honestly say we got the likes of you winged sons of bitches beat, hands down."

Tobias swiveled his stool from the counter to face the angels.

"You have some nerve coming after me," he said with

a snarl. "Has who gave me the horn to look out for slipped your divine minds? Let me refresh your memories—Gabriel himself."

Ronny had been silent until then but finally interjected. "All right, I can see where this is going."

Tobias caught the sound of something being pulled from beneath the counter—probably a baseball bat. "You guys take it outside or I'm gonna start swingin', and then I'm gonna call the sheriff."

The owner of Ronny's Diner and Grub moved around the counter, menacing with the bat. Tobias knew there was nothing he could do to help the man now. Ronny had had his chance.

But still Tobias tried.

"He's right. Let's take this outside." The blind man slid from his stool, and suddenly a powerful hand dropped hard upon his shoulder.

"You will give it to me," Geburah snarled.

Tobias heard a scuffling of feet, and Ronny's angry voice.

"Take your hands off him. I warned you."

A rush of air passed across Tobias's face and Ronny's words trailed off in a gurgle. The metallic odor of fresh blood filled the air, and Tobias imagined the damage an angel's wing would do as it slashed across an exposed human throat. The bat clattered to the linoleum floor, followed by the thump of a heavy body.

"You didn't have to do that," Tobias said.

"Think of it as an act of mercy," the leader said. "We have saved him from the pain that will follow the summoning of the Abomination of Desolation, when this sad world is finally brought to its end."

Geburah's hand was still upon Tobias's shoulder, its grip so tight that the bones beneath had started to ache from the pressure.

"The Abomination of . . . ?" Tobias couldn't believe what he was hearing. "You'd think you peacocks would have learned," Tobias said to them with a disgusted shake of his head. "Verchiel already tried something like this."

The angels gasped at the mention of their former leader's name.

"And he failed miserably."

The blow was fast and hard. It lifted the blind man from the stool, tossing him across the restaurant, where he struck a jukebox with such force that he shattered its glass front.

Tobias dropped to the floor, stunned. He'd always wondered what it would feel like to be struck by an angel's wing, and now he knew.

It hurt like hell.

The taste of blood was in his mouth as he pushed himself up on all fours, jagged pieces of glass digging into his hands and knees.

"The Archangel Gabriel gave me and all before me this

task," Tobias grunted, the entirety of his ancient body scream-ing from the punishment it had just received. "He said we would know when it was time to hand it over . . . that an emis-sary from Heaven would come to claim it."

He could hear the Powers moving closer.

"We are the emissaries of which you speak," the leader said. "Give me the instrument and fulfill your purpose."

Tobias felt dizzy, and instead of attempting to stand, he pushed himself back and simply sat upon the glass-covered floor, leaning against the jukebox.

"Nah, I don't think you're the guys he was talking about," he said with a shake of his head. He turned and spat a wad of bloody phlegm onto the floor. "In fact, I've been warned about the likes of you . . . angels that would want to use the instru-ment as a tool for their own purposes . . . angels that felt what the Lord God had accomplished on the earth didn't quite live up to their own standards."

Tobias wiped more blood from his lips with the back of his hand.

"The last fella to hold the horn told me I should have a plan in case I ever ran into angels like you."

"I tire of these games, ape," Geburah snapped, his voice booming like the thunder of a summer storm.

"It always comes down to name-callin', don't it?" Tobias said. "Well, you should know that I listened very carefully to what my predecessor had to say, and I took it to heart."

Tobias reached inside his jacket and carefully removed a horn.

"Is this what you're looking for?" the old man asked, holding the bugle-shaped instrument out to the angels that he knew were close by.

"I promise to be merciful," the leader said, glass crunching beneath his feet as he stepped toward Tobias.

"Here's a little something I call 'End of the Line,'" Tobias said as he placed the horn to his lips.

And began to blow.

Geburah and the others leaped back with horror, mighty wings spread wide to carry them away from destruction as he raised the instrument to his lips.

The horn could be used as a powerful weapon; one blast was enough to shake the restaurant to dust and pulverize even the most divine of flesh. If the full fury of the instrument was to be unleashed upon them, there was little chance that the Powers would survive.

The Powers' leader was about to enwrap himself in his white-and-brown-flecked wings, and flee this place and the devastation that would follow the blowing of the horn, when he heard the most surprising thing.

Instead of notes of sheer destructive force, there came a pathetic and flatulent honk.

Followed by the old man's laughter.

Geburah opened his wings and looked about. The other

five were still behind him, as confused as he but mesmerized by the sight of the old man sitting upon the ground before them, laughing, the instrument clutched to his chest.

Geburah moved closer, eyes locked on the horn in Tobias's hand.

"You've deceived us," the angel said, trying to keep his rising ire in check.

"I most certainly have," the old man said, tears of laughter running down his face.

"That is not the instrument."

"No, it is not the instrument," Tobias agreed. He held up the horn, which had been fabricated by mere human hands. "But it is a beauty. Cost me twenty-five bucks at a pawnshop in Michigan."

"If that is not the true instrument, then where . . ."

Tobias turned his milky white eyes from the horn to the angel; all traces of humor were now gone from his ancient expression.

"Now, do you seriously think I'm gonna tell you that?"

Geburah squatted down before the old man. "We will make you tell us."

Tobias smiled, his teeth yellowed from the passage of many, many years.

"You'll try," he said with a shake of his head.

The Powers' leader rose and looked toward the angel Shebniel, he who had always nurtured a more sadistic streak during his interactions with God's chosen.

No words were needed.

The lanky angel sprang upon the old man like some great predatory beast, using his powerful wings to beat the human, bruising flesh and breaking bone. Again and again the wings came down, until Shebniel's creamy white feathers were flecked with blood.

But the old, blind black man—one of the chosen of the Archangel Gabriel—remained true to his word. He did not tell them what they wanted to know. He did not tell them where he had left the instrument. And he died because of that.

It never ceased to amaze Geburah that anyone could harbor so much affection for this horrid place that he would be willing to die in order to save it. He gazed down upon the mangled body of the old man, the toy horn, crumpled and bent, lying by his hand.

His death was meaningless in the greater scheme of things. Tobias had only delayed the inevitable, not prevented it. It was only a matter of time until the horn made its presence known; an object of such power was not meant to be hidden.

And they would feel it.

And once it was in their possession, the countdown to the End of Days would commence.

CHAPTER THREE

Aaron could not get back to sleep. He was exhausted, but no matter how hard he tried, those last hours of rest eluded him.

Images of his foster mother and brother horribly burning replayed in his mind as their words echoed through his thoughts.

"It's going to get worse."

Beside him, Gabriel snored loudly, deep in the embrace of sleep. And finally Aaron had had enough. Carefully, he peeled back the covers. As quietly as he could, he slid from the mattress and padded to the window, opening it wider.

He chanced a look over his shoulder and was rewarded with the sight of the Labrador still fast asleep. He needed this time alone.

Aaron climbed up on the windowsill and willed his wings

to emerge. The black-feathered appendages emerged from under the skin of his back. It used to hurt, but now he felt nothing but the pleasure and excitement of the experience to follow.

He leaped out into the early dawn stillness, his wings fanning out to their full, glorious span before thrusting him skyward.

The school that the Nephilim had adopted as their new home grew smaller beneath him. For the Saint Athanasius School and Orphanage *was* their home—their Aerie—where they could live lives as normal as was possible for their kind. The previous Aerie had existed in a housing development, abandoned because of illegal toxic-waste disposal. Nephilim and fallen angels who had managed to escape the Powers hid in Aerie, but after Verchiel's death and the return of the fallen to Heaven, the remaining Nephilim had come here to the school.

Aaron pushed himself higher, and higher still, mighty flaps of his wings taking him up into the clouds. This was where he needed to be, to collect his thoughts, to reaffirm his purpose. If there was one thing he could never show the others, it was doubt.

He was their leader: the Chosen One.

Aaron was the offspring of Lucifer, at one time the Creator's most beloved of angels, and being the son of the angel who fell so far from grace made Aaron special. An angelic prophecy said that a child of humanity and the angelic would bring forgiveness to all the angels who had fallen from the grace of God, reuniting them with Heaven.

The Redeemer.

Aaron was that being, and in his hands was the power of redemption.

It had been his purpose to forgive the angels fallen to earth after the Great War in Heaven—which he had done—but now an even heavier task weighed upon his shoulders.

Aaron strained his wings, pushing himself higher into the atmosphere, as if to escape these obligations—these burdens. The clouds were pregnant with moisture, and his flesh tingled with the cool touch of pending rain.

Opening his wings, he slowed his ascent, riding the air currents, looking down upon the world below him. *From here, it looks so small . . . so manageable*, he thought, gliding above it all.

Up here, alone with himself, he was just Aaron Corbet, not the Chosen One, not the Redeemer. Up here, he was not the leader of the Nephilim in their war against the forces of evil that skulked daily from the shadows to plague the world. He was just Aaron Corbet—if only for a little while.

The currents of air whipped at his body, pushing him toward the land below, as if to say, *"You've had your peaceful moment. Now it's time to get back to work."*

Aaron pulled his wings tight against his body and angled earthward. The wind whipped at his hair, drying his cloud-dampened skin in his descent.

He tried not to think too hard about what might be waiting for him below, what new threat was ready to reveal itself. *Maybe there's nothing today,* he thought. *Maybe today will be the day the forces of darkness take a break.*

Aaron smiled at the thought as the winds of his descent beat at his face. That would be nice, but he knew it was a fantasy.

That sort of day didn't exist for him anymore. It had become a thing of the past the day he turned eighteen, and his birthright emerged.

Extending his wings as wide as they would go, Aaron slowed his fall, gliding down toward the open window of the dormitory room he shared with his girlfriend and his dog.

What was that old saying his foster father had often used when he had to work on the weekend? No rest for the wicked?

Images of his foster family and their burning fate appeared before his mind's eye once more, images he could never forget.

The man had been right, the wicked didn't rest, which meant neither could he.

No slacking off for the Chosen One.

Lucifer Morningstar could not help but feel that he was at least partially responsible for breaking the world.

He had been in tune with the planet for so many millennia that he could feel its rhythm was off, like a car with a flat tire barreling down the highway—almost out of control but holding on, trying to keep from going off the road, over a cliff, and into the waiting darkness below.

Lucifer stood outside the rectory of the abandoned school and orphanage in the hills of western Massachusetts, taking in the morning and wondering how much longer they had before it all went wrong.

How much longer he had to make things right.

It was up to him now, him and the Nephilim. It was up to them to save the world, a world left in a very bad way by the machinations of a renegade band of angels.

The Powers had been assigned to protect the earth, to keep God's favored world free of evil, of anything that might offend Him. But instead they had become preoccupied, obsessed with the halfling sons and daughters of fallen angels—the Nephilim.

To say they'd taken their eyes off the ball was an understatement.

Lucifer chuckled softly, recalling how wrong the Powers had been—how misguided.

The Powers, led by the insane Verchiel, had developed tunnel vision, seeing one thing, and one thing only, as the cause of all that was wrong with the world. The Nephilim were blamed for the ills of Heaven and Earth. And the Powers firmly believed that when they were exterminated, everything in the universe would be right again.

So while the Nephilim were hunted and murdered, the true threats to mankind waited in the darkness, untouched, strengthening, awaiting the time when they could emerge from hiding.

And that time appeared to be now.

Despite what Verchiel and the Powers believed, the Nephilim were never the problem. They were, in fact, the solution.

For had it not been for the Nephilim—for one Nephilim in particular—the world would have been consumed by madness long before now.

The Morningstar began to subconsciously rub at his stomach with his free hand. That was where he had been cut . . . opened.

Where Hell had been exposed to the world.

For Hell was not a place. Hell was the writhing, churning horror that Lucifer had caused when he'd turned brother angel against brother angel. It was all the misery, fear, and pain that he had been responsible for when he'd started the Great War in Heaven. Hell was the Almighty's punishment inflicted upon the Morningstar for his unforgivable impertinence. And it lived, trapped inside Lucifer, a constant, gnawing reminder of the danger of his ignorance, desperately needing to be kept under control.

Verchiel, in his insane zeal to see the Nephilim destroyed, had captured Lucifer Morningstar and had opened him up in an attempt to unleash the Hell that was inside him.

Lucifer could not help but think that exposing the world to his inner Hell, even for a brief amount of time, had hastened the emergence of the things of nightmare that had been patiently waiting for their time.

All life on the planet would have been brought to an end if not for a Nephilim whose coming was foretold in an ancient angelic prophecy. The prophecy spoke of one who would bring the Allfather's forgiveness to the fallen angels that had sided with the Morningstar.

Aaron Corbet was the Nephilim of prophecy.

And Lucifer's son.

The Morningstar smiled proudly at the thought. After being responsible for so much ill, it gave him hope to know that he had brought life to someone who was destined to do so much good.

Perhaps someday he would even be forgiven, although he was certain that day was still a long time away.

Lucifer felt something stir in the pocket of his sweatshirt, and looked down to see the tiny pointed snout of a mouse emerge to sniff and twitch at the air.

"Nice day, isn't it?" Lucifer commented to the creature that had been far more than a pet to him this last year or so. He'd named his tiny companion Milton, and although the little rodent seemed to like the name, Lucifer doubted he understood its literary connotations.

"Going?" Milton squeaked.

"Yes, we're going," Lucifer answered, placing his hand in his pocket, allowing the mouse to scramble up his arm and perch upon his shoulder. "I just was enjoying a moment of quiet before the inevitable."

"Death," said Milton.

Lucifer sighed, reaching up to stroke his tiny friend's head. Maybe he understood the significance of his name after all.

"There is always that, isn't there?" the Morningstar said sadly. "Even when we wish there wasn't."

Lorelei felt as though she were dying.

She splashed cold water from the sink on her face, and looked up at her reflection in the old mirror.

Were those dark circles under my eyes last week? When did my hair start to look so dry and brittle? She stared hard at herself, adding these latest concerns to the mental list of aches and pains she'd been experiencing since volunteering to help Aaron and the others with their new lives.

Since beginning to use Archon magick every day.

Lorelei was only twenty, but these days she felt much, much older. It was the effects of the ancient angel magick. Yes, she was Nephilim, but even her angel half wasn't enough to protect her from the corrosive rigors of the magicks developed and wielded by the angelic sorcerers, Archons.

If she were human, she would have died long before.

Aaron and the others had hinted that maybe she should slow down, to take it easy on the Archon spells, but there was just too much to do—too much for them to accomplish—and if they were to succeed, the use of the powerful angel magick was required.

She dried her face on a towel and left the bathroom, padding down the hallway of the abandoned school that had become the sanctuary for their small band of Nephilim.

She'd already been outside for her daily walk around the property to be certain that the magickal wards she had laid were still intact, keeping their presence secret from prying eyes, be they human or inhuman.

The Nephilim had needed somewhere new to rest and regroup after their battle with Verchiel and the Powers. This abandoned school complex in the middle of the Berkshires had offered the perfect place. Its remote location, and the magickal wards she provided, made certain that they were safe from nosy small-town officials as well as supernatural forces.

The magick that hid them was holding, as were they, even as the forces of darkness seemed to be on the rise. The fight was relentless, but they had never expected it to be easy. Every day Lorelei scoured the ether, searching for emerging darkness and sending the Nephilim to eradicate each threat before it could gain a foothold in this world.

And every day, as she used the gifts that her angelic heritage had provided her, she died just a little bit more.

As did something else.

Lorelei crossed the old science lab to the open door of a supply closet. Instead of test tubes and Bunsen burners, the small room now contained a wall of individual cages, each holding a delicate dove.

"I'm sorry, my lovelies," she said sadly to the birds as she entered. "But it's time again for one of you to give your life for the cause."

As if understanding her words, the doves fluttered wildly in their cages. She liked to think they understood the necessity of their sacrifice; it made her feel a little better about what she was going to do.

The one that fluttered the loudest was the one she chose.

"Shhhh," she whispered to calm the bird as she removed it from its cage. "I'll make this as quick and painless as I can."

Gently, she carried the dove to her workstation, holding it tightly to her chest with one hand as she pulled a copper bowl to her with the other. She picked up a finely sharpened scalpel and took a deep breath, steadying herself for the unpleasant task before her.

No matter how many times she did this, Lorelei still hated the fact that something had to die to fuel the power of Archon magick. But it was the only way to find the evil that threatened the world, and she was asking nothing less of the doves than she was willing to give herself.

"Thank you for your sacrifice," she whispered to the bird, as she had to countless others before.

Then, carefully, she turned it over in her hand to expose its downy white chest. Quickly and efficiently, Lorelei extracted its fluttering heart and placed it in the copper bowl.

She had to be fast now, and she added several other ingredients, then lit a match. There was a brief flash as flames consumed the contents of the copper bowl, and a cloud of thick red-hued smoke wafted up from the body of the fire.

Lorelei leaned in, filling her lungs with the red smoke as she recited an incantation that was already old when Adam and Eve first walked the Garden of Eden.

Jeremy Fox sat alone at the far end of the cafeteria, well away from his fellow Nephilim.

They were all laughing and carrying on as if they hadn't a bloody care in the world. As if they were normal.

They were so far from that.

Didn't they realize that they were likely the last of their kind? How many others just like them—kids fathered by horny angels without the common decency to keep it in their robes— had been murdered throughout the years . . . throughout the centuries . . . all because of what they were.

What was it that Aaron said the Powers had called them?

Abominations?

Yeah, that was it. And that was as good a description as any as to how he had felt when he'd turned eighteen. That was when something had come alive inside him, something that raged to be released.

Something dangerous.

Jeremy had thought he'd gone off his nut, sliding down that same slippery slope his own mother had traveled far too many times.

He remembered her stories about the angel that had visited her, and her stories about how special Jeremy would be one day. From time to time she'd be locked away, only to return to him with the declaration that she was cured and everything would be wonderful. And it was, for a time. Until the voices began to whisper to her again.

The memory of the last time he'd seen his mother flashed in Jeremy's mind, and he found himself feeling both sad and incredibly angry. His mother had been tied to the bed with thick leather straps—so she couldn't hurt herself, they'd said. So she wouldn't hurt him, or anyone assigned to care for her.

The doctors had talked a lot about breakthroughs with new medications, but Jeremy just saw her slipping away. Every day he would see less and less of her in her drug-induced haze. The lucid moments became fewer and further between, until they stopped altogether.

Jeremy had always feared for his own sanity, and had thought it was the end for him when dreams of murderous angels began on his eighteenth birthday. He knew—*somehow*—that they would be coming for him. The nightmares became worse and worse, and he felt as though there was something living inside of him, something furious, ready to explode from his body.

He couldn't—*wouldn't*—end up like his mother, tied to a bed and drifting away from sanity. He'd thought about calling it quits, walking into busy traffic at London's Piccadilly Circus, or maybe jumping from the Ferris wheel–like Eye overlooking the river Thames. Instead he took an old bottle of his mother's pills and left the flat he'd shared with her, hoping to find somewhere to quietly overdose—no mess, no fuss, no regrets.

And that was when Aaron Corbet and Lorelei had found him. It had taken no small amount of convincing, but eventually they had helped him understand that he wasn't going mad at all, that his body was simply changing.

Becoming something new.

Something special, like his mother had always said he would be.

And they promised to keep him safe.

The laughter of the other Nephilim reverberated through the room, jarring him from his thoughts. The angelic essence at Jeremy's core churned with annoyance. There was nothing to be laughing about; they carried the weight of a changing world squarely upon their shoulders, and Jeremy felt a spark of anger in him that had no other place to go but out.

"Would you please shut the bloody hell up!" Jeremy cried, standing and sending his chair clattering to the floor behind him.

The others quieted, their eyes upon him.

"Is there a problem?" William asked.

Jeremy and William had taken a dislike to each other as soon as Jeremy had arrived. William was tall, charismatic, and handsome, the type that all the girls flocked to, and the kind of bloke that Jeremy was the exact opposite of. The two had already exchanged words several times, and it was only a matter of time before it escalated into something else.

"Yeah, there is," Jeremy said, striding angrily around the table toward the gathering. "I can't bear the sound of your squawking anymore."

William met him halfway, and the two stood toe-to-toe. The pretty boy was a good inch taller, but Jeremy didn't care.

"Then maybe you ought to leave and go someplace else," William said, glaring at him.

This was it, the moment Jeremy had known was coming the first time the two teens set eyes on each other. Jeremy could feel the angelic essence clamoring to be free, and he decided what the hell, it was going to happen sooner or later anyway.

His skin began to tingle and a sudden bolt of pain at his shoulder blades made him hunch over as wings unfurled from his back.

William seemed shocked, glancing quickly behind him at his friends, who appeared equally surprised.

"So what's it going to be?" Jeremy asked through a snarl, his wings slowly fanning the air. "Are you going to shut your gobs, or do things have to get a bit more nasty?"

William glared as his own wings unfurled from his back. "Nasty is fine by me," he said, dropping to a crouch, then springing to attack.

"I was hoping you'd say that," Jeremy replied, his wings carrying him into the air.

He could no longer deny it; the angelic essence yowled at his core, thirsty for the blood of combat.

CHAPTER FOUR

Chicken fingers? Really?" Aaron asked the dog as they left what used to be the rectory and was now their living space.

"*I love chicken fingers,*" Gabriel said as he walked beside his master.

"Yeah, but are they really the thing you miss most about our old lives?" Aaron asked.

"*Well, that and Goofy Grape,*" the Labrador said sadly.

"Goofy Grape?" Aaron asked, stopping to look at the animal, totally confused. "What the hell is that?"

Gabriel stared up at him intently.

"*You don't remember Goofy Grape?*" the dog asked incredulously. "*It was only the best toy ever. I miss Goofy Grape.*"

Aaron didn't know what to say. He vaguely remembered a purple stuffed animal the dog used to play with, but he had never realized the intensity of the emotional attachment.

"Maybe we should try to find you a new one," Aaron suggested, disturbed by the dog's sudden sadness.

"Wouldn't be the same," Gabriel said, looking dejectedly at the ground. *"Lori and Tom gave me Goofy Grape."*

Then it all made sense to Aaron. His foster parents had been just as important to Gabriel as they were to him, and the Lab must have associated the toy with them. It had probably been destroyed when Verchiel and his Powers had killed Tom and Lori, burning their home to the ground in the process.

Gabriel became very quiet, and Aaron wasn't quite sure how to respond. Back when Aaron had first begun to manifest his abilities, Gabriel had been hit and nearly killed by a car. Aaron had first used his angelic power to bring his best friend back to life. Since then, the Lab had grown increasingly intelligent, no longer responding to things as a normal dog would. Aaron had to keep reminding himself that Gabe was different; no longer could he think of him as just a dog.

"I miss them too," Aaron finally said, stopping and reaching down to pat the dog's head.

"I think about them all the time," Gabriel replied, leaning forward to sniff at a patch of ground before turning his soulful gaze back to Aaron. *"Wondering if I could have done more."*

Aaron knelt down and gently held the Lab's face, looking directly into his dark eyes. "Don't torture yourself like that,

Gabe," he said. Then he put his arms around the dog and gave him a loving hug. "There was nothing more you, or I, could have done. Verchiel was way more powerful than us back then. And, besides, if something had happened to you, I'm not sure . . ."

Aaron didn't even want to think of it. Gabriel was everything to him, far more than just a best friend; it was as if he and the dog were connected at the soul.

"You would be lost without me," Gabriel finished Aaron's thought, leaning his head in to lick the young man's ear.

"You're right," Aaron answered, laughing. "I would be."

He gave the dog's side an affectionate thump as he stood. "Let's go and get some breakfast," Aaron suggested.

"Chicken fingers?" the dog questioned.

"I doubt it, but there might be frozen waffles," Aaron offered.

"Frozen waffles are all right," Gabriel grumbled, falling into step with Aaron as they continued to the cafeteria. *"But chicken fingers would be better."*

Aaron chuckled as the pair walked alongside the main building, which housed the cafeteria as well as the classrooms and the auditorium. "Maybe the next time we head to town, I'll buy you some—"

A window in front of them exploded outward in a shower of glass and flailing bodies, powerful wings beating furiously as two figures grappled in combat above the grounds.

Gabriel barked angrily, and Aaron felt the sudden rush of

fear and exhilaration that came with the potential for battle. His keen eyes locked upon the figures aggressively circling each other in flight, his mind already racing with possibilities. Had an enemy breached their security? Had one of the newer Nephilim lost control of his angelic nature? And then he realized that neither was the case. Two of his own were fighting each other: William Dean and Jeremy Fox.

Of course Fox is involved, Aaron thought, ready to end this nonsense.

"What the hell is going on here?" Aaron screamed at them.

A flaming sword spun through the air, plunging into the ground before him, just missing his foot.

"That was close," Gabriel growled, watching as the burning weapon dissipated with a sizzle and a flash of heat.

Aaron tensed, preparing to unfurl his own wings, spring up, and separate the pair when one of them was struck a powerful blow and fell to the ground.

William Dean struggled to stand.

"You," Aaron's voice boomed as he pointed to the youth. "You stay right there."

William wiped a trickle of blood from the corner of his mouth and averted his eyes, obviously embarrassed that his opponent had gotten the better of him.

"And you." Aaron turned his attention to Jeremy Fox, who had dropped from the sky in a crouch, his furious gaze still fixed upon his foe.

"No time for you, boss," the Brit said, approaching William with a snarl. "Got myself some more ass to kick."

"You'll do no such thing." Aaron reached out and grabbed the young man's arm as he passed.

Jeremy's eyes snapped to Aaron.

"Get your bloody hand off me or you'll be drawing back a stump," Jeremy warned, a sword materializing in his hand with a flash of heavenly flame.

That was all Aaron needed. He'd had issues with Fox before. The teen seemed to be having difficulty managing the angelic essence living inside him and the potential for violence it could ignite if left unchecked.

Aaron smiled tightly as his huge wings of shiny black unfurled, and the angelic sigils that were the names of all the fallen he had redeemed and returned to Heaven appeared upon his exposed flesh.

"Now, explain to me why I shouldn't take that sword and shove it up your—"

Gabriel's sudden barking interrupted Aaron's colorful threat, and the air began to shimmer and pulse near the gathering.

Someone was coming.

The scent of powerful magick hung thick and unpleasant in the corridor.

Lucifer wrinkled his nose and began to breathe through his mouth as he walked toward Lorelei's workshop.

The Morningstar carried coffee for the young woman as he had every morning since they'd taken up residence in the abandoned school and orphanage.

She should be wrapping up her scan of the ether, he thought as he approached the closed door. He knocked lightly, then turned the knob and pushed open the door.

He hoped that today's activities would be light, but he seriously doubted that would be the case. The things of darkness were becoming bolder, and more of them seemed to be venturing out into the world, their courage bolstered by . . . what exactly? That was a question the Morningstar was desperate to have answered.

Lucifer entered the classroom, stopping short as he witnessed Lorelei in the grip of Archon magick.

The poor girl was suspended limply above her workstation. The smoke wafting from the copper bowl had become like a living thing, throbbing, wrapping her in its embrace as it flowed into her body through her nose and open mouth.

The crimson cloud filling her with visions, visions of things that did not belong in this world.

Lucifer stood there watching, feeling absolutely helpless as Lorelei was assaulted by the ancient angelic spell. She twitched and moaned in the smoke's grip, and he could only imagine the intensity of what she was experiencing, what she was seeing.

The mist began to recede, withdrawing from Lorelei's body, dumping the girl unceremoniously on the floor as it returned in a flash of blinding light to the bowl from which it had been conjured. The copper dish spun noisily atop the Formica-covered worktable.

Lorelei moaned as she tried to sit up, and Lucifer knelt beside her, placing a strong arm at her back, helping her to rise.

She looked at him, eyes trying to focus. A small trickle of blood leaked from one nostril. Lucifer took a Kleenex from his sweatshirt pocket and dabbed at her nose.

"Hey there," he said with a smile.

"Hey," she answered, recognition filling her eyes. "Wow, that was a nasty one."

"Looked like it," he said. He stood and retrieved the coffee he'd brought for her, placing it in her hands. "Two creams, one sugar."

"Thanks," she said, holding the hot mug in both hands and bringing it to her mouth. She gulped greedily, not minding the heat. "Mmm," she said. "Just the thing to take the edge off having your ass kicked by angel magick."

"What did you see?" Lucifer asked. It seemed that time was always of the essence these days.

"It wasn't good," Lorelei said, holding out her hand. He reached down, grasped her hand, and pulled her to her feet.

"We're going to have to move fast on this one," she finished.

Vilma never really knew what she would find when she returned to the school: students learning how to summon weapons of fire or practicing aerial maneuvers above the orphanage grounds, her boyfriend and his dog waiting for her to appear, somehow always knowing that she was about to return.

That's what she hoped was awaiting her now. She needed Aaron, his powerful arms holding her close while he whispered in her ear, reminding her how much he loved her.

She never expected this: Jeremy Fox, British bad boy and Nephilim-in-training, holding a sword of flame, about to face off against her boyfriend, who was wearing his full-on, scary, I'm-going-to-destroy-you form.

Gabriel bounded over to her, barking wildly for her attention.

"What's going on here?" she asked as she marched toward them.

"Jeremy and Aaron are going to fight," Gabriel said excitedly, looking back to the pair.

"I don't think so," Vilma said. "What is going on here?" she repeated, feeling her anger rise. Her own angelic essence began to stir, but she held it back, reassuring the power that it wasn't needed for something this trivial.

Aaron opened his mouth to explain, but she was faster.

"I leave for a little while and this is what happens?" she asked. She glared at Aaron and then turned her icy stare to Jeremy, who was still holding his sword of fire.

"Put that away right now," she ordered, not even close to fooling around.

Jeremy sneered, but the sword dissipated in a flash.

The other students had gathered outside, standing near the building to watch the fireworks.

"Jeremy and William were having a bit of a disagreement," Aaron said. The sigils on his flesh began to fade as he furled his black wings, withdrawing them into his body. "Things got out of hand."

Aaron stared at Jeremy, waiting for the youth's response.

"Tempers flared," Jeremy said with a shrug. "It's all good now that we've had a chance to cool off."

Vilma folded her arms and cocked her head.

"And would it have cooled off if I hadn't gotten here when I did?" she asked.

Jeremy smiled, and his gaze moved to Aaron.

"Eventually, I'd wager," he said.

They all knew that Jeremy had some anger issues, that the angelic essence inside him was especially wild, but Vilma had never imagined that he would actually challenge Aaron's authority.

"Yeah, we're fine," Aaron said. "Nothing that a few weeks of generator duty won't solve, right, Jeremy?"

Ouch, Vilma thought. Since Saint Athanasius was officially shut down, there wasn't any electricity to the place. Their power was entirely supplied by industrial generators wired into the school's electrical system. The generators ran on gasoline and needed to be refilled quite frequently. It wasn't a favorite chore of those living at the complex, so it made a pretty decent punishment when necessary.

"No problem," Jeremy said, seemingly unfazed, but Vilma knew he was angry. "Perhaps your girlfriend would like to join me on my rounds. Make sure I'm doing it right and, y'know, keep me company and all."

Jeremy sure knew how to push buttons, and he was doing an excellent job.

Aaron start to lean forward, and Vilma reached out to touch his arm, squeezing it tenderly, encouraging him to dial it down, reminding him that the kid was just trying to get a reaction.

"Sorry, but you'll have to handle that particular chore on your own," Vilma said with a smirk. "A girl needs her beauty sleep, y'know."

"Not from what I can see," Jeremy leered. "Everything looks fine to me."

Vilma felt Aaron's muscles tense again beneath her fingers, but this time it was the Morningstar himself who put an end to things.

"Excuse me," his voice rang out.

They all turned to see the first of the fallen standing there. Even dressed in a hooded sweatshirt, jeans, and sneakers, he had something powerful about him.

And dangerous.

Thank God for Lucifer, Vilma thought, recognizing that

there was something most definitely wrong with that line of thinking but grateful for the reprieve he provided.

"If you'd all come to the auditorium," he said, gesturing for everyone to follow him. "Something has come up, and you're all going to need to be briefed."

He started to turn toward the building but quickly looked back to the group.

"That is, if you are quite finished here," he added, a glint of menace in his dark eyes that said he knew exactly what had been happening there.

And that he didn't approve.

CHAPTER FIVE

ONE MONTH AGO

Dustin "Dusty" Handy had always wanted to play the harmonica.

He stared at the harmonica lying harmlessly on the cracked, fast-food restaurant tabletop beside his bottomless cup of diet soda.

He'd told himself he was going to buy a book on how to play the mouth organ, and gradually teach himself to play before graduating high school.

Dustin had also always wanted to learn how to play the guitar, to ski, to make beer, and had even considered learning ballroom dancing at one time, but had never gotten around to doing any of it. Hell, he hadn't even finished school.

But the desire to play the harmonica had stuck.

Staring at the instrument, the teen wondered if it was that long-standing wish that had caused the horn to change, for it *had* been a horn when the blind old man had given it to him.

Dustin's brain felt hot. He imagined that all the information he was trying to process was about to go critical, making the gray matter inside his skull melt and run out his ears and down his worn leather jacket.

He removed the plastic cover on his cup and took a large gulp of soda and ice, hoping the caffeine would help him focus. Absently he crunched on the ice as he set the cup down, eyes still locked on the musical instrument.

There was a part of him that never wanted to touch it again, a part that wanted to leave it right there on the table of the fast-food joint and walk—no, run—away.

Yet another part of him would rather die than be separated from the harmonica.

For a moment Dusty wondered which part was stronger. Then he reached out and gently spun the harmonica on the table.

Round and round she goes, he thought. Memories of the night he'd found himself taking possession of the instrument flashed through his mind.

He'd been on his way from the bar and grill where he worked bussing tables to the tiny apartment he currently called home when he'd heard the commotion. Ordinarily he would have ignored the sound of struggle, preferring to keep his head low and not to get involved with other people's troubles.

But that night something had made him stop. Almost without thinking, he'd paused, and then backed up a few steps to peer down the trash-strewn alley. Three good-size guys appeared to be taking out their frustrations on someone a heck of a lot smaller . . . and a whole lot older.

Dusty remembered feeling afraid at first, but that fear was quickly overwhelmed by anger at the sight of three goons kicking the crap out of an old man.

Maybe it was because he'd spent most of his early childhood getting beaten within an inch of his life, or maybe it was the incredible injustice of the act before him—three against one—that spurred Dusty to action. Maybe it was both; he probably would never know.

Regardless, he'd found himself yelling into the alley in his loudest tough-guy voice, telling the thugs to leave the old man alone or he'd call the cops. His warning didn't seem to register. In fact, they seemed to start pummeling the man all the harder.

Dusty had tried to help, and it would have been perfectly fine if he'd just walked away. After all, what was he to do—take on all three? Certainly he'd been in his share of brawls since deciding to quit school at eighteen and take to the road, but three against one was practically suicide. And he'd never thought of himself as suicidal.

A loudspeaker announcement from the bus station next to the fast-food restaurant momentarily broke Dusty's concentration and returned him to the present. It wasn't the bus he was waiting for. He took another large swallow of his diet cola before immersing himself once again in the review of his folly.

A large broken pallet had been leaning against the wall of the alley, and Dusty had pried a piece of wood from its frame as he headed down toward the commotion.

"Leave him alone," he had hollered, hefting the wooden plank, making sure the goons could see that he had a weapon in case they chose to mix it up with him.

Dusty remembered the relief he'd felt when they actually stopped beating on the old man. He also remembered how fleeting that feeling was as the three thugs let the old man drop to the ground and turned their attentions to him.

The men had slowly advanced toward Dusty, and he had had to make a conscious effort to hold his ground. It had rained for most of the day, but the sky had just begun to clear, and as the three figures slowly stalked toward him, a curtain of thick clouds drew back from the moon, filling the alleyway with an unnatural light.

That was when Dusty realized that the men who were coming for him weren't really men at all.

Sitting at the restaurant table, Dusty closed his eyes. This was the part where he usually began to doubt himself, thinking that maybe he'd been mistaken, that what he'd really seen was a trick of the moonlight, or the effects of an empty stomach—he hadn't eaten anything that day except a stale bagel at breakfast—causing him to hallucinate.

But what had followed had proved that it was neither.

The men stood fully exposed in the moonlight. At first Dusty's brain had attempted to rationalize what his eyes were seeing, explaining away their awful appearance as horrible masks that made their flesh appear pale and glisten as if wet. But the closer they got, the more he realized that these men were not wearing masks or even makeup.

Their eyes were black, shiny, and unblinking, like a doll's. Their teeth were long and pointed, and there seemed to be far too many of them crammed inside their mouths.

They looked like dead men . . . or at least what he imagined long-dead men would look like. These men were something he wasn't supposed to ever have seen . . . something that would kill him to keep their secret safe.

"A hero amongst the sheep," one of them managed to speak through his many teeth.

"A sheep who believes himself a hero, brother," said another.

"But a sheep nonetheless," the final of the three monstrosities had offered.

Dusty had spent a large portion of his life being afraid. He'd always thought his abusive father to be the ultimate bogeyman. How wrong he'd been, for the terror he felt as the three creatures began to circle him made his father seem like a joke. His heart was hammering in his chest so hard that he thought his ribs might shatter. He had no idea why he hadn't simply turned and run. It was as if he was mesmerized by the nightmare that had been revealed to him.

Dusty shook himself from the memory and tried to collect his wits.

The harmonica had started to make a soft, tremulous moan, as if a faint breath were blowing through the instrument. It almost sounded as if it were growling in response to the memories of Dusty's fear.

As the monsters, for Dusty had no doubt that was what they were, had moved closer, he had noticed an odd smell about them. A smell that had made him think of every sad thing he'd experienced in his nineteen years, and *that* had made every hair on his body stand at attention.

He'd raised his weapon, bending forward ever so slightly as he prepared to defend himself.

"Now what would entice this sheep to come to the aid of the carrier?" one of the creatures asked his brethren.

Dusty tried to keep his eyes on them, turning to look at each of them as they circled him.

"Curiosity," the second suggested. "They are naturally drawn to the misfortunes of their own kind."

"As we have seen time after time, brother," the third said, "they seem to gain some kind of sustenance from the suffering of others. This one has come in for a little snack only to end up as a snack himself."

Dusty felt as though he might vomit as he watched a thick

black tongue slither from the monster's mouth and slide over teeth that seemed too sharp.

"Perhaps," responded the first. "But I suspect that there is something more to it . . . that there could in fact be some connection between—"

"And you'd be right," a new voice interrupted.

Dusty found his own gaze following those of the three walking nightmares to the far end of the alley, where the old man had been abandoned.

Only the man wasn't lying on the ground anymore. In fact, he seemed to be in relatively decent shape considering the thrashing Dusty had seen him take.

Dusty couldn't stand it anymore and took his chance while the three were distracted.

With a bloodcurdling scream, he'd swung the board in his hand as hard as he could. Visions of his freshman year in high school, when he'd played varsity baseball, danced before his eyes. He'd wanted to send that ball to the moon, and that was exactly what he'd wanted to do to the closest monster's head.

The board hit pale skin and skull with a strangely satisfying *thunk*, the monster's body going comically rigid as it dropped to the alley floor. Dusty's blow had cracked its skull like an eggshell, spilling its black, glistening contents upon the ground.

Something eel-like squirmed and flopped within the oily liquid, squealing horribly as it was exposed to the light of the moon. Dusty couldn't pull his eyes from the thing as it slithered across the ground, searching out a patch of darkness.

The monster's two comrades lunged at him, reaching out with long-fingered hands. Dusty swung at them, driving their distorted bodies back as he moved down the alley toward the old man.

"Stay behind me," Dusty ordered the old man once he reached him. He wasn't sure exactly what it was he was going to do. He was probably only delaying the inevitable, but he'd gotten this far and wasn't going to just lie down and die.

He'd glanced quickly over his shoulder to be sure the old man had heard him, and it was then Dusty had realized with surprise that he was blind, his eyes milky white in his dark brown face.

Dusty came out of his memory with a start, his hand flailing out and knocking over his soda cup, spilling the contents.

"Shit," he muttered, getting up from the table and leaving his bags, and the harmonica, to get some napkins to clean up his mess. He plucked paper napkins from the metal container, attempting to hold back his further recollections but having little luck.

"Give us the instrument," one of the monsters had hissed in the alley. "Give it to us and we'll kill you quickly."

Again there was that thing with the tongue, fat and slimy, snaking from its mouth.

Dusty had had no idea what they were talking about. At

first he thought the monstrosities were referring to his make-shift weapon, but then he heard the old man softly chuckle behind him.

"I think this has gone on long enough," he said, and Dusty couldn't have agreed more.

Then, as if things weren't already bizarre enough, the old man pulled a tarnished horn from inside his tattered suit coat. The absurdity of the action almost made Dusty break out in laughter, until he saw the monsters' reaction.

The pair stopped advancing, their glistening black eyes fixed upon the sight.

"The instrument," one of them hissed excitedly.

"Give it to us," demanded the other, holding out a twisted, clawed hand.

The old man chuckled again. "You don't have to ask me twice," he said. He turned his blind eyes toward Dusty, as if he could see, moving the horn up to his mouth. "You might want to cover your ears." He smiled, then touched the horn's mouthpiece to his ancient lips.

If he lived to be a hundred years, Dusty would never . . . could never . . . forget the sound that came from that horn. It was every horrible sound that he could imagine rolled into one.

He heard it again, in his mind, as he stood at the napkin dispenser. He heard it as he'd heard it every night since that bizarre encounter in the alley.

Dusty caught movement out of the corner of his eye, and he glanced over at the table where he'd left his things. A little kid stood there now, staring with great curiosity at the harmonica.

The harmonica that had once been a horn.

Dusty remembered what he'd seen that horn do, and he dove across the restaurant, screaming for the kid to get away from his table, to get away from the harmonica.

The instrument.

The horrible sound couldn't have lasted for more than a second. It had been a short blast, its shrillness barely muted by Dusty's hands as they covered his ears. But even more fantastic was the fact that Dusty could see the sound as it left the muzzle of the battered old horn. As the notes flowed down the alley, the air had shimmered like the waves of heat from a desert road.

The monsters had tried to flee, falling over one another in an attempt to be the first to escape.

Neither got very far.

As the note resonated, the disturbed air seemed to expand, enveloping the horrible pair as well as the body of their fallen comrade. Then it had torn them apart. It was as if they'd exploded, their malformed, corpselike bodies disintegrating into a fine black mist that coated the walls and floor of the alley. Even their clothing had been reduced to nothing.

As Dusty raced back to his table, he imagined that child, if he should somehow rile the instrument. . . .

But he needn't have worried. His scream had driven the little boy, crying, into the arms of his mother. "He wasn't going to touch anything," the woman huffed as she hugged the child and glared at Dusty from her booth.

"That's good," Dusty muttered, reaching out and snatching up the harmonica. He carefully placed it inside the pocket of his jacket. "Wouldn't have wanted him to get hurt."

The mother gave Dusty another disgusted look and returned her attention to consoling her wailing son, promising him an ice cream if he would only stop crying.

Dusty sopped up the spill with a large wad of napkins, and quickly gathered his things. He threw his knapsack over his shoulder and trudged toward the door. People were staring now, and he forced himself to look at each and every one of them, just to be sure.

To be sure they were people, and not monsters.

Monsters that wanted the instrument.

In the alley, the remains of his attackers had dripped from the wall while Dusty had listened intently to the old man's tale. Of course, at that point, the blind man could have been telling him Santa Claus was coming and Dusty would have believed him.

Tobias had explained that the Riders—he'd called them Corpse Riders—were after his horn, that they were hell-bent on getting it for a group of renegade angels called the Powers. There was a hint of relief in his voice as he told Dusty that he was getting too old to protect it. He had stared at the horn in his hands as if he could see it. He had been traveling, he had said, searching for someone to take on the burden, for a burden it truly was.

And that was when Tobias had turned his blind stare on Dusty and offered the horn to him.

Dusty left the restaurant, and went out to wait for his bus in the damp cold. But he barely felt it, as the instrument in his pocket radiated a heat that warmed his body. He put his hand into his jacket, allowing his fingertips to gently brush the metal of the harmonica, and felt an electric tingle race through his body.

He'd felt that same tingle when he had accepted the horn from Tobias, gasping aloud as the metal touched his flesh.

The old man had smiled at him then. "She likes you."

And Dusty had to wonder, *What if she didn't?*

That night in the alley had been the first and the last time Dusty had seen Tobias, although he had dreamed of the old man's death—feathered wings mercilessly pounding him into darkness.

The instrument had shown him many things during the ensuing days. He previously would not have seen those visions, but now that he was the instrument's carrier, they were images that he *must* see.

It was one of those visions that had brought him to the Seattle bus station tonight.

A bus pulled around the corner and into a space in front of the station. Its doors opened with a loud hydraulic hiss.

It was one of those images that had shown him where he needed to go. He was to go east, for *they* would be looking for him.

Dusty didn't know who they were exactly, and felt that perhaps it would be best that he didn't know. Images of the Corpse Riders appeared inside his head, and he quickly drove them away.

The driver stepped off the bus, fished a pack of cigarettes from his pocket, picked one out eagerly, and lit it up. Dusty climbed the stairs onto the bus and walked all the way to the back.

The instrument told him that they needed to keep moving, that it had much to show him before a decision could be made.

A decision for what? He wondered.

Hunkering down, and closing his eyes to the whispering voice in his head, he realized that he didn't have the courage to ask.

TWO WEEKS AGO

Geburah hated to be in the foul presence of the Corpse Riders, but he took great pleasure from the sounds of their screams.

He had ignited the fire of Heaven in his right hand and was bringing it closer and closer to the monster's pale face.

"You promised you would find me the instrument if I

spared your miserable life," the Powers' leader stated, his words lacking any emotion.

The demon squirmed beneath the holy light in Geburah's hand while the other denizens of the demon nest were held in place by the razor-sharp stares of Geburah's angelic brethren.

"We have done what you asked!" the Corpse Rider cried, cowering beneath the glow, his pale flesh blotchy in the cruel light of Heaven. "But since a new carrier was chosen—"

Geburah cut off its words as he pressed a burning finger down onto the bare skull of the demon, reveling in its pathetic wails.

"Why is it that what we ask has become so difficult?" the angel demanded, the smell of seared, dead flesh wafting up to assault his senses. "We have allowed you to live for this reason alone, and now you make us regret that decision."

The Corpse Riders were a loathsome race of demonic beasts that found their way from their world of shadow to God's earth through rips in the fabric of reality. Rips believed to have been caused by Verchiel's attempts to unleash the Hell contained within Lucifer Morningstar.

It was an unfortunate side effect of their previous leader's plan.

The Riders' natural forms could not survive the harsh, sunlit conditions of this plain, and so they chose to hide themselves away in an environment more hospitable to their needs.

They chose to live in the bodies of the dead, something

that the world had little shortage of. They animated corpses as if they still contained the glimmer of life, but instead of a spark of divinity, they held a vile worm of darkness.

The idea of working with creatures as foul as these made Geburah nauseous, but their numbers were many, and they did have an uncanny ability to track items of vast supernatural power, even when those objects endeavored to remain hidden.

Besides, once the instrument was in his hands, their kind would not matter anymore.

Nothing would matter anymore.

"We still search," the mewling creature said, face pressed to the floor of the basement chamber. "And our numbers are great," the monster continued in an attempt to placate the angel.

That bothered Geburah as well. Things such as the Corpse Riders should have been wiped from existence as soon as their presence was detected, back when the Powers safeguarded the world, before the coming of the Nephilim, but now . . .

The Powers' leader looked around the chamber and saw how the demonic beasts has assimilated themselves into human society. They had set up their nest in a mortuary, using the corpses that had been handed over to the funeral business for cremation and burial.

Monsters living right beneath the noses of humanity. It had gone too far, and it made him all the more confident that what he was attempting to do—what the great Verchiel had asked them to do—was the right thing.

"You will find the instrument for me, yes?" he asked the cowering demon, again touching the tip of his index finger to the creature's flesh.

"Yes!" it screamed. "Yes! We will find it."

"Our patience grows thin," Geburah said.

His brothers had begun to glow, throwing blinding light and intense heat across the room. The cries of the Corpse Riders were like music to Geburah's ears.

And if that brought him so much joy, he had to wonder how beautiful it would be when this entire blighted world was screaming.

ONE WEEK AGO

Dusty had started to doze, even as the trucker droned on and on. He knew it wasn't very polite. Jack had been nice enough to offer him a ride from Vermont to Boston, but Dusty was so damn tired he could barely keep his eyes open. The instrument had kept him moving west to east, now south. He hoped he wouldn't start snoring. If he could at least keep up the appearance that he was listening, it might be okay.

But the instrument had more visions to show him.

Eyes closed, the harmonica nestled, warm and pulsing, in his jacket pocket, Dusty learned of its origins.

And of its dire purpose.

Jack kept on talking as Dusty's mind filled with images he

could barely comprehend. He saw the creation of reality from nothing—a flash of brilliance when the Almighty gained consciousness and decided that the darkness would reign no more.

Dusty saw the creation of what could only have been Heaven, and the winged creatures that the Lord God had brought into existence to help Him with His chore.

From there it became a blur: he saw the Creator giving birth to the universe—the stars and the planets—and he witnessed the creation of all the life that would swim, slither, crawl, and walk upon the earth.

Dusty could feel the Creator's love for this place, and it was this love that led to the creation of the instrument. The Lord God loved His world, and dared not see it tainted.

There were things that had lived—still lived—in the darkness that had been banished with creation, evil things that would see the Almighty's world corrupted.

The Lord of Lords could not bear to think of this, and had fashioned a means to keep the world from falling into the clutches of evil. From deep within His being, the Creator took a portion of His wrath, and from it He fashioned an angel. He called this angel Wormwood. Wormwood would be called upon only in times of darkness and shadow, when the world He so loved was tainted beyond repair.

And then He fashioned an instrument—a trumpet—to summon this terrible angel . . . this Abomination of Desolation, for when the horn was blown, it would be too late.

The angel would come, and all that existed upon the world would end.

"So I ate 'em," a loud voice boomed, awakening Dusty from his apocalyptic vision with a start.

The boy looked around the cab, taking a moment to remember where he was and how he had gotten there. He turned his attention to the truck driver, to Jack, who was staring at him.

"What?" Dusty asked. It was obvious that the trucker hadn't known he'd been asleep.

"The doughnuts," Jack said matter-of-factly. "I ate all of them."

Dusty had no idea what the man was talking about, but he managed to put on a smile, pretending to be amused.

"Wow, that's something," he murmured, gazing out the eighteen-wheeler's broad windshield at the night stretched out before it.

Jack nodded and fell silent, having finished his tale of mass doughnut consumption.

Dusty's hand slipped into his jacket to find the warmth of the harmonica . . . of the instrument that could very well call down the apocalypse.

The end of the world right inside his pocket.

CHAPTER SIX

The first thing Aaron noticed was how pale Lorelei looked. She seemed sick, her blouse appearing too large upon her frail form.

The Nephilim magick user sat in a chair at the front of the room, bony hands clasped tightly in her lap. Lucifer stood at her side, glancing down from time to time, concern showing in his gaze.

Aaron felt Vilma's hand on his arm as she pulled him toward some chairs. The look on her face as she stared at the front of the room told him that she had noticed Lorelei's appearance as well.

The eight other Nephilim filtered into the room, choosing their seats. A nervous anticipation began to grow in the air. Jeremy Fox was the last to arrive, taking a seat against the wall, well away from the others. He glanced briefly over his shoulder and grinned smugly at Aaron and Vilma before turning his attention to Lucifer.

Aaron felt his anger flare but was distracted when his father began to speak.

"We're all here?" Lucifer asked, scanning the room.

Gabriel slunk in, head down, and went to where Aaron and Vilma sat.

"Sorry," the dog grumbled as he sat beside Aaron. *"Had to do my business."*

This got a laugh from the Nephilim in the room, but their mood quickly turned serious as Lucifer continued.

"We have a bad one, I'm afraid," he said, his gaze touching each and every one of them, ensuring that he had their undivided attention. "And we don't have time to waste. A group of miners in Kemerovo Oblast, Russia, have been trapped by a cave-in. They're running low on air, and it appears that they are not alone."

Everyone seemed to sit a little straighter in their seats with Lucifer's last statement.

"What kind of beastie are we dealing with this time?" Jeremy asked.

"For lack of a better name, I would say that they are trolls," Lucifer responded.

Laughter flared again in the room as the Nephilim made jokes about cartoons and fairy tales.

"Guys," Aaron warned, turning partially in his seat.

"Did I say something funny?" Lucifer asked sternly,

immediately quieting the room. "From what Lorelei has told me . . . shown me, there is nothing humorous about these creatures. These things are evil, and you'll be in their environment beneath the ground," he explained. "A creature is always far more dangerous when it's in its own territory."

He turned to Lorelei, who seemed to be looking a little bit better, a little color having returned to her fair features.

She rose to stand beside the Morningstar. "The vision came hot and heavy this morning; we're not talking about a lot of time if we want to save the miners." She took a deep breath, as if steeling herself for what was to come.

"So, are we ready?" she asked.

Aaron could see that Lorelei herself was still shaken by the effects of the vision. But as with so much of their lives lately, what choice did any of them really have?

Aaron knew what was coming and mentally prepared himself for the confrontation that was sure to happen, and for that he needed to be thinking not as a man but as something more than that, something more than human actually—*Nephilim.*

He glanced around the room at the others as they, too, readied themselves. Janice, Kirk, William, Melissa, Samantha, Russell, Cameron: he was proud of this group, proud of how far they'd come, and that they had been able to step up to the responsibilities that life had so cruelly dropped in their laps. With the Powers gone, they were the protectors of the world from darkness. Sure, some of them were still a little raw—he glanced at Jeremy Fox—but they were doing well. They were surviving. They were getting the job done.

At the front of the room, Lorelei closed her eyes and took another deep breath. Besides her ability to use the ancient Archon magicks, she was also able to psychically share her visions with the other Nephilim. Aaron wasn't sure if he or any of the others would eventually be able to do the same, or if this was just another of Lorelei's unique talents, but he did know that her ability had proven quite useful in carrying out their missions.

Aaron felt the girl's presence in his mind almost at once. It started as a dull pain that gradually intensified, followed by a flood of imagery and knowledge. He heard some of the others cry out as the information flowed forcefully into their brains.

And then it was done. Aaron blinked, then looked about the room. The others were recovering; some were dealing with small nosebleeds, while others had headaches that would eventually fade.

Now they all saw what she had seen: the troll-like things emerging from the darkness of the underground, and the innocents that were threatened.

And they knew where to go to face off against this threat.

Lorelei looked the worse for wear, leaning against Lucifer as she attempted to pull herself together.

"Are we set?" Aaron asked as he rose from his seat.

The others almost visibly shook off the effects of the psychic connection and stood as well.

"Do we all know where we're going?"

As one, they nodded, a certain grimness passing over them, not knowing if they would return from their mission.

Not knowing if they would survive.

"Then let's do this," Aaron said, wings beginning to unfurl from his body.

Wings of white, gold, brown, and copper began to emerge from the backs of the eight other youths. It was truly an awesome sight to behold, and it drove home to Aaron the importance of what they were doing on this world.

Vilma was ready beside him, her white wings slowly fanning the air. She gave him a wink, and he returned the favor with a smile.

"We'll be back as soon as we can," he told Gabriel, who watched him with serious eyes. "Look after things while I'm gone."

"Be careful," the dog said.

Aaron promised he would, then wrapped himself in a cocoon of feathers, as did the others, and one after the other they were gone, traveling to the place of darkness they saw inside their minds.

KEMEROVO OBLAST: RUSSIA

Anatoli Olegushka always knew that working in the Ulyanovskaya coal mines would probably be the death of him, but a certain sense of invincibility was developed when one descended into the bowels of the earth day after day and ascended again into the fresh air and gray Russian skies.

Certainly there were accidents—cave-ins, methane and coal-dust explosions—but those things happened to other people, and when they did, he knew he was safe for some short time, that the spirits that lived in the earth had taken their sacrifice and would be sated for a time.

For a time.

Anatoli lay upon a bed of broken rock, the lantern on his helmet shining upward onto the curved ceiling of the chamber. He struggled to remain conscious in the thinning air.

The day had begun just like any other: Anatoli, Pavel, Nikolai, Olik, and other members of the crew descended into the tunnels 885 feet below the surface. They couldn't have been working any more than twenty minutes—Olik had barely settled into his latest tale of woe about how fat his wife was becoming—when their world exploded in a flash of fire and the deafening roar of the end.

But it wasn't the end for all of them. Anatoli slowly turned his head, the beam of light from his safety helmet shining through the choking, dust-filled air as he sought out his friends. Bodies were scattered about, some partially buried beneath crushing rock, all of them lying horribly still. The sight of his friends stirred him to move. He carefully rolled onto his side, then slowly pushed himself up onto his hands and knees. Miraculously, he didn't think he had broken anything. He crawled across the rubble to the first of his comrades.

"Hey," he said, nudging the man who lay facedown. "Hey there, are you all right?"

Anatoli rolled the man over. It was his closest friend, Pavel, who now stared up at him with empty eyes, dark blood streaming from his mouth and nose.

There will be time for mourning later, Anatoli told himself, fighting back tears. For now, he had to concentrate on finding other survivors and holding on until he could be rescued.

He left Pavel where he'd found him and moved on to the others. He found Nikolai alive but barely conscious. Another worker—Vadim—who had begun working in Ulyanovskaya only a few weeks previous, was also living, although his legs had been badly injured, likely broken.

The rest of Anatoli's crew were not so lucky.

He appeared to be the most unscathed from the blast and ensuing cave-in, and was able to cautiously crawl about to investigate their surroundings. It didn't look good. They were trapped within a fairly large pocket, fallen rock surrounding them on all sides. The phone that was their only connection to the surface had been smashed beyond repair.

Anatoli half considered trying to dig out some of the smaller rocks to see if he could find his way into an adjoining passage, but he was afraid of loosening more stone and jeopardizing their small sanctuary.

"Looks like we're going to be here for a little while," he said, turning from the wall of rock to the other two survivors.

Nikolai moaned as he sank into the grip of unconsciousness, while Vadim began to sob.

Anatoli busied himself with trying to find the first-aid kit amid the debris, anything to help his two comrades with their pain. And that was when the screaming began.

It was Vadim.

Anatoli turned, illuminating the man's thrashing body with his headlamp. He crawled on his belly over broken rock to his comrade, and was ready to lay a comforting hand upon his shoulder when he realized that there already was a hand on Vadim's shoulder. In fact, there were two, one on either side of the man's head. And the hands were sticking out from the wall of loose rock behind Vadim.

Anatoli could not fathom what he was seeing, his brain attempting to rationalize. At first he thought it was one of their own, reaching through the rock wall from a pocket on the other side, but there was something not quite right about the hands.

They were large, the skin leathery and dark brown. The thick fingers were clawed, and they ripped through Vadim's heavy work shirt into his flesh beneath. Anatoli glimpsed the reflective shine of blood in his headlamp.

"Help me," Vadim begged, eyes wide with fear.

Anatoli reached out to grab Vadim's outstretched arms,

but he did not act quickly enough. The clawed hands yanked mightily upon Vadim's shoulders, pulling his injured body closer to the rock wall at his back.

Vadim cried out in pain and terror. Suddenly there were more hands pushing through the rock and grabbing at the injured man's arms and sides. They continued to pull on him, and Vadim shrieked all the louder, struggling to escape their clutches.

Anatoli grabbed one of Vadim's legs, which caused him to cry out in agony. On reflex, Anatoli released it, not wanting to cause his comrade any more pain than he was already feeling.

The inhuman hands weren't so considerate. They continued to pull on the man as he helplessly fought to escape them.

And that was when Anatoli noticed that the rock looked almost liquid. The entire wall of rubble at Vadim's back appeared insubstantial as whatever was on the other side drew him toward it.

"Help me!" the man screamed pathetically.

A spidery fingers emerged above Vadim's head and sank its talons into his helmet, crushing it like an eggshell as it yanked his shrieking head through the liquefied stone, muffling his cries.

Anatoli dove forward, grabbing hold of Vadim's booted ankles. It became a bizarre parody of tug-of-war as something on the other side of the wall pulled furiously on Vadim. Anatoli held on for as long as he was able, but whatever was trying to take his friend was too strong. One of Vadim's boots suddenly came loose, sending Anatoli falling backward upon the jagged rock.

Anatoli sat on the ground, clutching the empty work boot to his chest as he watched the sock-covered foot of his friend drawn through the liquid stone to the other side. All Anatoli could do was stare at the wall that now seemed solid. He was tempted to touch the stone, to test it, but he was afraid that the hands would be waiting and he, too, would be snatched away.

It was then that he recalled something his grandfather had said, way back when he'd first talked about working in the Ulyanovskaya mines. The old man had warned him that one day they would dig too deep and they would find themselves in Hell.

And as the hands clawed through the rock again, this time behind the unconscious Nikolai, Anatoli knew that his grandfather had been right.

They had gone too deep.

And Hell was now coming for them.

Nikolai was gone. He had disappeared through the wall of rock, and now Anatoli was alone with the corpses of his fellow workers.

The air had become thicker, and he was finding it harder and harder to breathe, but Anatoli did not—would not—take his eyes from the wall of black, glistening stone through which

Vadim and Nikolai had disappeared. His vision began to blur, his eyelids growing heavier with each passing minute.

Anatoli had pushed himself into the center of the chamber, as far away from the wall as he could, terrified that the moment he lost his struggle with unconsciousness, Hell would come for him.

But Hell was impatient; Hell was eager to take him now.

"No!" Anatoli screamed as the wall across from him began to shimmer. First the clawed hands dug through, followed by the most horrific faces, and then dark, skeletal bodies. One by one they crawled out of the wall and across the loose rock and rubble toward him.

From the corner of his eye he could see more creatures entering from the wall to his left, but they seemed to be focused on those who hadn't survived the cave-in, dragging the bodies away, one by one.

Anatoli kept his gaze fixed on the creatures before him, and attempted to push himself away from their relentless advance. Long, oily black hair hung in front of their faces, obscuring everything but their extra wide mouths, filled with razor-sharp teeth.

He wasn't a religious man, but Anatoli started to pray aloud; the Lord's Prayer swam up from the recesses of his childhood memories. It had been years since he'd last attended church, but something told him that if he was going to believe in Hell, then there must be room for Heaven as well.

THOMAS E. SNIEGOSKI

"Our Father, who art in Heaven, hallowed be thy name. Thy kingdom come. . . ."

Still the creatures came, reaching long, clawed fingers toward him.

"Thy will be done, on Earth as it is in Heaven."

And then there was a flash of absolute brilliance, a light so bright and searing that for a moment he believed there had been another gas explosion, only this one appeared to be lacking any sound.

The beasts hissed and wailed in the light, scrambling back across the loose earth toward the wall that separated this realm from their own.

Blobs of black caused by the sudden brilliance undulated before his eyes as Anatoli turned toward the warmth and source of the light.

Nothing could have prepared him for the sight before him.

Wings furled upon their backs and weapons of fire in their hands. Anatoli counted ten in all. Angels . . . what else could they be?

"We're here to help," one of them spoke to him in perfect Russian, and Anatoli's previous thoughts were confirmed.

If he was to believe in Hell, then there must be room for Heaven as well.

CHAPTER SEVEN

The trolls were gone.

The light of the Nephilim's arrival had driven the monsters away.

Aaron had caught a glimpse of the creatures as he'd first unwrapped his wings, skin like leather, shaggy hair, limbs thick and long, with clawed hands that looked as though they could do some serious damage.

Lucifer had been right. There was nothing at all funny about these trolls.

"Check for survivors," Aaron instructed the others as he knelt before Anatoli. Considering what he had been through, the man didn't look too bad, just some bumps and bruises.

"Are you hurt?" Aaron asked in Russian. The gift of tongues was inherent in all Nephilim, and it never ceased to amaze him when he opened his mouth and heard himself speaking a language he'd never studied.

The miner just stared at him, the tears from his eyes melting clean tracks through the thick layer of dust and dirt that clung to his face. Aaron guessed that the young man was in shock, with all he had just lived through—what he had seen.

"You're going to be fine," Aaron reassured the man, reaching down to grip his shoulder and give an encouraging squeeze.

"Am . . . am I dead?" the man asked, lips trembling. "Are you going to take me away?"

"We're going to take you out of here," Aaron assured him.

Vilma came to stand beside him.

"Get him to the surface, would you?" Aaron asked her.

She knelt down beside the man, taking him into her arms, allowing her wings to enfold them both.

"I'll be right back," Vilma said. And then they were gone.

One of the other Nephilim approached him. Janice was one of the more quiet of the group. She was petite and wore her hair in a boyish cut. She dressed always in black and had a tendency to keep to herself, blending into the background, never attracting attention. They'd found her in Michigan, living in a group home, zonked out on multiple forms of antipsychotic medication.

Janice hadn't needed pills to help her; she just needed to understand what she was, and to be with her own kind.

"There isn't anybody else," she whispered.

"Thank you, Janice," Aaron said. "The air in here is getting pretty bad. We might want to think about—"

One of the Nephilim screamed.

Aaron and Janice looked over to where the others had been standing, checking for survivors, when the first of the trolls returned.

The monster had thrust a spear out through the rock, impaling a Nephilim named Kirk.

"Damn it," Aaron roared, jumping to his feet.

There was a disturbance in the air behind him as Vilma returned from her errand.

"What's going on?" she asked, retracting her wings.

"The trolls are back," Aaron replied quickly.

Kirk stumbled back, away from the protruding spear, as the troll emerged from beneath the rock. Aaron had never seen anything like this. It was as if the rocks had turned to fluid, allowing the monsters to penetrate the stone.

"Get back," he ordered, as more of the trolls crawled effortlessly through the rock wall, wielding their spears, swords, and knives.

Vilma and Jeremy dragged the bleeding Kirk away from where the trolls had emerged, and the others formed a line of defense before the advancing beasts.

"What are you waiting for?" Aaron barked, summoning his sword of fire. "Let's get to it."

The others reacted as well, their own specialized weapons

forged from the fires of Heaven appearing in their hands.

The trolls hesitated momentarily, shielding their eyes, the monstrousness of their forms illuminated in the light cast from the Nephilim's weaponry. In the divine light of their weapons, Aaron saw how horrible these trolls actually were, skin like old leather, some of their flesh adorned with primitive tattoos.

They blinked black, beady eyes before attacking en masse.

The Nephilim acted as they had been trained, launching themselves at their attackers. Aaron spread his wings, joining the fray.

The warrior nature of his being surged forward, and all that he saw before him was an enemy to be vanquished. A troll with a raised sword came at him screaming, and Aaron blocked the descending blade expertly, sparks flying as divine weaponry met one forged in the depths of shadow. Drawing back, Aaron saw the troll raise its weapon to strike again. It was an opportunity, and he took advantage of it, slicing his blade across the round, protruding belly of his foe. The sword of fire sizzled as it cut the taut flesh, the monster's innards spilling out onto the cave floor, tripping another of the beasts as it bounded at Aaron, spear in hand.

This attacker met with a similar fate, his leathery body cleaved nearly in two from shaggy skull to midsection.

The trolls continued to pour from the liquid rock. There were far more of the ugly monsters than Aaron would have thought. When one fell, two more emerged from behind the rock wall. The trolls had little finesse to their attacks—lots of stabbing and hacking—but as primitive as their skills were, they were still dangerous, and he hoped that the others remained aware of that fact.

Cockiness could get them killed.

Aaron moved amongst his enemies, the warrior's lust for battle tingeing his vision of the darkened world around him scarlet, and he expertly dispatched the monsters as they came at him. From the corner of his eye he watched the others, impressed by what he saw. The Nephilim were doing well; certainly they had sustained injuries, but the bodies and appendages that littered the rocky floor belonged entirely to the trolls.

The ceiling of the collapsed chamber was low, no higher than seven feet in sections, and the Nephilim could not gain much in the way of altitude, but their wings allowed them to evade the trolls' furious attempts at maiming and dismembering.

But then the trolls adapted to their foes' superiority, dragging crude nets from behind the wall of rock and tossing them over the flying Nephilim, dragging them to the ground.

Janice was the first to fall. Frantically, she used her burning rapier in an attempt to cut herself free, but two trolls leaped upon her, one knocking her senseless with a club, the other stabbing her repeatedly with a trident.

Her screams echoed obscenely through the chamber. Aaron fought, as did some of the others, to get to the fallen Nephilim's side. He stabbed at the trolls who stood in his way, using his powerful black wings to sweep aside any who thought they might flank him. Cameron had reached Janice, but Aaron could tell by the look on the boy's face that he was too late to matter.

After seeing what had befallen their comrade, the Nephilim rallied to fight all the more savagely.

Through a mist of blood and flying limbs, Aaron saw the girl that he loved, and found himself suddenly both excited and disturbed. Vilma fought with the savagery of a creature whose entire purpose was to eradicate evil from the world. She moved amongst the trolls as if they were standing perfectly still, cutting them down one after another, like wheat beneath the scythe. Here was violence incarnate, wrapped in the form of the most beautiful girl he had ever known.

But he also remembered her before the angelic nature within her had matured.

Watching as she unmercifully moved through their enemies, striking them down in a flash of her fiery blade, Aaron could not help but miss the innocent girl that used to be, and feel great sadness for what had been lost.

"She's a sight, isn't she?" commented someone close by.

Aaron spun around, still in the midst of his berserker fury, to see Jeremy Fox standing there, his clothing and exposed skin flecked with black blood. At his feet was a dead troll, a burning ax blade still stuck in its back.

"Excuse me?" Aaron asked, not sure if he understood.

"Your woman, there," the British boy said with a lascivious grin. "She's certainly a beautiful sight."

It took nearly everything Aaron had not to forcibly wipe that grin from the boy's face. Instead he threw himself into combat against a dwindling enemy.

Though at first their number had seemed endless, many of the trolls were now retreating back from whence they came, leaving behind their dead and wounded as they passed through the now permeable rock.

Aaron found himself winding down, the throbbing of boiling hot blood through his veins slowing. He looked around. Some of their number had been injured, while others . . .

Vilma knelt before Janice's body, using a knife of fire to cut away the heavy netting that covered her.

Aaron approached them.

"Is she . . . ," Aaron began, knowing the answer but still wanting to ask the question, just in case there was a chance.

"Yeah, she's dead." There was a cold indifference in Vilma's tone.

He could feel the others' eyes upon him. They all were very aware that this could happen to any of them; it was stressed day in and day out. They were at war with the forces of darkness, and the forces of darkness could very easily take each of them down.

"What now, Aaron?" William asked, and Aaron turned to see him standing at the rock wall. "Are we going after them?"

There was a part of him that wanted to leave, to get away

from this cold, dark place. Since becoming Nephilim, he'd had his fill of death, enough to last him for years, but Aaron knew that wasn't what they were going to do. He was about to tell them his plans when another spoke up.

"Of course we're going after them," Jeremy Fox said, pulling his burning ax blade from the skull of one of his troll victims.

He advanced toward them, spinning his ax in hand, the blade spitting sparks that sizzled and hissed as they struck the puddles of blood that had formed on the ground.

Jeremy's eyes glistened in the twilight of the chamber as he stood before him, waiting for what Aaron had to say. Seeing a use for all that pent-up fury that the British boy still carried, Aaron stepped aside, gesturing to the wall.

"Yeah, we're going," he said. "Just as soon as we deal with this obstruction."

Jeremy glared at the wall of rock, a cruel snarl of a smile forming upon his face as he came to realize what Aaron wanted him to do.

"If you would be so kind," Aaron encouraged.

And Jeremy charged at the wall with a snarl, ax blade of divine power coming down upon the rock obstruction with a sound ringing like the end of the world.

He went wild, fueled by his anger, hacking unmercifully at the wall. Slivers of rock exploded outward with every hit of Jeremy's fiery battle-ax.

Aaron's wings unfurled reflexively, as did the other Nephilim's, as they shielded themselves from the flying debris.

Then, cautiously, Aaron lowered a wing and saw that Jeremy had made an adequate opening. "That should be good enough," he said.

But Jeremy continued to pound the pieces of rock into powder.

"Enough!" Aaron's voice boomed in the chamber. He flew beside the youth and grabbed his arm, holding him tightly so the ax could not fall again.

"Enough," he repeated, his voice softer.

Jeremy's eyes were wild with rage, but he obeyed, relaxing the tension in his arm and looking to the opening in the wall. "Well, what are we waiting for?" he asked, ducking through the hole.

There was an immediate commotion from the other side.

Aaron readied his sword and followed Jeremy's path through the hole and into a much larger chamber beyond. Jeremy was near the entrance, standing over the dead bodies of three trolls lying on the rocky floor.

"Everything all right?" Aaron asked him.

"Right as rain," Jeremy replied, an unnerving grin momentarily gracing his pale face as he turned away from them and headed toward a circular corridor of rock.

Aaron was about to tell the young man to wait for them, but Vilma appeared beside him.

"I'll keep him out of trouble," she said, using her wings to fly after Jeremy, gracefully flitting across the rocky surface of the chamber and into the shadowy corridor beyond.

Aaron turned toward the entrance to the cavern just as the last of the remaining Nephilim entered. "Let's go," he said, motioning to the others to follow Vilma.

Kirk was the last to stumble by, and Aaron reached out for the young man.

"Maybe you should stay here," Aaron suggested, eyeing the scarlet stain on the side of the boy's T-shirt.

"I'm all right," Kirk said, even though his face was pale and dappled with sweat. "I can do this."

"Are you sure?" Aaron stressed.

Kirk took a deep breath, nodded, and turned to follow the others.

They walked into the stone passage. At first it appeared that there had been no resistance, but then the troll bodies started to pile up as they continued farther in.

"Hmmm," William said so that everyone could hear. "Wonder if Fox happened to pass this way?"

There was some nervous laughter from the group.

"Stay focused," Aaron warned, wanting them to remain on guard. They had no idea what they were walking into, but there was no choice. They were Nephilim, and this was their job—their purpose.

They needed to be ready for anything.

And, as if on cue, the wall beside them seemed to melt away. A shaggy beast in all its twisted glory sprang at Aaron.

It let out a horrible, bloodthirsty cry, lunging at Aaron's chest with its filthy spear tip. There wasn't much maneuverability in the passage, and Aaron threw himself back against the opposing wall, raising his sword of fire to block the attack and willing the blade to blaze all the brighter.

The troll screamed, dropping its weapon to cover its injured eyes. Aaron didn't hesitate a moment. He slashed his blade down upon the monster and ended its life before it could recover.

"Watch the walls," he warned the others, in awe of the beasts' abilities to pass through stone and rock as if it were little more substantial than smoke.

A troll screamed from somewhere behind their group, and Aaron saw the blaze of a heavenly weapon followed by another unearthly cry.

"You guys good back there?" he called.

"We're okay," Cameron reported. "One just tried to come up from the floor. I took care of it."

They had to get out of the confined space of the passage, to find Vilma and Jeremy.

The tunnel before them suddenly dipped down, winding farther into the bowels of the earth, and from somewhere below there came a series of screams.

Something told Aaron that they'd found what they were looking for.

* * *

This is what it's all about, Jeremy reveled as he surged into the large subterranean chambers that housed what looked to be a troll village.

This was what he'd been waiting for, to let loose, to let the power flow through him and into the ax he carried. There was nothing the filthy beasts could do to stop him; he was a force to be reckoned with, the ultimate power of God made physical.

He was like a storm upon them; no matter how many they sent to fight him, they were struck down in death by his unrelenting fury. He could see the fear in their beady eyes as he came farther into their territory. *How do you ugly buggers like it?* he thought, enjoying the monsters' distress.

Deeper into the village he went; huts made of rock and dirt exploded into black clouds under the power of his ax.

From somewhere in the distance he heard his name.

"Jeremy."

But it didn't stop him. Nothing could stop him. He was a destroyer . . . a berserker . . . and there was nothing that would make him cease, until all their enemies were . . .

"Jeremy!" a voice cried all the closer.

He spun toward the sound, ready to destroy that, too, and came face-to-face with the girl—with Vilma Santiago. He had to pull back upon the fury that roared within him. He wouldn't want to hurt something as fine as that.

"Watch out," she cried out to him as she did battle with a group of trolls that sprang at her from the rubble of their dwellings.

He had no idea what she was talking about, for there was nothing that could stop him. It was she who needed to watch out . . . she, and their so-called leader, whom she called "boy-friend."

The blow came to the back of his head. Jeremy fell to his knees in an explosion of color and sound. Dazed, he glanced up, and through bleary eyes saw what Santiago had tried to warn him about: a troll wielding a hammer that would have made the God of Thunder himself weak with envy.

The beast raised its hammer once more, and Jeremy struggled to raise his weapon to block the hammer's descent. But his concentration was gone, and the blade of the divine ax exploded into sparks as it was decimated by the fall of the troll's war hammer.

Jeremy managed to roll out of the way just as the hammer struck the stone floor in an explosion of shattered rock. The chamber was spinning, and he was finding it hard to put together a coherent thought, never mind re-create his ax of fire.

The large troll saw that it had not yet claimed the life of its victim and, with a snort, again brought the hammer up, charging forward to finish the job.

Jeremy desperately needed a weapon, but try as he might,

he could not create one; his brain was still too scrambled from the force of the initial hammer blow.

He wondered if Nephilim were allowed nine lives, like cats, as he prepared to have his brains bashed in.

But the blow didn't fall. He looked up at the troll, which still stood above him but no longer held its weapon. In fact, it no longer had hands.

There was a flurry of movement near the beast, followed by the sound of something soaring through the air as the troll's shaggy head tumbled to the ground and rolled toward him. Jeremy could see the monster's beady eyes, wide with shock, peering out from beneath locks of black, greasy hair.

"I told you to watch out," Vilma said.

He looked up from the troll's dead eyes to see the striking young woman standing there, burning sword crackling in her hand.

She was a sight to behold. Even though her clothes were torn, and covered with dirt and blood, Jeremy wasn't sure if he'd ever seen another girl like her.

"That'll teach me to listen," Jeremy said as he raised a hand for her to help him up.

"Could anything possibly teach you to listen, Jeremy?" Vilma asked as she pulled him from the ground.

"Maybe I could surprise you," he said, looking into the dark spots of her eyes, far closer to her than he had ever been before. The angelic nature stirred within, but this time it did not hunger for violence but for something else entirely.

Vilma released her grip on his wrist, stepping back to look toward the cavern entrance.

Aaron stood in the opening to the chamber, and a perverse part of Jeremy hoped their fearless leader had seen them.

And the thought of this brought a sly smile to Jeremy's lips.

Aaron wasn't sure exactly what he was seeing as he entered the chamber, but he knew he didn't care for it.

The way Fox and Vilma had been standing there, so close together . . .

Stop, he told himself. He couldn't allow himself to be distracted from the job at hand. He was about to call down to them, to ask if they were clear, when he felt it.

Aaron's senses came immediately alert, his skin starting to burn and itch as the sigils of the angelic fallen began to appear there. It must have been something extremely dangerous to arouse their appearance. A quick glance around showed him that the others felt it too.

"What is it, Aaron?" Russell asked, his wide blue eyes darting around the stone cavern.

More attuned to his angelic abilities than the others, Aaron moved toward the source of the disturbance. He stepped over the bodies of the fallen troll soldiers, the sensation intensifying as he approached an area that looked as though it had been designated for the preparation of food.

He heard the others behind him gasp.

Two human bodies hung by their ankles from a rack, their throats cut and their blood drained into large stone bowls. There were gore-covered knives, and a primitive meat cleaver, lying beside smaller bowls that looked to be filled with dried spices.

It was a horrible sight, but not what had drawn him to this place.

Aaron sensed Vilma by his side and turned to look at her.

"Do you feel that?" Aaron asked her.

She nodded, stepping closer to him and gently touching his hand. The black sigils upon his flesh tingled with her touch.

Jeremy stormed past them, his fiery ax taking form in his grasp. "Looks like we interrupted their tea."

Aaron still couldn't put his finger on it, moving farther into the area, a sense of danger still present in the air. He noticed the stone handle protruding from the ground at his feet. At closer examination he saw that it was a handle to a circular stone cover in the ground.

As he bent to grab hold of it, he knew what had drawn them to this section of the troll habitat.

"Be ready," he ordered as he pulled the heavy lid from the ground, revealing a circular manhole-like opening in the floor.

Aaron dropped the heavy cover with a thud, and brought his sword to life to illuminate what was within the hole.

He gasped at what he saw below.

Vilma and Jeremy came to his side and peered down into the opening.

"Oh my God," Vilma said, bringing a hand to her mouth in shock at the sight.

"Bloody hell," Jeremy whispered.

Down in the hole were bodies—dried yellow bones, some still covered with leathery flecks of meat—but wedged into the corner, now looking up at them with hateful eyes, was a sight Aaron had never expected to see again.

He had thought them all destroyed, and if not destroyed, sent back to Heaven by his own hand to face the judgment of the Lord, but there was no mistaking the smell of its hate for him . . . for his kind.

An angel of the heavenly host Powers.

"Abomination," he hissed, a mere shell of its former divinity.

And seeing what had been done to the angel that had hunted the Nephilim nearly to extinction . . . Aaron actually felt a tinge of pity.

"That's one of the bastards that was hunting us, isn't it?" Jeremy asked, glaring down into the pit.

Aaron didn't answer, still stunned by the horrific sight.

"I say we leave 'im down there to rot." Jeremy leaned forward to spit into the hole.

Aaron's hand shot out, catching the fluid before it could fall upon the imprisoned angel.

"No" was all he said, the young man's spit sizzling in his hand as it heated, turning to steam. "We're not like them."

Jeremy glared and walked away in a huff.

Aaron then turned to William. "Help me get him out of there."

It wasn't easy, but they managed to haul the injured angel from the death pit. Lying on the ground before them, he was a disturbing sight. It appeared that the trolls had been gradually feeding upon the Powers angel, and the thought nearly made Aaron sick to his stomach.

The angel drifted in and out of consciousness, rambling when awake, cursing the Nephilim's very existence. He called them a blight in the eyes of God.

At least that was what this particular host of angels had believed.

Aaron thought of their leader and felt a chill of fear pass through him. Verchiel had been a formidable foe, and had almost succeeded in unleashing Hell on earth. He had planned to wipe out all life, and allow God the opportunity to start all over. Whether God wanted it or not.

But with the fate of the world hanging by a thread, Aaron had stopped Verchiel, forgiving him his sins and allowing him to return to Heaven to face the judgment of the Creator.

Aaron doubted that the Powers' leader had gotten off easy for what he had intended for the world, and for the many Nephilim that had been murdered over the centuries.

"What are we going to do with him?" Vilma asked, interrupting Aaron's thoughts. Even after what he had said to Jeremy, there was a part of him that wanted to leave the angel to rot in the cavern for all the evil it had done, but Aaron knew that wasn't the answer.

One of the angel's wings had been severed at the shoulder, while the other, which was missing most of its feathers, beat fitfully upon the ground, stirring up clouds of dust.

"He's dying," Aaron said as he knelt beside the trembling creature.

"Looks like he's been doing that for a very long time," Jeremy added from where the others stood. "Maybe we should help him along."

Jeremy's ax sparked and hissed as if eager for the taste of more violence.

Aaron could see the way the Nephilim looked at the Powers angel. Many of them had endured horrors that the hands of these angels had delivered to them, while others had certainly heard the stories. This was a creature whose sole purpose had been to exterminate them. How were they supposed to feel toward it?

"Maybe you're right," Aaron said, staring at the mangled angel on the ground before him.

"You're not going to hurt him . . . are you?" Vilma asked.

It hurt him to have her ask such a thing of him, to think that he might be capable of such an act, but the times they lived in had changed him—it had changed all of them—and he was sure she had seen him do things in battle that had given her pause.

"No," Aaron said with a slight shake of his head. "The exact opposite, really." He held up his hand and felt the power surge to life there. The power to forgive.

The power of redemption that was his gift as the Chosen One.

If the angel before him was filled with repentance, Aaron had the ability to send him back to Heaven.

The Powers angel continued to writhe upon the ground as Aaron placed a softly glowing hand upon his sunken chest. The angel was wearing little more than filthy rags, and Aaron felt the cool touch of his skin through his palm.

The angel stopped his thrashing and looked up into Aaron's face. One of his eyes was missing, but the other fixed upon Aaron intensely.

"What are you?"

"I can send you home," Aaron told him. "Back to—"

"Heaven," the angel finished.

"Yes."

"And what must I do to receive such mercy from the likes of you?" the Powers angel asked.

Aaron sighed, sensing the resentment, the disgust that the angel still held for his kind.

"You have to be sorry," Aaron said.

"Sorry?" the angel asked.

"Sorry for the sins you've committed . . . sorry for all the pain you have caused."

The Powers angel started to laugh, and it was an awful sound. Blood, like black tar, spurted from the sides of his grinning mouth, running down his face. Aaron recoiled.

"When I was taken by these . . . things," the dying angel croaked, blood still filling his throat, "I was searching for the means to see you . . . to see all of you dead."

An icy chill ran down Aaron's spine as he felt the hate that emanated from the angel in waves.

"We lost the battle," the angel said, nodding his head. "But we have not . . . have not lost the war."

Aaron had heard enough. "Verchiel was defeated, sent back to Heaven to face the wrath of the Almighty. The Powers were wrong, and the sooner you accept—"

"Accept?" the angel barked, blood-flecked spittle spraying from his mouth. "There will be no acceptance. As I lay there in the pit, as those beasts feasted upon my flesh, I waited . . . not for my brothers to come, but for the eventual end."

The angel's ignorance was maddening, and it took everything that Aaron had to hold it together. And he needed to hold it together. The others were watching.

"I can't help you. I can't send you home, unless—"

"I have done no wrong," the angel declared, straining with each word. "It was our mission to see the monsters that inhabited His world destroyed."

"And yet, here we are," Aaron said as he stood. He gestured to the other Nephilim. "No matter how misguided you were, your mission has failed."

The angel's one eye darted around as if searching for something.

"They're still out there," the angel whispered to the stone ceiling.

"Who?" Aaron asked. "The Powers? They're gone," Aaron told him again. "The Powers have all been sent back to Heaven to face judgment for their sins." His palm began to radiate a warm glow again, and he held his hand out toward the angel.

"I sent them there."

"Not all," the angel said, violently shaking his head. "Others . . . others still search for the solution . . . the solution to the problem at hand."

Aaron felt his insides twist into a knot. "I don't understand," he said.

"You will," the angel replied, his single eye twinkling maliciously. "But by then it will be too late."

Aaron knelt again beside the angel.

"What are you trying to tell me?" he asked, sensing that the angel was hinting at something very important.

The angel laughed again, sending new rivers of black blood from the corners of his mouth.

"Tell me," Aaron demanded, the power of forgiveness gone from his hands, the warm glow replaced by a far more destructive flame. He brought it close to the angel's face.

"Wormwood," the angel said through a ferocious snarl, batting Aaron's hand away with surprising strength. "Wormwood will take you all."

Then there came a flash of fire from the angel's filthy, mangled hand, as a dagger of heavenly design formed there, a dagger that he plunged into his own throat.

Aaron and the others gasped.

The angel's flesh began to burn, ignited by the blade forged from the fires of Heaven. And soon there was nothing more than smoldering ash, the angel's final words echoing through the underground cavern.

Wormwood.

CHAPTER EIGHT

G abriel was on his elbows, butt in the air, tail wagging furiously from side to side, as he barked at Milton, who scampered around in front him.

"Sometimes it feels like that," Lorelei said, her voice still sounding weak from the wear of Archon magick upon her form. She'd switched from coffee to tea, and was playing with her mug as they sat at one of the long tables in the old science lab, watching the animals.

"Hmm?" Lucifer questioned, looking to the dog and mouse at play.

"The tiny against the large . . . what we're up against . . . it seems so big," Lorelei explained.

"It does, doesn't it," Lucifer replied, now understanding. He brought a fresh cup of Earl Grey to his mouth.

Gabriel had dropped to his side upon the floor, his paws

waving about in play as Milton deftly evaded the dog's attempts to swat at him. The small creature darted through Gabriel's flailing limbs to poke at the dog's black snout with its own, before quickly running away, and then starting the game all over again.

"Our numbers are so small," Lorelei said. "And the threats get bigger and more dangerous."

Lucifer nodded. "More and more every day," the Morningstar said. "Far more than when we first began."

"It's going to come down to us having to pick and choose," the white-haired girl said.

"There was supposed to be more of us," he said sadly. "I'm sure the Almighty never expected the Powers to be quite so efficient with their hunting skills."

"Every week I cast a spell to be certain," she said, picking up her mug with trembling hands and taking a careful sip. "To make sure that there aren't any more of us . . . Nephilim . . . out there alone, needing to understand what is happening to them."

Lucifer didn't expect any more Nephilim would be found, but he guessed there was always a chance, however slim that might be.

He looked at Lorelei and smiled. "There's no harm in trying," he said, even though he knew that anytime Archon magick was called upon, it took its toll on her.

She smiled sadly. "I keep hoping," she said. "Even though deep down I know that we're the only ones left."

They sat in silence then, only Gabriel's heavy breathing filling the air. The Labrador had fallen sound asleep on the floor, the tiny mouse nestled in the fur of his throat, both exhausted by their playful antics.

If only the world could be as peaceful.

"What if we're not strong enough?" Lorelei finally asked.

Lucifer looked at her, not sure how to respond. It was a good question, and one that made him fear for the future.

For even though the Powers were gone, other supernatural threats intensified almost daily, and Lucifer could not help but remember the words spoken to him so very long ago, by a dark-haired child, in the ruins of a temple erected for the worship of some ancient god, long forgotten.

AN UNNAMED ISLAND IN THE AEGEAN SEA, BEFORE THE SINKING OF ATLANTIS

The Morningstar reveled in the silence and the cold dampness of the ancient temple. How long it had been abandoned, what god had been prayed to and sacrificed to here, were mysteries that did not concern him. He had had his fill of gods.

The fallen angel preferred these once-holy places, built to the glory of some heathen deity, the resonance of past worship acting as a kind of buffer, preventing the Powers angels that hunted him from picking up his scent.

He, as with all his fallen brethren, was drawn to the abandoned, the forgotten, finding in those haunted places the refuge that often escaped them.

Lucifer walked the hall of the sanctuary, pondering when last it had seen worshippers. At what appeared to be an altar, the Son of the Morning stopped to study a statue of the temple's lord and master. It was a loathsome sight, its body misshapen and its head adorned with multiple tentacles.

Who . . . or what . . . could worship such a thing? Lucifer wondered as he looked upon it.

"His worshippers called him name N'Ken-Thaa," came a voice from somewhere behind him.

The Morningstar whirled, wings of oily black spread wide in a defensive posture.

"Show yourself," the angel demanded, golden-flecked eyes studying the darkness but finding nothing.

Then a patch of shadow seemed to move as a small shape broke off and advanced toward him. It was a small human child, but something told the Morningstar that looks were deceiving.

"But I doubt that was his name," the child said cheerily. "Or whether or not it could be pronounced by human lips even if they knew it."

The child was barefoot and dressed in simple robes as he approached the altar.

"He was a silly sort," the child continued, staring at the monstrous statue. "Filled with delusions of grandeur."

Lucifer studied the child, or whatever it was. He sensed something unnatural here, and a large sword of fire grew from his hand.

"He was so sad when they stopped worshipping him, stopped believing in him," the child said, shaking his head in sympathy. "He actually thought this world would one day belong to him." He turned his inky-black eyes toward the angel. "Isn't that silly?"

"What are you?" Lucifer demanded angrily.

"Who, me?" the child asked innocently. "I'm nobody now, but someday . . ."

For a brief instant Lucifer saw the child for what he was, and it filled the Son of the Morning with revulsion—and fear.

The angel lashed out with his sword of fire. There was an explosion of searing flame as the sword hit the floor where the child had been standing, its force cracking the marble.

"I'm over here," the child's voice rang out playfully, and Lucifer spun to see the little boy strolling from the darkness between two pillars, completely unscathed.

"You should do something about that temper," the little boy said. "It might get you into trouble someday." He stopped, smiled, and placed a hand over his mouth. "Too late."

Lucifer came at him again, powerful thrusts of his mighty wings hurtled him toward the youth, his flaming sword cutting a swath across the child's throat in an attempt to decapitate him.

But it appeared to have little effect.

"Now is that any way to treat someone who has come to make you an offer?" the child scolded.

Lucifer landed in a crouch, his sword of Heaven's fire still crackling in his hand, still ready to strike.

"What could you offer me?" the Morningstar scoffed.

The child smiled sweetly and faced the altar.

"There will come a day," he began as he waved his hand in front of the monstrous idol of worship, "when the God that has abandoned you will have no power over the earth."

There were sudden snaps and pops as jagged cracks appeared upon the statue's form; pieces dropped off, crumbling as they hit the altar floor, where they then disintegrated.

Lucifer studied the child.

"The messengers of He who believes Himself most holy will no longer believe in Him, and they will attempt to exert their own beliefs on how things should be."

The idol had been reduced to a pile of dust. The object of worship, which once held great power, was now no more.

The child looked at Lucifer.

"And darkness will claim the world."

As the child spoke, Lucifer saw hints of things crawling in the darkness of the boy's mouth, things that wished to remain hidden.

For now.

"And when that time comes, I'll be there to claim what was

always mine . . . what was taken from me when the wretched Creator brought light to the universe."

The words left Lucifer's mouth before he could check them. "And what does that have to do with me?"

"I am the dark, and you are the Son of the Morning," the child said, spreading his arms. "What a world we could build together."

Enraged, Lucifer turned his back on the thing pretending to be a child. "A world that will exist only in your twisted imagination," he said, sensing the boy behind him.

"Perhaps," the child said. "But then again, perhaps not."

Lucifer felt something touch the armor that adorned his back, and suddenly he was so cold that his beautiful form began to tremble. The feeling was like nothing he had ever experienced.

"Time will pass, the world will change, and from the darkness my lesser brethren will emerge, heralds of a new age dawning."

"And then?" Lucifer asked, not turning around.

The child giggled mischievously. "Now that would be telling."

"We can't think like that," Lucifer told Lorelei. The memory of the boy child's promise of a world enshrouded in darkness still left him cold.

There was a time when he had been held captive by the

Powers' leader, Verchiel, when he thought *that* had been the future the child had predicted. Lucifer thought once Verchiel and his plans had been thwarted, the ominous future that had been foretold was moot.

But now he wasn't so sure.

"You look as worried as I feel," Lorelei said.

Lucifer shook his head and smiled, reaching across the table to place his hand upon hers. "We'll be fine," he reassured her. "The other Nephilim get stronger every day, and it won't be long until we're able to send them out individually to deal with some of these manifestations."

"I guess you're right," Lorelei said, forcing a smile of her own. "They can't stay students forever."

"No, they can't," he told her. "Eventually they will have to step up and claim their rightful place as protectors of this world." He gave her hand a squeeze. "Better?"

She nodded. "Thanks," Lorelei said. "When I'm tired, I have a tendency to embrace the doom and gloom."

"Perfectly understandable," Lucifer said. "Archon magick isn't something to be taken lightly. That's some heavy-duty stuff."

He was about to suggest that maybe it would be wise for her to stop using the angel magick so frequently, but never got the chance.

Gabriel sprang up with a loud bark and bounded for the wall of windows.

"*They're back,*" he growled, as Milton scampered back to his master and climbed swiftly up Lucifer's pants leg to take his place upon the fallen angel's shoulder.

The Labrador put his front paws up on the windowsill, peering out intently.

"*And I smell blood,*" the dog said, turning his worried canine gaze to them. "*Somebody is hurt . . . or worse.*"

CHAPTER NINE

Aaron was the first to reach home.

Wings slowly unfurling, he appeared behind the administration building, cradling Janice in his arms. The smell of her blood was overpowering, and it aroused the angelic-warrior essence that was part of him, stirring it to anger. It took everything he had to keep from summoning a blade of fire, and going off to kill something in a fit of rage, as he knelt to lay the girl's body down upon the grass.

But there had already been enough violence.

One after another the Nephilim appeared behind him. William was helping the injured Kirk to stand. They looked as though they'd been through a war, their clothes filthy and torn and spattered with blood, their enemies' as well as their own.

"Get him to Kraus right away," Aaron ordered.

Aaron didn't know the extent of the boy's injuries, but if anyone could treat him, it would be Kraus. The man who acted as their healer had once cared for the health of the Powers, but now he had come over to the side of the Nephilim, using arcane remedies, and perhaps a little bit of angel magick, to care for the ills and injuries of Aaron's small band.

Gabriel's worried bark filled the air, and Aaron glanced over his shoulder to see the animal and Kraus hurriedly moving toward them, Lorelei and Lucifer close behind.

"Take care of Kirk," Aaron said to the healer.

William was practically carrying Kirk, the youth barely conscious as he was helped toward the older man.

"What about Janice?" Lorelei asked.

"It's too late for her," Aaron said, his gaze fixed upon the dead girl on the ground before him. He wanted to look away but couldn't. He had to look at her; he had to remind himself once more of what death looked like.

They all needed to see it.

Lucifer suddenly appeared at Aaron's side, and an overwhelming sadness washed over him, threatening to break Aaron's fragile hold on his emotions.

"She wasn't ready," Aaron said, feeling the heavy responsibility of being a leader. "Maybe if she'd had more training . . . if we'd all had more training . . . I should have—"

His father gripped his shoulder tightly, stopping his words.

"Don't blame yourself," Lucifer said. "You can't second-guess yourself. We all had a hand in this."

Gabriel came up along Aaron's other side, bringing his cool muzzle up to lick his master's ear. *I'm so sorry.*

"I know, Gabe," Aaron said, ruffling the dog's velvety soft ears. "I just wish I could have saved her."

"We did what we could, Aaron," Vilma said. She knelt beside him. "We were in the midst of battle; all of us were fighting for our lives."

"And she lost hers," Aaron said.

"It's going to happen, Aaron," Lucifer said. "Despite what we hope and want."

Aaron wished he could argue, but he knew his father was right. They were at war, and the sad truth was that people died. No matter how young they were, or how special they were supposed to be, they weren't invincible.

And that made him very angry.

A gasp, followed by a familiar chuckle, caught Aaron's attention. Cameron and Jeremy were huddled off to his right, and Cameron was looking at something that Jeremy was showing him. The expression on Cameron's face was one of surprise—and perhaps disgust.

"What is that?" Aaron roared, getting to his feet, pushing past his father, and striding toward the pair.

Cameron immediately stepped away from Jeremy, and Jeremy tried to hide what he was holding behind his leg.

"It's nothing," Jeremy said defiantly, chest puffed out.

"Then why are you hiding it?" Aaron demanded, reaching for Jeremy's wrist and pulling his hand up.

It was a bloody ear from one of the slain trolls.

Aaron couldn't control himself. He lashed out, punching Jeremy in the face and driving him to the ground.

"Is that what you think we are?" Aaron demanded. "Savages taking trophies from the enemies we kill in battle? What were you going to do with that, Jeremy? Make a necklace? You make me sick."

Jeremy, red-faced with fury, threw the bloody ear to the ground. His wings sprang from his back, and sparks of heavenly fire crackled at his fingertips.

"Go ahead," Aaron taunted. "Keep trying to prove that I was wrong about you . . . that you'll never control the power inside you."

The battle-ax flared to life in Jeremy's hand.

"That's enough," Vilma ordered, moving to stand between them.

Always the referee, Aaron thought, recalling that she had been there the last time he and Jeremy had almost come to blows. And then he remembered the sight of the two of them as he'd entered the trolls' chamber, their hands entwined—and the way they'd been looking at each other.

After the day he'd had, Aaron was done with the nonsense.

"I think you should get out of the way," Aaron warned

Vilma, his eyes never leaving Jeremy's. He flexed his shoulders, releasing his own wings.

"Aaron, I know you're upset but—"

"He's been asking for this since he came here," Aaron interrupted.

Vilma seemed taken aback by the cruelty in his voice, and she looked at Aaron in such a way that he felt ashamed.

But not ashamed enough to back down.

"Fine," she snapped angrily. "If you won't listen to me, maybe he will." She turned her back on Aaron to face Jeremy.

"Jeremy, please," she pleaded.

Jeremy's mouth moved, as though he was trying to say something but had trouble forming the words.

"Do you know how hard it is?" he finally blurted out. "How hard I have to work to keep it bottled up inside?"

The ax disappeared from his hand as his wings began to enfold him.

"Every last one of you can go to hell for all I care" were the last words Jeremy spoke as he disappeared within his wings. He was gone.

Vilma turned on her heel, storming past Aaron without even looking at him.

"Something has to be done about him," Aaron said coldly. "He's too unstable . . . dangerous."

"Like I wasn't?" she asked, stopping short. "If I remember correctly, I tried to kill you."

Aaron had nothing to say, choosing not to think about how untamed and extremely dangerous Vilma's angelic nature was when awakened, and how he'd feared that it just might kill her.

He avoided thinking about anything that could possibly take her from his life.

"I'm going after him," she said, and her tone told him that her decision wasn't up for discussion.

Aaron knew he'd been wrong, that anger had gotten the better of him, and he opened his mouth to apologize to her. But she had already spread her wings, wrapping them about her. And then she, too, was gone.

Aaron stood there alone, embarrassed. He saw that Lorelei and the others were seeing to Janice's body as his father came to stand beside him.

"I guess I could have handled that better," he mumbled, watching the others carry the body of the girl toward where they'd decided to store their dead.

Lucifer shrugged. "Do you want to talk about it?"

"I guess that's probably not a bad idea."

It had started to rain, that kind of rain that seemed to bleed through the skin and into the bones.

Dusty felt as though he were ninety, trudging along the lonely side road where his last ride had dropped him.

He'd finally made it to Boston, and was now heading west.

He had no idea where he was going, but the images that played inside his head told him the instrument knew exactly where to take him.

At the faint sound of tires hissing on wet pavement behind him, Dusty turned quickly, sticking out his thumb and hoping that the driver was feeling charitable on such a miserable evening.

A number of cars, vans, and trucks had already passed him by, and he couldn't really blame them. What sane person was out walking the roads in godforsaken weather like this?

Only someone who could summon the end of the world with his harmonica was the insane answer.

As tired as he was, Dusty hated to sleep. His dreams had been filled with the most horrific of sights, almost as if the instrument were showing him how bad the world had become, and that maybe it was time to use the heavenly doomsday device for its rightful purpose.

The world is filled with so many monsters, he thought, pulling the collar of his jacket tighter against the back of his neck in an attempt to keep the water out. He could feel the instrument in his pocket grow warmer in agreement.

Too many monsters.

The old, blind black man hadn't bothered to tell him what a struggle it would be to carry the instrument, that it had a mind of its own. It was a struggle Dusty hoped he could continue to win. That was all he needed—to be responsible for the end of the world.

He passed a particularly dense section of woods and felt cold tendrils of dread vibrate down the length of his spine, and he wondered what could be watching him from the darkness.

He'd noticed that the longer he held the instrument, the more heightened his senses became, making him more aware of the things that hid in the shadows, watching . . . waiting.

Dusty stopped walking, squinting his eyes to peer through the trees, searching for signs of movement. His hand hovered over the harmonica in his coat pocket, ready to take it out, and use it if he had to.

If there really was something there, he couldn't see it.

Again he heard a vehicle approach. Dusty greeted it with his thumb in the air. It was raining harder now, and the cold made his feet feel numb and set his entire body to trembling. *Maybe I'll get a nice bout of pneumonia out of this,* he thought, watching as an old Buick passed him. A doomsday instrument in his pocket and pneumonia in his chest, he couldn't imagine life getting any better than that.

Dusty came to a stumbling halt as the Buick's brake lights flared in the darkness ahead and the old car pulled over to the side of the road, waiting for him.

It took some effort to get his frozen feet moving again, but Dusty managed, running toward the car, hand reaching for the passenger-side door.

It was locked.

Half expecting the car to suddenly peel out, spraying him with gravel and mud, Dusty was tempted to pull the harmonica from its nest and let the old car have it. But the car door clicked, then opened, the ceiling light illuminating the driver, who had leaned over to push open the passenger door.

Dusty angled himself inside.

"Thought you were gonna take off on me," he said, taking a good look at the driver before closing the passenger door and plunging the inside of the vehicle into semidarkness.

"Didn't realize it was locked," the old man said, sounding as though he gargled with broken glass.

His appearance was almost as pleasant as his voice. His hair was a sickly yellowish white, and it looked as though he hadn't had a haircut in quite a few years. His beard was the same yellowish color, stained dark around his dried-looking lips. Dusty guessed that the discoloring was from cigarettes, but the car didn't carry the clinging smell of smoke, only the heavy soup-like aroma of severe body odor.

The old man put the car in drive and maneuvered the vehicle back onto the rain-slick road.

"Thanks for stopping," Dusty said, settling his damp body into the seat to get comfortable. He wedged his duffel bag between him and the passenger door. "I really appreciate it."

"Not a fit night out for man, nor beast," the old man said, glancing quickly at Dusty with a huge smile of large, healthy-looking teeth. "The name's Fred," the man said, taking a hand from the steering wheel and holding it out toward Dusty. "Fred Leclaire."

Dusty returned the smile and took the man's hand. "Hey there, Fred Leclaire," he said. "Dustin Handy, but call me Dusty."

The old man's hand felt like a piece of tree bark, hard and calloused, with an amazing grip.

"Nice to meet you, Dusty," Fred said, finally releasing his hand from the bear-trap grip. "What brings you out here on a night like this?"

"Just traveling," Dusty said, not wanting to get into it. "Going from here to there is all."

Fred grunted with a knowing nod.

"I remember those days," he said affectionately. "It's been a long time since I prowled the back roads."

"You look like the type that might've seen the world," Dusty said. "Am I right? . . . And please feel free to tell me to mind my own business if I'm getting too personal."

The old man laughed, a loud barking sound, like he was about to cough something up. "I have been around a long time and seen this old world go through quite a few changes."

"I'm sure you have," Dusty agreed.

It was raining even harder now, and Fred turned the wipers on faster. Their staccato beat as they passed over the glass was strangely mesmerizing, and Dusty found himself beginning to relax.

Fred laughed that horrible laugh again. "I know I'm gonna sound like the typical old fart, but it was better in the old days."

Dusty smiled. He knew that would be coming. He wanted to keep the old man talking, to help keep him awake. Between the heat in the car and the rhythm of the wipers, he was beginning to feel drowsy.

"How so?" Dusty encouraged him. "What made it so much better?"

Fred seemed to think about the question a bit before answering.

"The food," he said after a moment. "The food was better . . . not as many chemicals." He smacked his lips as if trying to rid his mouth of something foul. "And these days everybody knows everybody's business."

Dusty had to agree with that.

"Cell phones and cable TV, and those computers with the interwebs."

Dusty chuckled at Fred's distaste for technology.

"In my day you could slaughter two or three drifters in a week, and nobody would be the wiser."

It took a second for the words to register.

Slaughter drifters?

Dusty carefully turned to face the old man. His heart was suddenly pounding.

"Don't get me wrong, there's a lot to be said for modern technology," the old man said. "Hell, I would never'a known about you if it wasn't for me having one of those prepaid cell phones."

"Known about me?" Dusty repeated, trying to process Fred's words. He noticed then that the instrument inside his pocket was becoming warmer, as if attempting to warn him of something.

But the warning was too late. The old man changed before his eyes. The crazy yellowish hair turned into a kind of lion's mane; a snout like that of a dog—or better yet, a wolf—slid out from the center of his face.

Before Dusty could even react, Fred lashed out.

A hairy fist struck him square in the face, knocking him violently against the passenger door. The pain was excruciating, and an ocean of darkness threatened to pull him in.

He was trying to turn, fumbling with the door handle to try to escape, but his hands had suddenly lost their bones, becoming like rubber.

"You're a tough one," Fred said, holding the steering wheel steady with one clawed hand as he leaned across and drew back a hairy fist to punch Dusty again.

There was another brief explosion of agony and color, followed by the bliss of nothing.

The darkness claimed him.

Fred kept glancing at the boy as he drove, looking for signs that he might be still awake, but Dusty was out cold. The smell of the boy's blood, which streamed from his nose and split lip, was maddening as it filled the car. Now in his true form of a beast, Fred was tempted to take just a taste but thought better of it. He didn't want any trouble from the Corpse Riders, just their reward money. So with regret, he left the boy intact.

Fred pulled the car off to the side of the road and put the Buick in park. He tilted his large bulk to one side, fishing in his pocket for the cell phone. He pulled out the foul piece of technology, snarling as he tried to remember how to make a call, then placed the phone to a pointed ear.

There was a click followed by an eerie silence, but Fred knew there was somebody on the other end.

"I have him," Fred said.

The response that followed was like the cries of infants being thrown into a meat grinder, and Fred quickly pulled the phone away from his ear.

He wasn't sure about the noise, but he guessed they were happy with the news.

It took Vilma a second to figure out exactly where she was. She'd appeared before Jeremy, who crouched atop an egg-shaped capsule that was part of the giant Ferris wheel called the London Eye.

The weather was quite miserable, but the view through the fog and rain was still both breathtaking and a little bit terrifying as the wheel slowly turned. She watched a barge carrying multicolored storage containers move leisurely along the river Thames below. Vilma had seen pictures of the Eye, and had always wanted to go on the ride that provided such a spectacular view of the old city.

In an odd way, now she was getting her wish.

"This is nice," she said, wings fluttering as she tried to maintain her balance atop the slick glass-and-metal oval. The sightseers inside the pods had a spectacular view of the city and the river below but thankfully couldn't see her and Jeremy as they stood on the metal roofing. If she strayed too close to the side though, there was a chance some tourist would see the bottom of her foot. That was something she didn't need right now.

"You shouldn't have followed me," Jeremy said. He sat on his haunches, hugging his knees to his chest, looking straight ahead and squinting through the rain.

"We need to go back," Vilma said. She raised her wings ever so slightly to protect her face from the wind and storm. "Lorelei's spells won't hide us this far from home."

"Home?" Jeremy scoffed. "You must be joking." Then he wrapped himself in his wings once again, and was gone, the sudden displacement of his weight causing the Eye's capsule to pitch and roll.

Vilma tumbled backward, her sneakered feet sliding from the slick metal roof of the egg, but she remained calm, closing her eyes as she fell, and feeling the trail left by the Nephilim she was following. Her wings hugged her tight, and she disappeared as well.

She reappeared beside Jeremy on a residential street. From the looks of the buildings and the cars, she guessed they were still in England.

Jeremy stood on the narrow sidewalk, staring at a building across the street; the houses were built extremely close together, one seeming to blend into the next with little separation.

"Jeremy, please," Vilma said.

"This was home," he told her, nodding his head toward the building. "Well, as close to one as I can remember, anyway."

She didn't know what to say, sensing a melancholy coming over him to replace the anger from before.

"I wish I could be back there again."

Vilma understood. She, too, remembered a better time . . . an easier time, before her angelic heritage reared its head and changed her world.

"But it wasn't real," Jeremy continued, turning his troubled gaze to her. He smiled sadly and shrugged. "It was just as mucked up then; I just believed what she was telling me."

She was about to ask *who* was telling him when he was gone again.

With an exasperated sigh, Vilma followed, to a sprawling lawn of green in front of an old stone building. A white sign, lit by twin spotlights, read STEWARD PSYCHIATRIC FACILITY.

"Let's see if she's in," Jeremy said. Then he disappeared as his wings enfolded his body.

Suddenly they were beside a hospital bed, in the quiet of a darkened room. The muted sounds from the hallway filtered through the closed door as they looked down on the tiny form of an older woman sleeping fitfully in the bed.

Vilma was about to ask Jeremy who this woman was, when she stirred, and fixed them both in a wide-eyed stare.

The woman looked as though she might scream, and then a toothless smile spread upon her aged features.

"Jeremy?" she asked with a croak, moving to sit up in her bed while clutching the nightgown at her throat.

"Yeah, Mum, it's me."

CHAPTER TEN

An angel of the Powers . . . really?" Lucifer asked from his seat behind the large metal desk. He scratched his cheek in thought as Milton perched upon his shoulder sniffing his ear. "I thought we had killed most, and you sent the rest back to Heaven."

"I did too," Aaron said. He was feeling overwhelmed. It was turning out to be the kind of day that he'd been hoping against. "But there was no doubt what he was."

So much for evil taking a skip day.

His father seemed deep in thought. "I suppose the trolls could have had him for a while."

"I guess," Aaron answered. "But he seemed to know about Verchiel failing, and he mentioned something about Wormwood . . . whatever the heck that is."

Aaron suddenly noticed Lucifer staring at him intently.

"What did you say?" his father asked.

"I said he seemed to know about Verchiel."

"After that," Lucifer demanded, pulling his chair up tight to the desk and leaning forward.

"He mentioned something about Wormwood."

"Are you sure?" Lucifer pressed.

"Yeah," Aaron answered. "It was definitely Wormwood. Why? What is it?"

"Something very bad . . . something I did not want to hear," Lucifer said, reaching up to take Milton from his shoulder. "And it's not a what, it's a who." He absently stroked the mouse's head and back with his finger.

"A who?"

Lucifer slowly nodded, staring past Aaron into space.

"A terrible angel," he said. "A terrible angel with a terrible purpose."

Lucifer's eyes shifted back to Aaron's, locking on them with a frightening intensity.

"A purpose to bring about the end of the world."

Their sadness summoned Gabriel like a whistle. He was drawn to it. He padded down the hallway in the building that served as the group's makeshift hospital, under the supervision of the human called Kraus, heading toward the Nephilim.

Gabriel considered all of them a part of his pack. Now he could sense their sorrow, and had come to provide them solace.

The remaining Nephilim were standing in the hallway outside the room where Kraus was tending to the injured Kirk. Their grief was nearly palpable, washing over Gabriel in waves as he watched them.

Since he had been struck by a car and Aaron had fixed him, Gabriel had found himself changing more and more as time passed. He was smarter now, able to understand more complicated concepts and situations, and he had the unique ability to help take others' pain away. His presence was a comfort to those feeling physical pain, as well as mental pain, and he had come to alleviate the suffering of his pack.

Many of the Nephilim were crying, others attempting to hold on to their pain. Some stood off by themselves, while others attempted to console one another.

Walking amongst them, Gabriel fixed them each with his dark, soulful stare, willing them to surrender their worry for Kirk's injuries and their sorrow at Janice's death.

Gabriel had liked Janice. She often gave him part of her lunch, and when they were alone, she would read him poetry that she had written. He, too, would miss her, but would honor her by helping the other pack members to surrender their sorrows.

William held back his tears as Gabriel looked up and stared into his eyes. Haltingly, William reached down to stroke Gabriel's blocky head, and then the tears came, flooding from the teen in pitiful sobs.

Yes, that's it, the Labrador thought. *Let it out. It's not good to hold all that sadness inside.*

William was but the first. As each of them sensed why Gabriel was there, they came to him, one after another, patting his head or wrapping their arms around his thick neck to hug him, burying their tears in his yellow fur. Cameron, Melissa, Samantha, and Russell: they tried to hold back, to keep their sadness, but it was too much for them.

And Gabriel took their burden willingly.

They were all petting him now, their souls soothed by his presence.

Gabriel looked toward the closed door, sensing that his work was not yet done. He left the attentions of the others, heading to the door. He reached out and scratched the door with his front paw, before turning his gaze to his pack.

Samantha approached, her eyes still moist with tears, and she opened the door to Kraus's place, where he was caring for Kirk.

But the Lab could sense that the boy was beyond Kraus's help, and that it was time for Gabriel to do what he could.

What he had to do.

For most of his life, Kraus had been blind, but a miracle in the form of the Powers' insane leader, Verchiel, had been given to him, and now he could see.

But there were times such as this that he wished he couldn't.

Kraus could see that the boy's life was slipping away. Kirk's flesh grew paler by the second as the blood from his wounds saturated the bandages. No matter what he did, Kraus could not stop the bleeding. They'd told him a troll spear had pierced the boy's side, and he had to wonder if the metal of the blade was in some way enchanted, preventing his skills—and even some of his own medicinal magicks—from working upon the injury.

Kirk was dying.

"I'm not going to give up on you," the healer said, quickly moving away from the table and toward the back of the room, where he kept some of his stronger medicines.

He had once cared for the wounds of the Powers, full-blooded angels of Heaven, and some of the medicines that he had in his possession had been concocted for their supernatural constitutions. They were far too strong for humans, and even Nephilim, but if there was the slightest chance . . .

He studied the jars upon the shelves, remembering their purpose, before grabbing hold of a particular glass container. The doctor returned to the youth, hearing with disturbing acuity his shallow breaths but also seeing that he was no longer alone with the boy.

Gabriel stood there, below the table.

"I think I can save him," Kraus told the dog.

Gabriel whined sadly as if to say it was too late.

"The medicine contained within the jar is a supercoagulant," he explained to the animal. "It's able to stop the bleeding of the most severe of wounds."

Kraus leaned in close as he twisted the lid from the jar.

"Hang on, Kirk," he said. "I think I have something here that will fix you up."

Kraus dipped his fingers into the noxious-smelling ooze and was about to bring it toward the open puncture wound in the boy's stomach when Kirk stopped him.

The grip on his wrist was weak, but Kraus understood its intentions.

Kirk himself knew there would be no saving him from his injuries, that he had fought it long enough and was ready to rest.

"Are you sure?" Kraus asked, already knowing the answer.

Gabriel stood on his hind legs, his front paws resting on the table's edge, and brought his face close to the boy's, licking his cheek.

Kraus sensed a change in the energy of the room; a certain calmness radiated outward from the young Nephilim as he accepted his fate.

"I'm . . . scared," Kirk said, his voice sounding as if it were coming from the far end of a very long tunnel.

"Don't be," Kraus said. "Nothing is going to hurt you anymore."

Gabriel brought his snout down the boy's arm and burrowed his nose beneath so that Kirk's hand rested upon his blocky head. Kirk feebly began to pet the dog, the act seeming to take away his fear.

And Kirk let go. All of his pain, all of his fear, gone in an instant.

"I tried," Kraus murmured, reaching out to grasp the boy's other hand in his, but he knew that sometimes it wasn't enough.

That sometimes surrender was the only answer.

THE ARDÈCHE DEPARTMENT OF SOUTHERN FRANCE
THE CHAUVET—PONT—D'ARC CAVE
1312 FEET UNDERGROUND

There were monsters in the earth.

Geburah and his brothers could feel them all around, slumbering in the cold, wet depths, waiting for their time to rise.

"Why have you brought us here?" the Powers angel Huzia asked, a look of absolute revulsion upon his perfectly chiseled features.

A thing of beauty amongst the ugliness of the subterranean chamber, Geburah thought of his brother.

It was indeed a nasty place, not fit for any life molded by the hands of God. But he had not brought them here for anything to do with beauty.

It was an unpleasant task before them . . . unpleasant, but necessary to their goals.

"We should be out searching for the instrument," Anfial

added, fluttering his mighty wings before drawing them tight upon his back.

Geburah understood their impatience, but there was a method to his madness, a reason he had brought them deep within the bowels of the earth.

"The instrument hides itself from us," Geburah said, placing his hand upon the cool wet stone of the underground chamber. "It does not wish to be found."

"All the more reason why we should be searching for it," Huzia snapped.

Geburah could feel the presence within the walls and beneath their feet. The *things* there were stirring, roused by the presence of the Divine.

"The Corpse Riders have sworn that they will find it," Geburah said. The words felt dirty upon his tongue, but the alliance with the repellent creatures had proven itself a necessity.

"Corpse Riders," Tandal roared, heavenly fire sparking from the tips of his long fingers. "I cannot believe that we do not choke upon their loathsome name. Messengers of Heaven allied with such foul things—it appears that we have fallen far lower than the creatures we once hunted."

Geburah sympathized with his brother's distaste, but things were different now. With Verchiel gone, a new dynamic had been introduced to the planet. A new dynamic to which they must adapt, or risk failing in their mission.

"War creates strange bedfellows," Geburah stated with

finality, turning to fix his men in an authoritative stare. He understood their unrest, but he was still their superior, and they would follow him without reproach.

"Though the instrument can mask its location, it cannot alter the purpose for which it was created."

His brothers were now paying less attention to their vile surroundings and more to him.

"It was fashioned by the Lord God to bring about the end of this world," Anfial informed. "An instrument to summon Wormwood, the Abomination of Desolation, to perform its final task."

Geburah nodded ever so slightly and began to pace slowly in front of his soldiers.

"A powerful tool, with a certain degree of sentience," the Powers' leader explained.

The angels listened, curiosity twinkling in the depths of their predator eyes.

"The instrument is reactionary," Geburah went on. "Responding to the world in which it lives."

He paused to see if they would catch on to what he was planning, but they showed no spark of recognition.

"We must show the instrument a world ripe for destruction," he told them.

The Powers angels looked at one another, still not quite registering what it was that Geburah proposed.

"Whoever possesses the instrument holds sway over its

destructive potential," Suria said. "It is he who must sound the call to summon the Angel of Destruction."

Geburah smiled, pleased that at least one of his soldiers seemed to be following the right train of thought.

"Yes," he said. "And what have we learned about the latest guardian of the instrument?"

"A human male," said Tandal.

Geburah nodded. "A lowly human male who had this great responsibility thrust upon him only weeks ago. A lowly human male without the centuries of fortitude needed to fight the will of the instrument."

Shebniel smiled cruelly, beginning to understand. "The instrument must know what we already know," the sadistic angel said.

"That it is too late for this world," Suria added.

Geburah concentrated briefly, summoning a mighty blade of divine flame. The gases within the air of the cavern ignited as the sword grew to life, filling the chamber with roiling fire.

The angels reveled in the divine inferno, the intensity of the heat having no effect upon them, but having an effect upon the subterranean environment, and the life-forms that slumbered there.

The walls began to crack; the stone floor beneath their feet started to bubble and roil as what lay hidden below began to awaken.

"We must show the instrument a world rife with evil,"

Geburah said as he spun the sword around in his hand until the blade was pointing down toward the ground. "And in order for that evil to flourish"—the Powers' leader knelt and plunged the divine blade of fire into the floor of the cavern—"we must awaken it."

The chamber of fire shuddered and shook, the ceiling above the angels' heads crumbling, as things not seen upon the earth for countless millennia emerged.

From the floor, something ancient, powerful, and larger than all the rest pushed itself up from the depths.

Something reptilian was roused from its slumber by the prodding of a heavenly blade.

CHAPTER ELEVEN

Jeremy's mother attempted to reposition the pillows at her back. She was having quite a bit of difficulty, but Jeremy did nothing, choosing instead to watch her struggle.

"What's wrong with you?" Vilma asked, moving closer to the bed. "Why aren't you helping her?"

Vilma reached down and slid her hands beneath the woman's spindly arms. "Here, let me help you," she said as she assisted the frail woman to a sitting position. Then she slid two pillows behind her back and allowed her to recline.

"How's that?" Vilma asked with a smile.

Jeremy's mother returned the expression, her moist eyes twinkling.

"Oh, you're pretty," the old lady observed. "Wings of snow white is what you have . . . beautiful wings."

Vilma stepped back, startled by the woman's observation.

"How does she . . . ?" Vilma began.

"She's always seen things," Jeremy said. "It's just that sometimes they're actually there, while others . . ." He shook his head and then shrugged.

"Can she see yours?" Vilma asked.

The old woman was looking at him now, smiling a toothless grin.

"I'd imagine," he answered.

Jeremy looked his mother in the eye. "Isn't that right, Mom? You can see my wings, right?"

"Oh, yes," she said happily. "Yours are pretty too, dear, no need to be jealous."

She looked down at her withered hands resting atop her blanket and gasped.

"Rings," she said, holding up her empty hands. "So many rings."

"What's wrong with your mother, Jeremy?" Vilma asked.

"What isn't wrong with her?" he replied. "She was diagnosed as schizophrenic when I was a kid, and that's just the tip of the iceberg."

"I'm sorry," Vilma said. The old woman was still admiring her many invisible pieces of jewelry, muttering to herself about how they would need to be cleaned if she was to be presentable for the ceremony.

"No bother," he said. "It's just how she is."

His mother stopped looking at her imaginary accessories

and let her hands drop to her lap. A strange look came over her face.

"Have you come to take me home, baby?" she asked. "Mummy's all better now. We can start again, nice and fresh, just the two of us."

Jeremy laughed, but there was no humor in it.

"Sorry," he said, glancing at Vilma before looking away. "That's what she always used to say when I visited as a lad. She always said that she was better, and that things would be different." He stared at the woman, his anger and hurt almost palpable. "But they never were."

The woman's mood seemed to change suddenly, a near feral sneer appearing upon her gaunt features. "You put me here," she accused. "You put me here, and you can take me out."

Jeremy slowly shook his head as he stared at her. "No, Mum, you put yourself here."

She looked around the room as if suddenly hearing something, and her expression changed from one of anger to one of fear.

"There isn't much time," she said nervously. "They're waking up and coming into the light. What chance do we have?"

Vilma reached down to lay her hand over the woman's. "It's going to be all right," she said in an attempt to comfort her.

Jeremy's mother stared into her eyes momentarily.

"Oh, no, dear, you're wrong," she said. "It'll never be all right again."

"Can you imagine what I went through?" Jeremy said.

Vilma glanced from the woman to him.

"When this . . ." He pointed to his chest, moving his finger in a circular motion. "When this thing inside me came awake?"

Vilma said nothing, choosing instead to listen.

"I thought I was losing it," he said, his voice tight and filled with emotion. "I thought I was becoming like her."

His mother laughed as if he'd just told the funniest joke in the world.

"But then your boyfriend showed up and proved me wrong," Jeremy said, glaring at his mother. "And now I don't know which is worse." He brought a trembling hand up to rub his face. "To be completely insane, or to have something inside you so powerful that it threatens to eat you alive."

Vilma left the woman and moved to stand beside Jeremy.

"And that's why you came with us," she said quietly. "We're helping you to learn to control your angelic heritage."

"Some days," he said. "Some days it feels like it's going to explode out of me, and there isn't anything I can do to stop it."

Aaron had always sensed that the angelic essence inside of Jeremy was one of the wilder they'd encountered, and would require special guidance. They'd thought he was doing better, but she now realized that they had been wrong.

Vilma reached out and took hold of Jeremy's elbow.

"We're not giving up on you," she said.

Jeremy looked at her. "Does your boyfriend feel the same way?" he asked. "Or is he just waiting until he has an excuse to put me out of my misery—and his, too?"

Occasionally, when a young Nephilim's power ran out of control, when the angelic influence overwhelmed the human conscience, and the Nephilim became a danger, it had been necessary to kill the Nephilim. It was always a last resort, and none of them ever talked about such things.

Although they all knew it happened.

"You know we wouldn't do that unless . . ."

"Unless I was out of control," Jeremy said. "Like how I was in the mines today . . . like when I cut the ear from a dead troll's head."

"We'll help you," Vilma stressed, giving his arm a gentle squeeze. "But you're going to have to let us."

He'd closed his eyes and was standing perfectly still.

"I so want to believe you."

"What do you have to lose?" Vilma asked.

Jeremy's mother tossed back her covers, exposing her skeletal frame.

"What does it matter?" his mother asked, throwing her bare feet over the side of the bed. "Once the darkness falls, there won't be anyplace for the likes of us."

Jeremy acted then, intercepting the woman before she could stand.

"Now that's enough of that," he told her, gently maneuvering her back into bed.

His mother was becoming agitated.

"It doesn't matter what you do . . . what we do. . . . It'll all end the same!" she cried.

Vilma looked toward the small glass window in the door for signs of a nurse or an orderly, certain they were going to be discovered. "We should probably leave now."

Jeremy reached down and took hold of his mother's ankles, picking her legs up, swinging them back onto the bed. Then he pulled the blankets up and covered her.

"I want you to stay in bed," he instructed her firmly.

She reached up to cup his cheek in her hand. "You're really a good boy, at heart," she told him. "It's too bad that doesn't matter . . . that we're all going to Hell."

And with that, she squirmed down beneath the covers, pulling the blanket tightly under her chin.

Jeremy seemed shaken by his mother's message as he went to stand beside Vilma.

"Are you all right?" she asked him.

He stared at his mother, who looked back from the bed, her wide eyes twinkling with madness.

"Couldn't be better," Jeremy said as his wings emerged, then closed about him.

Vilma summoned her own wings, giving Jeremy's mother one final glance before she, too, took leave.

"See, beautiful wings of snow white," the woman whispered as her hand sneaked out from beneath the blankets to wave good-bye.

With the angels gone, Jeremy's mother slipped from her bed and padded across the cold floor.

She stopped for a moment where her son and the girl had just been standing and stuck out her tongue. She smacked her lips, tasting the magick of their departure which lingered in the air, and then, as it faded from her mouth, she turned her attention to the door to the room.

She'd sensed the arrival of the new patient, a girl, as soon as she'd entered the building, like somebody eagerly tickling her, only from the inside.

The woman tiptoed up to the door and peered cautiously through the small window at the darkened hall outside her room. It was empty except for a small table and chair, where an orderly usually sat, listening for sounds of nighttime distress from behind the closed doors that lined each side of the hall. The fluorescent light in the ceiling flickered like a strobe light, casting everything in dancing shadows.

Dancing shadows, she mused. *The world will soon be engulfed in dancing shadows.*

Jeremy's mother waited, sensing that it wouldn't be long now. And she was right.

She heard the girl's cries like a distant memory. They were

so familiar, they could have been her own. But they grew louder as they came closer to her room.

Ducking to the other side of the doorway, she could see down the opposite end of the corridor. There was a flurry of activity, doctors and nurses surrounded a wheelchair that was being pushed by one of the larger orderlies. In that chair sat a young lady. The one that she'd sensed. A young lady who moaned and cried as she clutched her pregnant belly.

"I don't know what's happening," the girl wailed as she was wheeled down the hall. The staff ignored her as they talked amongst themselves, studying clipboards of information.

"I'm only sixteen. I've never . . . how can I be having a baby?"

Jeremy's mother crouched under the window as they passed her room, only standing again when they'd gone by.

It's happening sooner than expected, she thought.

The doctors and their patient disappeared through the swinging doors on their way to the hospital's basement level.

That was where it would happen.

That was where *he* would arrive.

She felt a sudden chill pass through her skeletal frame, and she walked back to her bed. It would be warm there.

Crawling beneath the covers, she imagined how it would soon be, lulling herself quickly to sleep with thoughts of a world filled with shadows.

Dancing shadows.

* * *

The Morningstar hadn't thought of the mysterious dark-haired child in more than a millennium, and now here he was, thinking of him for a second time today.

"There will come a day," the child had said, *"when the God that has abandoned you will have no power over the earth. The messengers of He who believes Himself most holy will no longer believe in Him, and they will attempt to exert their own beliefs on how things should be."*

Lucifer felt a cold, painful knot forming in the pit of his stomach as he heard the child's voice echoing from the past.

"And darkness will claim the world."

"Father?"

Lucifer spun toward the voice, his imagination conjuring the dark-haired child, a telling smile upon his beatific face.

"You okay?" Aaron asked.

"I'm fine," he answered, attempting to shake off the effects of the chilling memory.

"We were talking about the end of the world, and you got sort of quiet." His son paused, considering what he'd just said. "I guess that's kind of appropriate." The boy smiled weakly, attempting to lighten the pall of foreboding that hung about the room.

"You don't think the Powers are still around, do you?" Aaron asked him.

"Possibly a smaller faction," Lucifer replied. "Separated

from the rest perhaps. Sleepers, ordered to fulfill a specific task if Verchiel should fail."

He saw a look of desperation appear upon his son's face.

"What is it with them?" Aaron asked angrily. "They'd rather end the world than have us in it? I just don't get it."

Lucifer could understand his son's frustration but could also identify with the Powers' obsession, for he, too, had acted upon his own beliefs—though wrong—starting a war in Heaven with his Creator.

Only, he had learned the error of his ways, while the Powers just became more fixated. So beset, they were now willing to end the world in order to prove that they were right.

"They believe the Nephilim are a blight upon the planet, an insult to the Lord God, and have concocted a plan to see themselves victorious even if it means destroying all life upon the planet. Insane? Most definitely, but they see this as a final way to steal victory from defeat."

Aaron considered his father's words.

"I still don't see how they believe that they're carrying out God's will by destroying the earth."

The ball of tension grew tighter in the Morningstar's stomach.

"Perhaps they no longer serve the Lord of Lords, feeling somehow betrayed by the fact that He initially allowed them to fail. Perhaps now they serve their own selfish purpose."

"The messengers will no longer believe in Him," Lucifer heard the childlike voice echo in his mind.

Is this what the dark-haired boy foretold? Lucifer pondered. *Is this the beginning of the end of the world, a prologue to dark times to come?*

"We're going to stop them, right?" Aaron asked.

"Of course," Lucifer agreed, shaking off the distraction.

He pushed his chair back and moved around the desk, sitting on its corner as he thought about their situation.

"In order for Wormwood to be awakened, the Almighty created something called the instrument, which, when played, will signal the Angel of Desolation."

"The instrument," Aaron repeated. "Do you mean like Gabriel's horn?"

"That's exactly what I mean," Lucifer said. "It started off in Gabriel's possession but then found its way into the hands of different owners. Their job has been to watch and wait for a sign that it is time for the world to end."

"Any idea who has it now?" Aaron asked.

Lucifer shook his head. "No. But if I don't, then there's a good chance that the Powers don't either. And that will hopefully buy us some time."

"We're going to have to find whoever has it before they do," Aaron said.

Lucifer slid from the desk. His brain felt like a nest of hornets, so much information flying around, buzzing for his attention.

"Something that divine . . . that powerful . . . must leave

some kind of trail," Lucifer said. He stroked his chin in thought.

"If that was the case, wouldn't the Powers be able to track it as well?" Aaron asked.

"Good point," the Morningstar said. "But if they had been able to trace it, wouldn't we all be dead by now?"

"So it doesn't leave a trail," Aaron said.

"Or it does, and it's masked in some way."

"Then if it's masked, how would we find it?" Aaron wanted to know.

"Only the most sensitive could track something with the kind of power that instrument possesses," Lucifer said. He went to the window and gazed out over the school grounds. Everything appeared so peaceful, but under the surface . . .

"Powerful magick is needed here," Lucifer said, though the statement made him sorry. Lorelei didn't need this added on top of everything else she was doing.

"Archon magick," he said, turning from the window.

From the look on Aaron's face, he knew his son understood the ramifications of what he was about to ask.

"We have to talk to Lorelei," Aaron said.

Lucifer nodded sadly. "She's the only one with the talent to help us."

Vilma followed Jeremy's trail to the school, and as she unfurled her wings, she found herself back where they had started.

Jeremy was just standing in the grassy area, head down, his

hands hanging loosely by his sides. His wings were growing smaller now, disappearing into his shoulders.

"Jeremy?" she asked, and as the word left her mouth, he turned and stepped toward her, his hands suddenly on her shoulders, drawing her gently closer.

He was about to kiss her, and she felt herself responding, reacting to the moment as if on some sort of autopilot. Vilma wrestled with these instincts, pushing them aside before things could get out of hand. She turned her face away from his, and Jeremy released her, stepping back.

"I'm sorry," Jeremy stammered, instantly embarrassed. "That was bloody stupid, and inappropriate. I'm really, really sorry."

"It's all right," Vilma answered awkwardly. She felt ashamed, even though nothing had happened. *But what if it had?* She had no idea why she had reacted in such a way. It was as if something had taken her over, like some sort of switch had been thrown, and she was doing what she was supposed to do.

But that shouldn't have been it at all. Jeremy was a close friend, and she'd never really thought of him in any other way. She felt her body break out in a warm, tingling flush as the image of his lips coming closer to hers appeared in her head again.

"I never was really good with my emotions," he attempted to explain. "And this business with my mum . . . damn it, I can be so dumb sometimes."

"It's fine," Vilma told him, still flustered and wanting to pretend that it hadn't happened . . . but could she? "A misunderstanding that's already forgotten."

"Forgotten by you," he said with a weak laugh. "I'd be lying if I told you that I didn't want it to happen . . . that I didn't want to kiss you."

"Jeremy . . . ," Vilma began. She felt it again, that twinge of heat, the beginning of desire. She didn't like it, not one little bit.

"I was hoping for a better outcome, but it is what it is. You're smitten with our fearless leader, which is fine. But you can't blame a guy for trying."

She forced herself to laugh. The emotionally damaged guy, true to form, returning to the protective armor of his edgy cockiness.

"If Mr. Tall-Dark-and-Chosen ever disappoints . . ."

"Stop," she said, wanting him to quit before she forgot that she'd actually felt sorry for him not that long ago. They started to walk toward the classroom building to find the others when they saw Aaron standing there.

"Speak of the Devil's son and he appears," Jeremy said with a smirk.

"Aaron," Vilma said, trying not to feel guilty but having a tremendously difficult time. "We were just heading in to find everyone."

How long has he been standing there? She would have to

talk to him later, try to explain what Jeremy had shared with her while they were away—and what he might have seen moments ago.

But could she explain it without hurting him in some way? It was complicated, and Vilma wasn't even sure if she could explain it to herself.

"I was on my way to see Lorelei," Aaron said. "Why don't you come with me and I'll fill you in as to what's going on."

Vilma cringed as she joined Aaron, half expecting Jeremy to throw out some wiseass comment to add more tension to the situation.

But Jeremy remained strangely quiet, although she could feel his eyes upon them, even after they were out of view.

CHAPTER TWELVE

Fred carried the unconscious Dusty up the back steps and into the kitchen of his home.

The place was a mess and stank of rot. The sink was piled high with dirty dishes; a cloud of flies buzzed around the bare ceiling bulb. He'd never quite gotten a handle on keeping a clean house, believing it to be women's work.

And every time he tried to find that special someone to help take care of him and his home, well, his more bestial nature had always gotten the better of him.

A full belly always won out over a clean kitchen.

Still maintaining his animalistic form, Fred hauled Dusty into the living room and dumped him on the filthy floor.

He looked around the house with his feral eyes, sniffing the air with his long snout to be sure he was still alone.

There was nothing unusual in the air, only the scent of the

boy, the stink of decay, and his own familiar musky smell. The Corpse Riders had yet to arrive.

Fred returned his attention to the young man at his feet.

"Don't look too special to me," the beast growled, a thick pink tongue snaking across his sharp teeth.

But the boy was special. Word had gone out through the unnatural community, to all the denizens of the dark. The Corpse Riders were looking for a lone boy who stank of ancient power.

Fred sniffed at the boy again. The smell was most certainly there. There was no mistaking that he had hit the jackpot.

The Corpse Riders had put out the cry, claiming the boy could be the key to the community's continued existence upon the planet. Fred had even heard rumors that the peacocks—those winged cretins, the angels—were somehow involved.

Fred coughed up a wad of phlegm and spat it on the floor.

But there was no doubt; if the peacocks were involved, then it had to be pretty darn important, especially if they were rubbing elbows with Corpse Riders.

Dusty twitched and moaned, still held in the grip of oblivion, and Fred considered getting some rope to tie the kid up, just in case he awoke.

With a clawed hand he stroked his hairy chin. *What to do?*

The kid's heavy leather jacket was open, and he could sense something powerful from somewhere inside the coat. It was probably what everybody was looking for, whatever that was.

The beast-man tilted his head, trying to see into the darkened folds of the jacket, hoping for a glimpse of something that might shed some light on the mysterious possession.

Fred couldn't see a thing, but whatever was inside that jacket was giving off a kind of aura, a steady heartbeat of power that made the air around the unconscious boy thrum.

The wind howled outside, the heavy rain pattering against the side of the ramshackle house. There was the steady *drip, drip, drip* from a leak in the dining room ceiling behind him. The house was falling down around his pointed ears. He could certainly use the reward money that was promised.

Fred figured his parents had still been around the last time anything was done to this house, and he had killed them almost twenty-five years ago.

"What do you have?" he asked the young man on the floor with a curious growl. Using the toe of his boot, he kicked at Dusty's side, hoping to feel something. Getting no satisfaction from that, he again looked around the room, extending his preternatural senses outward to test his surroundings. As far as he could tell, he was still alone.

Nervously Fred knelt beside the boy. A tiny voice in his head that sounded an awful lot like his mother warned him not to attempt what he was about to do, but he'd never paid much attention to his mother. Hell, she'd had relations with a werewolf. Why would he ever even think about listening to a word she had to say, never mind the fact that she'd been dead and gone for a very long time.

"Just a peek," he grumbled. He could feel the pulse of power from within the folds of the jacket; it made the yellowish, coarse hair on the back of his hands stand up as if charged with static electricity.

Plunging his hand inside, he fished around, searching for a pocket. When he found it, he reached in, his clawed fingertips brushing against something hard. He eagerly grabbed hold and pulled it out so he could see.

For a moment he was holding a harmonica. *Is this what everyone's so fired up about?* he wondered. Then what appeared to be a simple mouth organ became something else entirely. Fred was suddenly holding a piece of the sun. It burned like nothing he'd ever felt before, worse than silver—and silver was the most painful thing of all.

The beast-man shrieked, trying to let go, but he couldn't. The flesh of his hand melted into a giant, dripping ball—the source of the most intense agony he'd ever experienced trapped within it.

Fred thrashed his hand about, attempting to loosen the object, but his hand was aflame now, burning like the head of a torch doused in gasoline. The pain was too much, and he dropped to the floor beside the unconscious Dusty, trying to put out the fire.

"This is your fault!" Fred cried as his hand blackened

and thick oily smoke started to fill the air. A spastic movement caused his hand to bang against the wood of the living room floor, and the wolf-man watched in shock as the hand crumbled to ash. The harmonica that glowed white with the intensity of Hell dropped harmlessly to the floor.

Fred clutched the oozing stump of his wrist, staring in wonder at where his hand used to be. He had been warned not to touch anything, but did he listen?

His mind racing, he was thinking about running to the bathroom upstairs for bandages, or at least some kind of anti-bacterial ointment, when he heard the sounds. Hugging the stump to his chest, Fred listened to feet thumping up wooden steps. The smell of rotting flesh and decay permeated his nostrils, eclipsing the smell of his own burning flesh. He knew he was no longer alone in the house.

His guests had made their way up from the cellar.

The Corpse Riders had arrived.

For a moment Dusty thought he was awake. He wasn't sure where he was, exactly, but he knew he wasn't alone.

He felt as if he was lost in a fog; the air was thick with a roiling, moist smoke that swirled about his face, blinding him to his surroundings. He was trying to remember what had happened when the fog lifted and he found himself standing in front of a diner.

He knew this place, but he didn't really know why. It didn't

THOMAS E. SNIEGOSKI

look at all familiar to him. He dug through memories of all the little restaurants where he had worked or visited for a quick bite, but he couldn't quite place this one.

It looked crowded, but as he approached the large plate-glass window, he saw a figure sitting in a booth, and that figure waved him inside.

Dusty moved closer, realizing that he knew the old black man.

It was Tobias, the man who had given him the instrument.

He found the door through the fog and pulled it open, a bell ringing in welcome. He walked down the aisle toward Tobias.

"Hey, Dusty," Tobias said. "Have a seat." The old man gestured across from him.

Dusty slid into the booth and realized that he was really happy to see the old man.

"How are ya, kid?" Tobias asked.

Dusty didn't know how to answer.

"Well, I guess I'm a little confused," he said, looking around the diner. There were other people sitting in booths, and they all seemed to be looking at them. They were all dressed so strangely. Some wore robes, some wore what looked to be leather armor. . . .

Is that a Viking?

"You're probably wondering where you are," Tobias said, pulling Dusty's attention back to him.

"Yeah," Dusty began. "I don't remember how I got here and . . ."

The image of the strange old man with the Buick suddenly flashed before his mind's eye . . . a man who suddenly looked more like an animal.

"You're nowhere really," Tobias explained. "You're someplace that the instrument has created. That I've created. That *they've* created."

He motioned with his chin to the others sitting around them. "Someplace where you'd feel safe."

There was suddenly a steaming cup of coffee in front of each of them.

"I still don't understand," Dusty said, again looking around the diner. It was like looking at a sampling of people from every time period in the world's history.

"Which is why you're sitting here with me," Tobias said. "There are things I didn't have time to share with you before giving you the horn."

"Harmonica," Dusty corrected, sampling the strong brew.

Tobias cocked his head ever so slightly, his milky white eyes moving quickly from side to side inside his skull.

"It's a harmonica now. It changed."

"Interesting," Tobias said with an understanding nod. "However it appears now, there were things that I didn't get to explain. I figured since you're currently lying unconscious on a werewolf's living room floor, it was as good a time as any to fill you in."

Dusty remembered the old man who had given him a

ride—*Fred*—changing, his face contorting into something inhuman, snarling as he lashed out, punching him, before everything went to black.

"A werewolf," Dusty said. "Is that what he is?"

"Just one of the beastly things that hide in the deep shadows of the world," Tobias said. "You'd be surprised what's lurking around out there."

Dusty found his attention again drawn to the people around the diner. They were still staring, watching him with desperate eyes.

"Who are they?"

"They were like you once," Tobias explained. "Like me."

Dusty looked back to the old man across from him, puzzled.

"We've all held the instrument for safekeeping," Tobias said.

"All of them?" Dusty asked. He turned in his seat, eyeing the other customers. No wonder they were so oddly dressed; thousands of years must have been represented there.

"The instrument takes a piece of us before it's passed on," Tobias went on. "The longer we hold it, the stronger our presence becomes here."

"Wait a minute, you're dead," Dusty said, facing the old man again. "I felt you die."

Tobias nodded. "You're right. It happened not too long after I gave you the instrument."

"How?"

"Let's just say the folks who want the instrument want it so badly that they're willing to do just about anything to get it."

"The werewolf?" Dusty asked. "And those worm things we faced in the alley before you gave me the instrument?"

"Yeah, they want it," Tobias said. He turned his blind eyes toward the window and appeared to be looking out at the unnatural fog. "But not for themselves. They want it so they can give it to someone else. I'm sure the instrument has already shared its purpose with you."

"It's to be used to summon the end of the world," Dusty replied.

"Yeah," Tobias said. His hands felt across the table for the sugar dispenser. He took it and brought it over to his cup, pouring sugar onto his spoon and stirring it into his coffee.

Dusty picked up his own cup and noticed that the coffee never went down; their mugs were always full.

"I should probably apologize for dropping that in your lap; it's a huge responsibility, and I should'a asked you first," Tobias said.

Dusty agreed; he should have been asked if he could handle the responsibility.

"But I was desperate," Tobias said. "And you did come to my aid, exhibiting the kind of character necessary for one who holds the instrument."

Tobias pointed his dripping spoon out into the restaurant. "They all did at one time."

Dusty nodded, even though Tobias could not see his response.

"So, who are those . . . things trying to get the instrument for?"

"Angels," Tobias said.

Dusty made a face, thinking maybe he'd heard the man wrong. "Angels?" he repeated, to be sure.

Tobias nodded. "Angels of the heavenly choir Powers. Or those that have survived, anyway."

"Why would angels want the world to end? I thought they were all nice and working for God and stuff?"

The old black man chuckled.

"You don't know much about angels, do you?" he asked.

"Well, I thought I did," Dusty answered. "Since when did they get to be bad guys?"

"They're not bad guys per se," Tobias started to explain. "It's just that they have a different view of this world, and of God's favorite creations."

"Let me guess. They don't like us."

"They're jealous," Tobias said, holding his cup of coffee halfway to his mouth. "It was the Powers' function to protect humanity from the various creatures that hide in the shadows, but they got distracted by something that they thought was more of a threat."

"Something bigger than the worm things and wolf-men?" Dusty asked.

"Yeah, ever since angels started visiting the world of man, there has always been a complicated relationship with humanity. Some fallen angels loved us . . . a little too passionately, if you know what I'm saying."

"Fallen angels were getting busy with us?" Dusty suggested, just to be sure he was getting it right.

"That's it," Tobias said. "And in some cases, babies were born. Nephilim. And the Powers saw these babies as a bigger threat than the monsters hiding around the world."

"The angels were killing babies?" Dusty couldn't believe what he was hearing; his whole perception of what angels were, and did, was being completely turned on its head.

"When they could," Tobias answered stoically. "Most of the time they couldn't tell until the child turned eighteen; that was when the angelic nature that was part of them usually woke up."

Dusty clutched his still-full coffee cup, absorbing the information.

"And did they succeed?"

"No," Tobias answered. "They were stopped by one of the Nephilim they hunted . . . a special Nephilim."

"So a Nephilim kicked their asses? Good for him."

"You would think," Tobias said. "But here's where it gets sticky. It appears that their leader, Verchiel, had a backup plan."

"This Verchiel sounds like a real dick," Dusty observed colorfully.

"Yeah, you're not too far off with that description," Tobias agreed. "But Verchiel had Powers angels hidden around the world, waiting to carry out his final wishes."

"And let me guess. It has something to do with the instrument."

"See, I knew there was a reason you got picked," the old man said.

"These Powers angels want to end the world to wipe out the Nephilim?"

"Let's just say they want to hit the restart button on the whole planet."

Dusty suddenly realized the enormity of the responsibility that was in his hands. "Well, I won't let them have it," he promised the old man. "I'll use it against them if I have to, but they won't take it from me."

"That's all well and good, but you might not have a choice," Tobias said.

"What do you mean?" Dusty asked. "You gave it to me. . . . It's my responsibility now, and I'm telling you that I won't give it to them, no matter what."

"And I'm saying that you might not be strong enough to deny the instrument."

"I don't get it."

"The instrument was created to summon the End of Days and call Wormwood," Tobias started to explain. "It reacts to the world in which it exists."

Dusty listened, still not quite understanding what the old man meant.

"If the instrument senses a world gone to hell in a hand-bag, it's gonna *want* to be used to bring the curtain down," Tobias stressed.

"But I would never do that," Dusty attempted to reassure him. "No matter how bad the world looks."

"You're not listening, kid," Tobias said. "You might not be strong enough to fight it yet. We've all had hundreds of years to learn to discipline the instrument's rather dominant personality. You've only had it for a few weeks."

Dusty recalled how powerful the instrument could be, how insistent.

"If it wants to end the world, there's a good chance that you might not be able to stop it."

Dusty considered the possibility.

"Then I'll just have to make sure that I'm stronger," he said bravely, although he had no idea how he would manage that.

"Good to hear," Tobias said. "But I think you need some help."

"What do you mean?"

"Remember that Nephilim I mentioned? The special one that took out Verchiel? He's still out there, fighting the good fight along with some other Nephilim survivors."

The restaurant began to tremble; it was as if a squadron of trucks was passing by the diner.

"What's happening?" Dusty asked, gripping the edge of the table as he looked around. The panes of glass in the windows vibrated and the light fixtures started to sway.

"We're done here," Tobias said.

"Done?"

"You're waking up."

"But I don't know what I'm supposed to do," Dusty said as the shaking grew more intense and the large panes of glass began to crack in their frames.

"Find the Nephilim," Tobias ordered calmly. He didn't appear to be concerned that the diner was crumbling around them. He just sat, sipping at his undrainable mug of coffee.

"And, oh yeah," he said, as if just remembering something of grave importance.

The windows shattered, and the thick fog drifted in. The bench beneath Dusty's rear was shaking so violently that he could barely remain upright, but he held on tightly to the edge of the table, desperate to hear the old man's final words of advice.

"Stay alive" was all Tobias said as he disappeared into the fog.

Then the ceiling of the mental construct came crashing down and the floor opened up, and Dusty tumbled down through the fissure to be swallowed by the darkness below.

Lorelei felt herself dying.

She sat in the quiet of a classroom on an overturned metal trash barrel, looking at the blanket-draped corpses of two she had considered more than friends. She had been connected to Janice and Kirk. The Archon magick that she used to show the Nephilim to where they needed to travel had bonded her with the pair, as well as the other soldiers.

Lorelei knew Janice had had a crush on Cameron but that she hadn't had the courage to share that with him. She knew that Kirk found monkeys hilarious and would often surf the Web looking for pictures of what he believed to be his totem animal. Janice had been afraid of heights and always got a jolt of terror when she'd been about to spread her wings and take to the sky. Kirk had been afraid that he would go to Hell when he died, and even though Lucifer had explained that Hell didn't exist, he'd still been afraid that he was going there.

Lorelei felt those memories dying, one after another, the longer they were dead. And as the memories faded, she felt herself dying as well.

She got up and grasped the ends of the blankets, pulling each of them down to expose the Nephilim's faces. She couldn't stand to see them covered; she wanted to see them as they had been, not as enshrouded lumps upon a classroom floor.

She was heartbroken, but she didn't have any tears left. Lucifer had said there were always casualties in war, but it didn't change how much it hurt her to see them like this.

How many more friends would she have to lose in the battle against the forces of darkness? Images of Vilma, and even Aaron—*dead*—flashed before her mind's eye, and she gasped.

No, something had to be done.

They needed help. It was obvious. And the prayers that she said almost daily appeared to be falling on deaf ears, or maybe her pleas just weren't loud enough.

She'd had an idea, and had quickly pushed it aside as insanity, but it was back, scratching at a door within her mind like some starving creature desperate to find its way inside.

The Archons had been powerful enough to speak directly with the Lord God, using complex spells and magicks to actually talk to the Creator in Heaven. Lorelei wanted to talk to Him too, to tell Him how hard they were fighting, but the enemy was growing stronger, and their numbers were faltering.

She could only imagine how Lucifer would react to such an idea, which was why she wouldn't tell him . . . wouldn't tell any of them. The risk was great. She understood that. But it was a risk she was willing to take.

Lorelei stood, making a conscious decision to find the spells necessary to open up direct communications with God. She knew it wouldn't be easy, and that it would require extensive time in the library, but it had to be done. She said her good-byes to her friends, then covered their faces again.

As she walked out of the makeshift morgue into the hall, Lorelei heard her name called.

Aaron and Vilma stood by the door to her workroom.

"We need you," Aaron said.

There was a nervousness to his voice, an uneasiness to his

posture. She knew that her plan would have to wait. Her special talents were once again required.

But once she was finished with whatever it was that Aaron needed her for, Lorelei had an appointment to speak with God.

CHAPTER THIRTEEN

Jeremy found his fellow Nephilim in the television room. It had once been the school library, but any books had long ago been removed, leaving behind a large room of scuffed hardwood floors, some badly scratched and carved upon heavy wooden tables, and some floor-to-ceiling bookcases containing nothing but dust.

It was the perfect place to hang the large flat-screen television that let them glimpse the human world outside the one in which they functioned.

He stepped into the room unnoticed. Some were reading, while others' attention was glued to a news broadcast of some kind.

Russell turned his head slightly to look at Jeremy before quickly turning back to the television screen. There was a look in the boy's eyes that sent a jolt of fear through his system. Something wasn't right.

"What's going on?" Jeremy asked, moving closer to the gathering.

Somebody shushed him—most likely Samantha—and he started to pay attention to the television correspondent on the screen.

The woman was reporting from somewhere in France, from what appeared to be the scene of a natural disaster. It took Jeremy only a few moments to realize that there was nothing natural about what she was reporting at all.

Something had come out of a limestone cliff near a place called the commune of Vallon-Pont-d'Arc, above the former bed of the Ardèche River.

Blurry still images—probably from somebody's phone— were flashed on the screen as the woman talked. They were images of something rather large—an animal of some kind— crawling from the crumbling limestone cliff. Other, better pictures were exhibited next, showing what appeared to be something very dinosaur-like, with bat-like wings spread as it took to the air.

Jeremy knew immediately what it was.

The reporter kept referring to it as the "unknown animal," or the "unclassified species."

"Bloody well say it," he found himself speaking.

The others all looked at him.

"It's a dragon." Jeremy gestured toward the TV. "Anybody with eyes can see that."

"There are no such things as dragons," Melissa said, though the tremble in her voice told him she knew otherwise.

"Right," Jeremy scoffed. "And there aren't any trolls, or Nephilim either, for that matter."

The news report shifted from France to the United States, where a reporter was talking about reports of unusual phenomena. A video clip from an Iowa school teacher's cell phone showed the disturbing image of human figures floating in the sky above a three-mile-deep sinkhole.

Human figures with obvious wings.

"That's not us," Jeremy noted.

"Yeah, but who are they?" William asked.

Jeremy said nothing as the hair prickled upon the back of his neck in warning. He thought he knew who those angelic figures where.

They were supposed to be dead.

But clearly they were still very much alive.

Lucifer breathed in the state of the world and was very disturbed.

It was all happening far too quickly. He could feel it in the tips of his fingers, upon the hair of his scalp. Things stirred the darkness. The Morningstar knew that it must have something to do with the surviving Powers and their plans to awaken Wormwood.

But he also suspected that it went much deeper than that.

The haunting memory of a dark-haired child and a world that it foretold tormented his thoughts.

A world that was now coming to be.

Milton stirred from his spot on Lucifer's shoulder, sensing his vast unease.

The Morningstar reached up, gently taking the mouse from his shoulder and holding it in his hand.

"I think I'm going to have to go," he told the small animal.

Milton squeaked in his primitive tongue, head tilted to one side in question. He stroked the rodent's head with his finger.

"There's someone I have to see about," he said, placing the mouse down on the desktop. "Someone I should have been paying more attention to over the years."

Lucifer knew that he shouldn't blame himself, but it didn't change the fact that a dark future had been predicted to him, a future that he had been invited to share.

He needed to know more about this prophecy, to see if it was somehow connected to the situation unfolding; was the mysterious child manipulating matters like some secret puppet master behind the curtain?

He had to know this enemy so, if need be, he could destroy it.

Lucifer had seen much during the Great War in Heaven, and learned equally as much during his time upon the earth, and he had sworn off violence, using it only as an absolute last resort. Now it appeared that there was little choice. A return to an old way of thinking was in order.

He closed his eyes in the middle of the office and remembered the armor he had worn in battle. The clothes that he wore began to smolder and burn, falling from him as the golden armor manifested upon his body, gleaming as if made from the flares of the sun.

Milton squeaked noisily from the desk, and Lucifer smiled sadly.

"There's no choice, little friend," the Morningstar said.

What he had to do next saddened him most of all because he knew that if this was done, it would be difficult to return to the way things had been.

Lucifer extended his hand, which shone with divine metal, and thought of the sword that he had wielded in battle against his brothers, against Heaven, against God Himself, so very long ago, when he was arrogant and stupid and jealous.

The great blade began as a spark and grew in intensity, until it became as the weapon he both feared and missed.

During the war this weapon had been like a brother upon the battlefield. In his arrogance he had called it Light Giver, an extension of his own Son of the Morning, and holding it now, he was nearly overwhelmed with a strange combination of sadness and joy.

"It's been a long time," Lucifer said, hefting the mighty

blade aloft. Light Giver hummed and crackled as if in response, eager to be put to use.

Standing in the middle of the office, armored for war, the Lucifer Morningstar of old appeared to have returned. And a disturbing tremble went out through the ether, as the world of God's man inched that much closer to the End of Days. It was a progression that the Son of the Morning swore he would do anything in his power to halt.

Fred wasn't sure how many bodies he had stored inside his basement larder, but the number of them standing in front of him now told him that he had far more than he'd thought.

The Corpse Riders had found their way into his food stash and were taking the dead for a spin. Several fully animated bodies ambled into the living room, and Fred could hear more still making their way up the stairs from the cellar.

A female corpse, missing half her face and with a large jagged bite taken out of her neck, shuffled closer, staring at him with her one good eye. He didn't remember killing this one but guessed it must have been during the spring or summer because she was wearing a yellow sundress, now stained with dirt and dried blood.

"What has happened?" the woman's corpse gurgled.

Fred tried to hide the blackened stump where his hand had been.

"Nothing," the werewolf said.

The half-faced woman must have been their leader, seeing as she was doing all the talking.

"What do you hide behind your back?" the corpse pressed.

"I'm not hiding nothing," he protested, but then he sensed—smelled—one of the other corpses behind him.

A heavyset man with a straggly beard grabbed his arm and yanked it up for the head Corpse Rider to see.

"Let me go!" Fred growled, pulling his pain-racked arm from the corpse's grip. "I ain't done nothin' wrong."

"You touched it," the woman's corpse said matter-of-factly. "You were told not to touch it."

"Yeah, well, I was never very good at doing what I was told," Fred said with a toothy snarl. "There it is, right where I dropped it."

The woman lurched toward where Fred was pointing.

"Where?"

"Right there on the floor in front of you."

The woman's head bent at an odd angle, fixating on the harmonica.

"This?" she asked. "You believe *this* to be the object of vast supernatural power we seek?"

"Well, if it isn't, why else would a harmonica burn my hand off?" Fred replied.

The corpse seemed to think about what he said for a moment, then she turned her attention to one of her other walking dead companions.

"Pick it up," she ordered the animated body of a skinny youth dressed in a bright red jogging suit that hid most of the bloodstains. He wore only one sneaker, the other foot bare, as he awkwardly lumbered to where the harmonica lay innocuously on the living room floor beside the unconscious teen.

The corpse stared for a moment before bending at the waist and reaching his long, spidery fingers, which were missing bits of skin, toward the harmonica. He snatched up the prize and was preparing to present it to his leader when his body suddenly exploded into flames. The Corpse Rider worm inside cried out as it sizzled in the unnatural fire.

"I could'a told you something like that would probably happen," Fred said.

The flames extinguished as the body disintegrated. The harmonica sat amidst the ashen remains, appearing as harmless as it had before.

"Silence, wolf," the Corpse Rider leader warned.

A corpse missing his legs dragged his ragged torso across the floor with his spindly arms toward the leader.

"If we cannot touch the instrument, how will we deliver it to the Powers?" the half corpse asked.

The leader pondered this question for some time, her one good eye focused upon the harmonica. But finally she seemed to know what had to be done.

"If we cannot bring the instrument to the Powers," the

Corpse Rider leader said, "then we shall have to have the Powers come here."

Fred cleared his throat loudly.

"Peacocks," he said, spitting onto the floor. "This night just keeps getting better and better."

Aaron didn't want to ask Lorelei for help, but he had no choice.

"Is there an Archon spell that would allow you to find the instrument?"

Lorelei's normally pretty features were drawn and her white hair hung loosely about her face. She looked as though she had aged another ten years since he'd last seen her.

She didn't answer right away, and Aaron began to think she might say no. A part of him hoped she would.

"Yeah," she finally said with a nod and a sigh. "Yeah, there might be. I don't think it's too different from the spell I use to identify our everyday missions."

"So it's not that complicated of a spell?" Vilma asked.

"I didn't say that," Lorelei responded with a tired laugh. Even her teeth looked older, more yellowed.

Aaron couldn't help but feel guilty, knowing what the spell casting would do to her.

"Then maybe there's another way," he suggested.

"Maybe an approach that won't take as much out of you?" Vilma added.

Lorelei headed toward a stack of books on the edge of one

of her worktables. "The problem is that many of these objects of power don't want to be found. That's how they protect themselves, to keep from falling into the wrong hands."

She picked up one of the old volumes and began to thumb through it.

"And I'm going to have to disturb them all to find the particular object we're looking for."

Lorelei closed the book with a dusty snap.

"I might need your help with this one," she said.

"Sure," Aaron and Vilma agreed, both nodding, eager to be of any assistance that they could.

"Where's Lucifer?" Lorelei asked.

That was a good question. "I left him back at his office," Aaron said. "I thought he was going to join us."

Lorelei thought for a moment. "Well, you two will probably do," she said, walking toward the door. "We'll have to go to the library."

The library had once belonged to Scholar, a former angel of the angelic host Principality and keeper of knowledge for the Nephilim's old home in Aerie, the one in the abandoned housing development built upon a toxic-waste dump.

This had been where Lorelei had grown up, learning of her special affinity to angelic magick, and where she and the others had waited for the special Nephilim—the Chosen One—who would arrive to save them, and fulfill the prophecy.

Aaron had come, and that prophecy had been realized.

The fallen had been forgiven and had returned to the kingdom of Heaven. And the Nephilim that had been hidden in Aerie, living in fear of discovery, were allowed to return to the world they'd been forced to abandon in order to survive.

Although the old Aerie was no longer needed, it still stood, a testament to those who believed in the prophecy, to those who lived and died to see it become real.

Scholar had collected books, papers, scrolls, stone tablets; if it contained information—no matter how small—he had wanted to possess it. The angel had lived in the world for a very long time, and throughout those long years he had amassed quite the collection. He had built his special library in one of the abandoned homes of Aerie.

And that was where they were going.

At the end of the long corridor outside Lorelei's workroom was a heavy wooden door that did not seem to belong in the old school. Behind that door was a magickal passage to Scholar's home and library, left for Lorelei to look after since Scholar had returned to God.

Lorelei stood in front of the door, placing her hand upon the glass, diamond-shaped doorknob and turning it.

The door came open with the sucking of air, and they all crossed over.

They entered another long hallway and proceeded forward to the closed door of the library.

Lorelei threw open the door to the enormous room, far

bigger than it had the right to be for the space allotted. But Archon magick was at work here, and the library space was close to limitless.

There were shelves as far as their eyes could see, with more books than could be read in a lifetime—twelve lifetimes. Scholar had loved his books, and the secrets and knowledge that he had found within them.

Lorelei disappeared into the stacks, and Aaron and Vilma waited for her near the door. Aaron imagined one could get lost in the maze of bookshelves, never to be found. He looked around, hoping that there might come a day, in the near future, when he could read some of what Scholar had collected for his own enjoyment, and not have the fate of the world hanging on information he needed to find there.

"Are you all right?" Vilma asked quietly, interrupting Aaron's thoughts.

"I'm as good as can be expected with what's going on," he said.

She stepped closer and gently touched his hand. "I have to tell you something." She paused a moment, then blurted out, "Jeremy tried to kiss me."

Aaron's angelic side, which he had to keep firmly in check, wanted to emerge, and to fight for what it believed belonged to it . . . but Vilma didn't belong to anybody, especially his jealous, angelic nature.

"I know. I saw," Aaron said, his voice strained.

She closed her eyes and sighed.

"I was hoping you hadn't," she said. "I can explain—"

"No, it's okay," Aaron interrupted quickly. "At least you didn't kiss him back."

"I didn't know he was going to try that," she told him.

"Did you want to?" Aaron didn't want to ask, but he had to know. "Did you want to kiss him?"

There was a flash of emotion in her eyes. Was it shock? Fear? Guilt? He couldn't say.

"Aaron," Vilma started to speak as Lorelei came around the corner, a selection of old-looking books and scrolls filling her arms.

"Could you give me a hand with these?" she asked. "Thanks," she said as Aaron and Vilma reached out to help with the books and scrolls. "We'll head back to the lab and get started."

Aaron chanced a glance at Vilma out of the corner of his eye as he followed Lorelei to the library exit. There were many things that still had to be said. Needed to be said.

If only the end of the world wasn't getting in the way.

CHAPTER FOURTEEN

The Corpse Rider leader did not care for the rotting carriage it currently inhabited. It always preferred the newly dead to the long dead, but this would have to do until it could take possession of a fresher host.

Perhaps the unconscious human male on the floor of the wolf's home, the Rider considered, but that, too, would have to wait for the Powers to decide whether or not he was needed to help them achieve their goals.

The Corpse Rider waited, along with others of its ilk. They were all of one mind, psychically connected, and the leader had sent out a summoning for one of their own to find Geburah and the Powers and inform them that their prize had been found, that they should come at once.

"I'm hungry," the wolf called Fred whined, still clutching the blackened stump where his hand had once been to his chest. "I'm thinking I'd like to take a little bite from this one," he said, pointing to the young man—the carrier of the instrument—on the floor before him.

"No," the Corpse Rider said with a shake of her head. "It is not yet known if that one has any importance to the Powers' mission. Only after they arrive will the fate of the youth be determined."

"Just a small bite?" the wolf pleaded.

"Do not test me, animal," the leader warned.

Her single eye kept falling to the instrument on the floor. She was fascinated with the simplicity of it but also feared its destructive potential. She had to admit that she was mildly curious as to why the Powers were so intent on locating it, so intent that they would actually seek out the assistance of the Corpse Riders.

But she guessed that it didn't really matter. The only important thing to her was that the persecution of the Riders would cease once the object—this instrument—was in the possession of the angels. A truce had been promised, and the Corpse Riders would be allowed to flourish upon this world.

She was about to mentally urge the Riders to make haste in finding the Powers when the wolf acted.

"Nobody is gonna tell me what I can and can't do in my own house," the beast roared, lunging for the still-unconscious youth, mouth poised to bite.

The other Riders acted with the speed of their leader's

thoughts. The shambling corpses fell upon the beast-man, dragging him to the ground and away from the carrier.

"Get your rotten hands offa me before I—"

The air in the living room thickened. It was as if a powerful storm was forming right there in the middle of the room. The air was charged with an energy that roused the leader's survival instinct, but she held her ground. Turning toward the new disturbance in the room, they all watched as the air shimmered, and something, accompanied by a disturbing and deafening sound, began to push its way into their reality.

One by one the angels of the Powers appeared, their mighty wings opening to reveal their fearsome countenance.

The angel Geburah was the first to manifest, his attentions instantly drawn to the struggle between the Riders and the wolf.

Fred stopped struggling long enough to witness his own demise.

The Powers' leader raised his hand, tongues of holy fire leaping from the tips of his fingers to engulf the hungry wolf, along with the Corpse Riders holding him. The flames were so intense that their cries roasted in blackened throats before their release.

"I felt the need to deal with that," Geburah said, wiggling the still smoldering fingers on his hand. "I hope you don't mind."

The Corpse Riders' leader felt it best to keep her mouth

shut, bowing her head ever so slightly in the presence of the divine creatures.

"Now," Geburah said, his huge wings closing upon his back. "Let's pray that is the only situation I'm forced to deal with in such a way."

The angel stared down at the mangled features of the corpse.

"The instrument," Geburah demanded. "Give it to me."

Lorelei was a little nervous about this spell, and perhaps a little distracted. She would rather have been putting her best efforts toward her own little project.

Communicating with God.

She studied the pages of the ancient book again, deciphering the strange text written in the language of the Archons. Even the act of reading required such concentration that it was exhausting; *anything* pertaining to the angelic sorcerers always required great reserves of strength.

Aaron and Vilma stood patiently nearby, ready to help, which was good; without their strength added to hers, the spell would be impossible, and Lorelei would be left practically drained of life.

The sound of claws clicking on the old linoleum floors distracted her, and she looked up to see Aaron's dog entering the old science lab.

"Hey, Gabe," Aaron said as Vilma knelt to pet the animal.

"Where's Lucifer?" the dog asked them.

"He's in his office," Aaron answered.

"No," Gabriel said, shaking his head.

Lorelei noticed movement from under the lab's collar, and the gray shape of the Morningstar's mouse emerged.

"Went to the office and found Milton alone," Gabriel continued.

"I can't imagine he went far," Aaron said. "We're in the middle of something important and—"

"Milton said he went to deal with something he should have dealt with a long time ago," Gabriel explained. The mouse squeaked in agreement as he walked along the Labrador's muscular back.

"Do you know what he's talking about?" Vilma asked, looking to her boyfriend.

Aaron just shrugged. It was a mystery he would have to worry about later. Right now there was a spell to cast, and an object of power to locate.

"I'm just about ready here," Lorelei said.

"What's going on?" Gabriel asked.

"We're going to help Lorelei with one of her spells," Vilma answered.

"I want to help," Gabriel barked, looking at all of them with his soulful eyes.

"That's all right, boy," Aaron said. "You just sit. As soon as we're done here, we'll find Lucifer and—"

"He can help if he wants," Lorelei interrupted.

Aaron looked concerned. "Is it safe for him?"

"He'll be fine," Lorelei answered. "He'll only add his strength to yours and Vilma's. The stronger the anchor, the better."

Gabriel barked excitedly, his tail wagging, the happy movements nearly causing Milton to fall from his perch upon the Labrador's back.

"Okay," Lorelei said, placing her hands on either side of the ancient text. "Are we set?"

"Ready," Aaron said.

"What do you need us to do?" Vilma asked.

"Nothing yet," Lorelei said. She reached out to the two covered dove cages she'd brought out from the closet and slid them over. She threw back the towels and the doves fluttered their wings and cooed, frightened by the sudden reveal.

"This isn't going to be too pretty," she warned her companions.

Then she drew the copper bowl close and opened the door of the first cage, capturing the dove. Lorelei acted quickly, dispatching the little bird, removing its heart, and placing it in the bowl. She did the same with the second dove, placing its body beside the first atop a towel, and folding the ends over the bloodied remains.

She picked up the bowl with one hand, and the book with the other, and carried both over to a corner of the room where she had drawn a circle in white chalk near the windows. Surrounding the circle were strange angled shapes—angelic sigils of power—also drawn in white chalk.

"Come on over here," she called to Aaron and Vilma as she stepped into the circle, careful not to disturb the chalk lines. She sat down in the center, watching as they gathered round.

"Is this good?" Aaron asked.

"That's fine," she said. They had spread out before her, following the curved line of the circle. Lorelei took in a deep breath through her nose, getting comfortable before arranging the bowl in front of her. Believing herself ready, she opened the book in her lap. "The circle will focus the spell and you three—"

Milton squeaked to be heard.

"Sorry, you *four* will provide me with the additional strength I'll need to maintain the spell."

"So we just have to stand here?" Vilma asked.

"That and lend me some of your physical and mental vitality," Lorelei said.

"I think we can do that," Vilma said, smiling nervously.

"Okay then." Lorelei focused on the pages of the book. "Just so you know, this spell allows me to psychically see objects of power. Each and every one of them gives off its own unique energy, and I'll be able to focus on that signature and hopefully find the location of the one we're looking for."

She looked up from the book to stress this next part.

"Some of these objects might prove hostile, not appreciating that I'm attempting to find them. That's when I'll need you guys. Your strength will be necessary to keep me from being attacked."

They all seemed ready, looks of nervous anticipation upon their faces. Even the dog looked prepared for anything, and Lorelei probably would have found it funny if she wasn't so afraid.

From her shirt pocket she retrieved a pack of matches, lit one, and dropped it into the bowl with the two dove hearts. She'd already laced the copper container with the other ingredients, and the mixture immediately ignited, creating a heavy gray cloud of smoke that did not disperse but billowed around her head, forming a kind of crown.

A crown of sacrifice.

Lorelei looked down into the book. She could feel the power of the Archon words drawing her in as she began to read them aloud. The words filled her being, wrapping her in their meaning and power. The air around her began to crackle, and she felt the hair on her head stand on end, but the power stayed contained within the circle of protection.

From the corner of her eye she saw that Aaron, Vilma, Gabriel, and Milton waited to be needed. It made her feel a little bit better about what she had to do.

The words flowed from her mouth, seeming to grow incredibly loud within the circle, and suddenly she felt herself begin to float away. Below, she saw herself sitting cross-legged within the circle, and she saw the others watching her with

urrent Check-Outs summary for O'Doherty
Thu Jun 10 13:28:11 BST 2021

ARCODE: 30011004670346
ITLE: Aerie and Reckoning.
UE DATE: 01 Jul 2021

ARCODE: 30011006059324
TITLE: The private life of the brain / S
UE DATE: 01 Jul 2021

BARCODE: 30011006016563
TITLE: Infinite days / Rebecca Maizel.
UE DATE: 01 Jul 2021

BARCODE: 30011007732929
TITLE: I Was Here
DUE DATE: 01 Jul 2021

BARCODE: 30011007732317
TITLE: An abundance of Katherines / by J
DUE DATE: 01 Jul 2021

BARCODE: 30011006118047
TITLE: The Fallen : End of days / Thomas
DUE DATE: 01 Jul 2021

cautious eyes. Then her very being—her essence—was propelled through the ether, hurtling off in multiple directions.

But with a single vision.

With one set of eyes, she scoured the world, Archon magick
carrying her to the locations where objects of vast supernatural
power lay hidden. Beneath the sea, a crown of gold and jewels
pulsed with an unnatural desire to again control a king and
raise an empire. Under the floorboards of a Serbian church, an
ancient book, bound in the flesh of holy men, awaited a day
when its forbidden text would be read again, and its master
would rise. On a dusty shelf in a Portland thrift shop, a wooden
chalice imbued with the power of healing sat forgotten. In an
old farmhouse, a musical instrument sat nestled amongst the
ashes of the dead, surrounded by angelic and demonic forces.
In a crumbling Vietnam temple, the egg of—

Wait.

The objects—*so many objects*—continued to rush past her.
Lorelei was caught in a current of power, but she believed that
she might have found what they were searching for.

She struggled against the flow with great exertion, turning
her attentions back the way she had come.

The old farmhouse . . . the musical instrument . . . *the
instrument* . . . lying in the ashes. *Are those angels around it?*

The instrument felt her presence, and it did not care for
it. She could *feel* its displeasure, like the growl of some great
primordial beast. She tried to communicate with it, but it

didn't want to listen. It felt the pain of the world, and so Lorelei felt the pain of the world.

And for that pain to end, the world had to die.

For the first time ever, Dusty saw the world for what it truly was.

Lying in the darkness, curled up in a fetal position, he was bombarded by his thoughts. Nothing was held back, it was all revealed to him, and he was glad that he was safely hidden from the terrors that abounded. Ghastly things were everywhere, gradually emerging from their hiding places to claim a world that once stood as the Creator's crowning achievement. Now it was a world tarnished and dirty, rotting from within. A world rife, not with the potential of good, but one exuding a noxious cloud of evil.

Dusty felt the warm tears spill from his eyes as he lay in the darkness. The world once held so much promise, but the taint of the monstrous had left it sick.

Dying.

He remembered his family's dog, a mutt by the name of Spenser. He was sure there had never been a better dog, and none since. That dog was the closest he'd ever come to having a brother, and he'd loved him more than anything imaginable.

Loved him enough to know when it was time to put him down.

Spenser had become sick, and every day that he had struggled to stay alive had been an affront to the love that

Dusty had for him. That poor sick animal wasn't the four-legged friend he'd once run with through summer fields.

Spenser had become a shadow of himself . . . a shell.

Dusty hadn't come by the decision lightly; it was probably the most painful one he had ever had to make, but he knew it was for the best—the best for Spenser.

He needed to be put out of his misery, and that was *his* job, as Spenser's owner, Spenser's brother, to be merciful and to take away his pain.

That was what Dusty had done for his dog, and what he now had to do for the world. The world had to be put out of its misery, before the evil could infect anything else of beauty. The earth needed to be put down, and Dusty had just the tool with which to do it—the right instrument for the job.

Dusty opened his eyes to the ocean of black around him, feeling the pull of the waking world. Far off in the distance he saw a pulse of light. It was calling for him to come nearer, for him to embrace his purpose.

Dusty swam through the shadows, fixated upon the light that grew stronger . . . brighter . . . as he moved closer.

The light praised him for what he was about to do, for making the right decision about the sickness of the waking world.

Hovering above the circle of light, Dusty gazed down at the instrument. He watched it as it refused to hold a particular shape, morphing from one musical instrument to the next—a flute carved from bone, a golden trumpet, a set of drums, the harmonica, another more ancient-looking horn—all the shapes that it had assumed throughout its many millennia.

Dusty listened to its soothing voice as it gave him instructions on how to begin the end.

Take me up, it called from its circle of light.

And Dusty regretfully did as he was told, for this was his job. He reached down, his fingers entering the warmth of the light that encircled the instrument.

And know in your heart, there was nothing more that could have been done to save this once holy place.

His fingers closed around the object as it continued to change in his grasp, and he pulled it from the warmth of the circle. Holding the means with which to call down the Angel of Destruction, Dusty felt his mind continue to fill with images of a devastated world, convincing him that he was doing the right thing. For the mercy of the world, and all the good people suffering upon it, there was no other way.

Holding the instrument to his chest, Dusty was about to close his eyes and will himself back to consciousness when he heard an unfamiliar voice. It echoed from the blackness, and he experienced a sudden shiver of fear that seemed to emanate from the instrument itself.

"You don't have to do that," said a woman's voice.

The instrument grew hot in his hand—practically burning his flesh. It commanded him not to pay attention. But Dusty, desperate for another way, was willing to listen.

"Who's there?" he called out.

An orange flame ignited, revealing the one who had spoken to him. She was not alone.

The woman drew closer, and he realized that she was no older than he was, though her hair was the color of snow. There were two others with her, a pretty, dark-skinned girl and a boy—and in their hands they each held a sword of fire.

There was a dog with them also, a yellow Labrador, and perched atop the Labrador's head was a mouse. Dusty would have been amused if it all wasn't so darn strange.

The instrument tried to show him that there was no other way. Horrible images cascaded through his mind, but there was something in the light thrown by the swords that calmed his panic. And made it possible for Dusty to wrestle control from the instrument, to hope—*believe*—that maybe there was another answer.

"Who are you?" he asked the mysterious figures invading his inner mind.

"Think of us as your conscience," the woman with the white hair said. "We're here to keep you from doing anything stupid."

CHAPTER FIFTEEN

Lucifer had believed himself prepared for just about anything—but not this.

Remembering the ancient temple where he'd first encountered that ancient, prophetic evil, he had wrapped himself within his cloak of feathers and had departed the school.

He had doubted that the tiny island was even there anymore. It had likely been swallowed up thousands upon thousands of years ago by the same cataclysmic event that had submerged the kingdom of Atlantis. But he had had to see if there was something to his strange resurgence of memory.

Prepared to materialize beneath waves, Lucifer was stunned when he had opened his wings to find himself in a vast underground chamber. The walls, thick with ice, glistened in the warm glow thrown by the Light Giver. It was freezing, but as was the case for all angels, the Morningstar did not experience differences in temperature.

The original island had been but a tiny spot in the Aegean Sea, and Lucifer could sense that he was nowhere close to the Mediterranean. Somehow he had been transported someplace else.

The icy ground beneath his feet slanted downward, and Lucifer began to walk. Raising his sword of fire, he illuminated the ceiling of the chamber, marveling at the enormous stalactites, like teeth hanging down from above.

Lucifer held his burning blade close to the frozen wall.

"What is this?" he spoke aloud, reaching out with his hand to wipe away a thick layer of frost that partially obscured what was petrified within.

What he saw suspended there in the ice made him step back in revulsion. Lucifer had been on the planet for quite some time but had never seen anything quite so . . . monstrous.

He was reminded of the idol he had seen within the temple, only this was not a thing carved of stone but of twisted flesh. Its shape was barely human, its face—if that was indeed what it was—covered in round, bulbous eyes, a slash in the mottled flesh beneath the organs of sight filled with thousands of needle-like teeth. It had multiple limbs, some thick muscular tentacles while others resembled the segmented legs of an insect.

Lucifer had no idea what was imprisoned within the

confines of ice, or where it had come from, but it was not of this earth. Its yellow eyes seemed to stare at him, boring into his being, silently commanding him to set it free.

The Morningstar slowly stepped away from the wall. Willing the weapon of fire to burn all the brighter, Lucifer saw more of the icy chamber and the horrors it held.

Monsters, even more horrible than the one he had just beheld, of every conceivable size and shape were frozen within the cavern walls. It was a chamber of horrors, and he wondered why he was there.

"Because you were looking for me," said a child's voice. "Because I brought you here."

"Show yourself," Lucifer demanded, experiencing a fear the likes of which he had not felt since standing before an angry God.

The child stepped out from behind a wall of ice, looking no older than he had a few millennia ago, only this time the robes that adorned his slight frame were far more elaborate and royal.

"Hello, Lucifer," the child greeted. "I wasn't sure if I was ever going to see you again, but I hoped that I would."

"What is this place?" Lucifer asked. "Where have you brought me?"

"A place of waiting," the child said. He rested a small hand upon the wall, gazing at the beast trapped on the other side.

"Waiting?" the Morningstar asked. "Waiting for what,

exactly? The dark times you told me about when we first met?"

The child laughed. "Yes, the dark times. They're almost here." The little boy's eyes danced mischievously, excited by the prospect.

It was as Lucifer had feared; *this* was the time that had been prophesied.

He was mesmerized by the horrors frozen around him. "What are they?" He gestured toward the walls of ice.

"They are my brothers and sisters," the child explained as he advanced toward Lucifer. "When the Almighty brought His damnable light to the universe, my family and I fled to the pockets of shadow where the Creator's light couldn't reach, and we watched Him and all His light had wrought from afar."

"You are far older than you appear," Lucifer said, realizing that he was in the presence of a power older than creation itself.

The child admired his reflection in the icy wall.

"I like this shape," he said, looking at his small hands, adorned with rings. "So small and innocent looking . . . but, really, so much more."

The child smiled, and Lucifer was again treated to a brief flash of the creature before him, and its true form. It was even worse than he remembered.

"We watched as He created the stars, and the planets, and the earth. . . . We liked the earth."

The child moved to another section of wall and gazed at the enormous figure frozen within.

"Didn't we, sister?" he spoke to the thing. "We liked it so much that we came here to hide, and to plan our eventual return."

The child returned his gaze to the Morningstar.

"The Lord of Lords didn't even know we existed. He never bothered to consider that something might have existed before His light, and so long as we kept from His attention . . ." The child's voice trailed off, and he spun playfully around to head back from where he had come.

"But my family was impatient," he continued, "and every so often they would spread their malignant influence."

The child faced Lucifer, putting up his hands as if claws and baring perfectly white teeth in a parody of a snarl. "From ghoulies and ghosties and long-legged beasties and things that go bump in the night . . . good Lord, deliver us," the child recited in a singsong voice before breaking out in laughter.

"Your family created the monsters of the world," Lucifer stated.

"Initially," the child answered. "But then some of those monsters produced monsters of their own, and so on, and so on."

The child cocked his head as if a thought had just come into it.

"It's like your fallen angels," he suggested with a smile, "creating the Nephilim."

"The Nephilim are not monsters," Lucifer snapped defensively.

"Really?" the child asked, a slight hand going to his chin. "That wasn't what I was led to believe." He clasped his hands behind his back and he began to pace. "I had a nice conversation a very long time ago with one of your brethren," the child went on. "And we discussed these creatures. He was an angel of the Powers, I believe. What was his name again?"

The child looked toward the stalactite-covered ceiling, tapping his tiny chin, goading Lucifer.

"Verchiel," Lucifer said quietly, a weight forming in the pit of his stomach.

"That's it," the child said, pointing happily. "Verchiel. I suggested he might want to focus on those Nephilim."

"Instead of focusing on your brothers and sisters, and the creatures *they* created," Lucifer said, as things suddenly became more clear.

The child nodded. "Exactly," he said. "Having angels on the planet poking into every dark corner was becoming quite annoying. The Powers needed a distraction, and by whispering sweet nothings into their leader's ear, I had found the perfect one.

"But, my family did not approve of my efforts," he sighed. "They were tired of hiding. They wanted to wage war against the Creator and His angelic forces. I couldn't allow them to do that. We weren't ready . . . yet."

He shook his head sadly.

"Which is why you see them like this," the child said, gesturing to the creatures frozen about them. "I needed my siblings to be more patient than they were willing to be, so I put them to sleep, giving myself the chance to steer the world in a direction that would benefit me."

"You?" Lucifer questioned.

"Me, and my family, of course," the child offered quickly, but Lucifer saw who was the true master behind this scenario.

"Won't they be angry with you?" the Morningstar asked. "For having imprisoned them? I know I would be," he said, the Light Giver sparking brightly in his hand.

"Perhaps," the child said, his gaze traveling over the ice walls that imprisoned his family. "But they'll come to realize it was for their own good."

"Or not," Lucifer suggested.

The child fixed him in a stare far colder than the ice of the cavern.

"Why did you come here, Morningstar?" the child asked. "Have you come to accept my offer?"

Lucifer gripped his sword tightly as he regarded the horrors trapped within the chamber walls, horrors that would soon be unleashed upon the world if what the child said was true.

He saw no other choice. Lucifer dropped to one knee before the child and bowed his head.

"I have," the Morningstar answered.

The child's eyes twinkled happily, and the world slid that much closer to eternal darkness.

Geburah extended his hands, letting the power of Heaven leak from the tips of his fingers.

The rotting body of the Corpse Rider averted its single milky eye from the brightness of the angel's divinity.

"Give it to me now," Geburah demanded.

"I cannot," the Rider gurgled. "If I do, it will be the end of me."

The Powers' leader bore down upon the female corpse, forcing himself to contain his fury.

"Explain," he demanded.

"I gather that the object will not permit itself to be picked up by one it does not see fit to touch it," the leader of the Riders explained.

"Do tell," Geburah said. "Where have you put it?"

The corpse pointed to the pile of ashes on the floor. "There . . . resting in the remains of one who attempted to retrieve it."

Geburah walked closer to the ash, studying the instrument. It certainly didn't appear dangerous.

"Show me," the angel commanded.

The leader hesitated, her blind eye searching the room for a volunteer, and of course there was none.

"You!" the leader commanded one of the other corpses.

A girl wearing cutoff shorts and a large shirt tied at the waist strode forward. On legs barely covered in flesh—yellow bone peeking out through tears in what little skin remained upon them—she approached her leader.

"Pick it up," the leader commanded her.

The corpse turned her gaze to the instrument but did not move.

"But I will perish," the corpse whined.

"Yes," the leader acknowledged.

The dead girl did not move from where she was standing, weighing the command she'd been given by her leader.

Geburah could stand it no more, his patience at its lowest ebb. The angel surged toward the corpse, grabbing her by the back of the neck and throwing her atop the instrument.

The corpse landed awkwardly, emitting a high-pitched squeal as she momentarily thrashed before exploding into flame.

"Fascinating," Geburah said. He turned his attention to his brothers, who were watching with cautious eyes, and he knew what they were thinking.

They were creatures of the Divine, and should have no worries at all about retrieving the holy object, but what if things had changed? What if the instrument no longer recognized their divinity; what if their time upon this accursed planet had left them tainted? What if the instrument knew their plans for the world, and did not agree?

Those were questions that only served to infuriate Geburah. Here he was, so close to fulfilling Verchiel's final solution for this wretched world, and still it eluded him.

Geburah was almost considering prayer to seek his answer when the unconscious teen lying on the floor started to move.

The young man slowly crawled to his feet with a strangely blank stare.

The Powers' leader found it odd that the carrier did not react in any way to the sight of walking corpses and winged angels standing before him as he rose unsteadily to his feet. He looked about the room, and seemingly beyond it.

"It is a pathetic place," the carrier said with little inflection.

Geburah watched with a growing anticipation as the human turned his attention to the instrument nestled in the ashes of the unholy, and bent to retrieve it.

"And one that must be brought to a close," the carrier continued, as he brought the instrument toward his mouth.

Geburah smiled broadly.

He could not have agreed more.

Aaron opened his eyes, and the cracked and water-stained plaster ceiling of the classroom gradually came into focus. He couldn't move just yet, every nerve in his body numb from the psychic assault.

Something had gone wrong . . . something had gone terribly, terribly wrong.

At first everything had seemed to be going well. Lorelei's magick had allowed them to enter the subconscious of the kid with the instrument. There had been a bit of a struggle going on there, the kid seeming to have some control issues with the device.

They seemed to have arrived just in time though, giving the kid what he needed to muster some control and override the instrument's desire to start the countdown to the apocalypse.

But the instrument proved to be stronger than they'd anticipated.

Lorelei had been in the process of explaining to Dusty— the longer they stayed within his mind, the more they seemed to know about him—that evil forces were at work, attempting to get him to trigger the End of Days.

Aaron guessed that they might have let their guards down just a little.

Lorelei had been encouraging Dusty to be strong until they had a chance to reach him physically. She told him they would protect him against those forces that were trying to steal the instrument, as well as against the instrument itself.

Yeah, everything had seemed to be going just fine, until Dusty had attacked. Although Aaron was pretty sure it had been the instrument asserting its control, not Dusty.

Finally feeling as though he could move again, Aaron mustered his strength and rolled onto his side. Vilma lay on the floor beside him. There was blood on her lip.

"Vilma," he called to her. She seemed so incredibly still, and he couldn't see if she was breathing. His heart began to hammer painfully in his chest with worry as he reached out, grabbed her arm, and gave it a shake. She moaned, and he gasped with relief, the rapid-fire beating of his heart starting to slow.

Gabriel lay on his side, legs straight out, his thick pink tongue lolling from his mouth to curl on the floor.

"C'mon, Gabe," Aaron said. He forced himself into an upright position, feeling his head go light. He focused, taking in deep breaths through his mouth, exhaling through his nose.

Milton appeared to be all right, peeking out from beneath Gabriel's floppy golden-yellow ear, squeaking for the dog to wake up.

Aaron placed a hand upon the dog's side, feeling a powerful heartbeat.

Vilma groaned louder, and then began to cough. She rolled onto her side, choking, and Aaron slid himself closer, taking her into his arms.

"Hey," he said. "You're going to be all right. . . . Slow, steady breaths, that's it."

She was tense as he held her, but she soon relaxed and her breathing came under control.

"What happened?" she managed groggily.

"I think we were forcibly removed from Dusty's subconscious," Aaron said.

Gabriel was sitting up now too. The mouse sat atop his head, cleaning himself.

"You all right?" Aaron asked his best friend.

"I'm hungry," the dog said.

"Guess you're fine," Aaron said, relieved that they all seemed to have survived relatively unscathed, when—

"Lorelei," Vilma said, pushing herself from his arms.

The instrument had gone after Lorelei first, knowing that she was the anchor holding them all there. The attack had been savage, like razor-sharp claws being raked over their exposed brains as an inhuman voice screamed for them not to meddle in the affairs of God.

Lorelei lay within the circle, curled in the fetal position.

Aaron crawled across the floor into the circle, not worrying about preserving the chalk lines.

"Lorelei," he called to her.

She remained perfectly still as he carefully rolled her over onto her back. Vilma gasped at what they saw. The girl, who was only a couple of years older than he and Vilma, appeared to have aged another ten years. Her skin was a sickly gray, and dark trails of blood ran from each nostril.

"What's happened to her?" Gabriel asked, pushing between them.

"It's the magick, I think," Aaron attempted to explain. "It's too much for her to control."

Vilma held Lorelei's wrist, feeling for a pulse.

"Her heart seems to be all right," Vilma said. "Gabriel, go and get Kraus," she told the dog.

Gabriel, Milton still riding atop his head, spun around and galloped from the classroom in search of their doctor.

"Hang on, Lorelei. Help is coming," Aaron said, soothingly. He supported her head on his thigh and was gently stroking her snow-white hair when her eyes fluttered open.

"I'll be fine," Lorelei said weakly as she struggled to sit up.

"Lie still," Vilma ordered, gently pushing her back. "I just sent Gabriel to get Kraus. Let's make sure."

"No time," Lorelei said.

Ignoring their attempts to have her rest, the girl managed, with their help, to climb to her feet. She held on to the windowsill to steady herself.

"Don't know how much longer we have," she said, panting as if she'd just run a race. Her nose was still bleeding, and she brought the sleeve of her blouse up to wipe at the steady stream.

"There's still a chance," she said. "Gather the others . . . get to Dusty before the Powers . . ."

"The Powers," Aaron interrupted. He'd been hoping that Lucifer had been wrong. "Are you sure?"

Lorelei nodded. "I caught a glimpse of Dusty in the waking world before the instrument torched my brain, and I saw angels, beautiful-looking things but with murder in their eyes. There was no mistaking what they were."

CHAPTER SIXTEEN

It was the harmonica burning the tender flesh of his lips that helped him break the instrument's hold.

But for how long? That was his worry.

The instrument was strong, constantly vying for control of him.

How did Tobias and the others do this? Dusty wondered fitfully. *It is exhausting, like fighting against an ocean current.*

He stood there, instrument of the apocalypse still pressed to the bubbling flesh of his lips, and eyed the sights before him. It all seemed like some sort of bad dream, like something he might've dreamed while having a severe fever.

The angel leader stared with eyes like polished black stones, a twitch of anticipation dancing at the corners of his mouth.

How can something so beautiful be so terrifying? he reflected, his eyes darting to the five other angelic beings that were waiting for him to call the end of the world.

"Do it," the leader of angels commanded, his voice filled with so much power and authority that Dusty almost felt compelled to do so, *almost.*

The instrument fought him, thrashing wildly against his psyche. He couldn't blame it, really; the instrument just wanted to fulfill its purpose. But Dusty wasn't ready to call down the apocalypse on an unsuspecting world. So he fought it, fought it with everything he had. He needed to show it who was boss; he had to take control of its divine power and use it to escape the situation he found himself in now: surrounded by bloodthirsty angels and zombies.

"Do what you were created for. . . . perform your purpose," the angel leader commanded, voice booming.

Yeah, he needed to take the bull by the horns. Dusty had to use the instrument, not for what it was intended, but to save his own skin.

Dusty tried to remember what Tobias had done on that rainy night in the alley, hoping that he wasn't about to accidentally do something he might regret.

"You want me to blow on this?" Dusty asked them, watching the angel's expression turn from anticipation to surprise. Dusty was back in control.

The zombies just stood there, waiting for something to happen, but the angels spread their wings. Dusty wasn't sure if they were going to attack him or fly away, but he didn't want to give them the chance to do anything.

Taking a deep breath in through his nose, he blew into the instrument, the air passing across multiple chambers, each of them containing two small metal reeds that vibrated to emit a hauntingly beautiful sound.

A sound that made all hell break loose.

Vilma walked faster to keep up with Aaron.

"We'll need to find the others and let them know what's happening," he said, wearing that determined look she'd become so familiar with since he'd accepted his purpose as leader of the Nephilim, and all that it meant.

"I'm not sure how much time we have, but we're going to need to leave right away if we're going to get Dusty and the instrument away from the Powers and—"

Vilma stopped short, reaching out to grab hold of Aaron's sleeve. It was all going so incredibly fast, and she had things to say to Aaron . . . things she *needed* to say.

Just in case.

"Wait," she said, trying to slow things down for just a moment.

Aaron kept walking, the fabric of his shirt slipping through her fingers.

"Back in the library you asked me if I wanted to kiss him," she said. "If I wanted to kiss Jeremy."

Aaron stopped. "We don't have to talk about this now," he said, not looking at her. "There are more important—"

She spread her wings in a blink, leaping up into the air to drop down in front of him, blocking his way.

"No, there's nothing more important right now, right this second," she said to him, her eyes blazing. "We need to take a minute," she said, "just a minute, to remember us. Not the mission, but *us*."

Aaron looked as though he was going to argue, but she was on a roll now, desperate to get it all out.

"'Cause if we don't remember us, what's it all for, really?" she asked.

She moved closer to him and wrapped them both in her wings.

"Sometimes we need to be reminded of what we have," she said, raising her hands to hold his face. "What we're fighting for."

She kissed him then, softly, gently, nervous that he wouldn't kiss her back. But he did. And that made everything that was going on in her head and in the crazy world bearable.

"We really need to find the others," Aaron said, breaking their kiss.

Vilma debated telling him about the weird attraction she felt with Jeremy, but decided that it wasn't the right time. She needed to think about it more, to understand what had gone on between her and Jeremy Fox.

"I love you, Aaron Corbet," she said, kissing him again. "Now and forever."

"Now and forever," he repeated, returning her kiss.

They were quiet for a moment, basking in the love they shared. There would be time for confessions later, when Vilma could think things through, but not now.

"That's it," she said, releasing him from her winged embrace. "We now return to our regularly scheduled craziness."

He laughed softly, taking her hand as they continued toward the building where the others were likely to be, but they didn't get far. As they turned the corner on the brick path, they came face-to-face with the others, Jeremy Fox in the lead.

"The world's suddenly gone mad," the Brit said, moving his finger around at his temple. "Just saw on the telly that the planet's being overrun with all manner of beastie, and we were wondering what we intend to do about it."

Vilma squeezed Aaron's hand, letting him know that she was there for him, always, forever by his side.

"Nothing," Aaron said calmly.

Jeremy looked as though he'd been slapped, and the others exchanged worried glances.

"For right now, anyway," Aaron clarified. "There's another situation that we have to deal with first."

"What? Something more important than saving people from monsters?" Jeremy asked in disbelief.

"If the world comes to an end first, there won't be any reason to save them."

Vilma had to hand it to her boyfriend; he certainly did have a way of making a point.

Geburah should have been dead. His flesh was blackened and moist, most of it burned away to reveal the soft angelic muscle beneath.

Rising up from the rubble, the angel fluttered his mighty wings, stretching them as he shook away rock, dust, and dirt. He looked about and saw that nothing of the structure remained standing. The home had been leveled in the destructive release of divine energies when the carrier had used the instrument.

Pieces of bodies that had once been animated by the Corpse Riders littered the grounds. Broken limbs stuck up from beneath the shattered walls and roof, but he had no care for them or the foul creatures that had made them move after death. Geburah wanted to know the fate of his brothers. Fearing that he may have been the only survivor, he walked through the remains of the home searching for a sign.

Suria emerged, throwing aside a still-burning piece of furniture. Tandal and Huzia pushed up from beneath the wreckage like flowers seeking out the rays of the sun.

He found the remains of Anfial and Shebniel, the pair having met the full brunt of the instrument's release. They were entwined in each other's arms, as if comforting one another in death.

Feeling the eyes of his living brethren upon him, Geburah turned to them.

"As long as one of us survives, we will continue with our mission," he said, experiencing discomfort as his divine flesh healed. He used the pain to focus himself, to plot their next move.

There was a chance that the carrier would again use the instrument's power against them, but that was a risk they would have to take. Geburah spread his charred wings and leaped into the sky. The act itself was one of sheer agony, but he needed to see where their quarry had gone. The angel dropped back to earth, exhausted, still not healed enough to pursue his prey, but in the distance he had seen something that gave him an idea.

Kneeling upon the shattered remains of the dwelling, Geburah bent down close to the debris and listened. He could hear things slithering in the patches of shadow cast by the rubble. The surviving Corpse Riders were attempting to hide from the rise of daylight.

"Can you hear me, foul beasts?" Geburah asked, the sounds of many appendages skittering beneath the rock growing louder in intensity with the question. "Now is the time to prove your worth. Not far from this spot there is a burial place that will provide you with the conveyances you require. Traverse the shadows in pursuit of the holy relic. Stop the carrier before he is lost to us again."

CHAPTER SEVENTEEN

Though normally he did not notice changes in temperatures, the Morningstar was suddenly very aware of the cold.

"I'm actually going to miss all this when it's over," the child said over his shoulder, as Lucifer followed the little boy deeper underground.

"Where are we?" Lucifer asked, amazed by the vastness of the subterranean chamber, and disturbed that something with the propensity for so much evil could be hidden there . . . waiting for so long.

"Isn't it wonderful?" the child asked, gesturing with his tiny hand at the immensity of it all. "We're beneath an Antarctic lake, which is in turn located twelve thousand feet beneath the polar ice cap."

The child turned.

"I've actually heard a rumor that some Russian scientists are very close to piercing Antarctica's frozen crust in order to reach the lake." He smiled, a nasty twinkle dancing in his eyes. "Can you imagine what they'll think if they ever find my family?"

He giggled, the sound strangely ominous as it echoed about the icy chamber.

"But we need not worry about that, am I right?" the child said. "My brothers and sisters should be up and around long before the scientists can find them."

Lucifer felt his pulse quicken. Just the thought of those things he'd seen imprisoned in the ice walking the earth was enough to send him into panic.

But he had to remain calm. He needed the evil child to trust him with his secrets. He thought briefly of Aaron and the others, but quickly pushed those thoughts aside. They would deal with Wormwood while he handled this monster. He only hoped he had the strength to see this through.

Lucifer found himself suddenly alone. He raised the Light Giver, its crackling glow illuminating yet another trapped monstrosity. But this one was different.

He felt drawn to this one, pulled by twin yellow eyes that glowed eerily bright, even from beneath feet of solid translucent ice. He was the Morningstar, once the Lord God's most powerful angel, and what he saw froze him as still as the petrified figure he now looked upon.

It was huge, its flesh the color of blood. Two enormous horns sprang from its head. Its eyes glowed like two search-lights, and its muscular, fur-covered legs revealed not feet but black cloven hooves. A thick muscular tail snaked out from behind the creature, and, seen on closer examination, leathery wings, like those of a bat, were folded at rest upon its back.

Devil.

The word sprang to the forefront of Lucifer's mind, for there was no other way to describe it.

This was how the world believed the ultimate evil should look, how earth's old legends and myths had portrayed *him*.

Lucifer was both fascinated and repelled by what he saw.

The child was suddenly beside him, staring up at the fro-zen Devil with rapt attention.

"What is this thing?" Lucifer demanded.

"It's me," the child said. "Or, what will be me as soon as everything is in place."

Lucifer stared at the frozen nightmare and then at the child.

"I made this," the child explained, pointing to the frozen Devil. "This will be the form I wear when I emerge to rule."

"You . . . made this?" Lucifer asked, eyes locked on the monster's yellow gaze.

"I gave up my corporeal form millennia ago, choosing instead to exist in spirit," the child explained. "But now that the time grows near for my plans to reach fruition, I shall need a body again."

All Lucifer could do was stare at the monstrous horned shape within the ice.

"I wanted to give them a shape that was familiar," the child continued. "Something that would put fear in their hearts."

He looked at Lucifer again and smiled.

"I will give them the Devil they know."

Kraus could not communicate with him like the Nephilim could, but Gabriel knew that the human healer understood how important it was that he accompany him.

He'd even brought along his bag of medicines.

Kraus hurried to keep up with him, walking beside the dog as he led him to Lorelei.

There was a distant rumble of thunder, and Gabriel could not help but pause. Milton moved nervously from the top of his head down his neck, then back to his head again. The mouse was frightened, and Gabriel wished he could have reassured the small animal, but even he wasn't too sure anymore.

The Labrador lifted his snout to the air, sniffing, and he did not like the scents he found there. Without really knowing why, he began to growl, a low rumbling sound that ended in a kind of anxious whine.

"What is it, boy?" Kraus asked, still standing beside him.

Gabriel knew that the healer was only human, but he wondered if Kraus could feel what he did, sensing that there was something bad in the air.

Gabriel started off again, and Kraus obediently followed. At the front door to the science building, Gabriel barked impatiently.

"All right, I've got it," Kraus said as he reached for the handle and pulled the door open so they could enter.

The building smelled funny. It always did. That was just how magick smelled, Gabriel guessed.

"It's Lorelei, isn't it?" Kraus asked worriedly.

Gabriel barked, and the mouse squeaked, but the man did not understand. So Gabriel quickly trotted down the hallway to where he had left his friends.

At the classroom Gabriel paused, looking around. No one was there.

"Lorelei?" Kraus called out as he entered the room.

Gabriel warned the mouse atop his head to hold on, then dropped his nose to the floor. Finding her scent almost immediately, he began to follow it through the doorway and down the hall. He stopped at the door that stank of magick and led to the room filled with books.

If Lorelei had gone through the special doorway, then that's where they would need to go.

Gabriel barked at the door, signaling for the healer to hurry up and let them in.

"Ah," Kraus said. "She's in the library."

The healer opened the door, and Gabriel bent his nose to the ground and started to track the missing Lorelei. He sneezed, the magick—mingled with the aroma of old paper, parchment, and leather—making the inside of his nose tingle and burn.

He turned around to make certain Kraus was following, which he was, the older man walking along the rows upon rows of books.

Gabriel managed to get ahead of the man but barked once to let him know where he was, then continued on in search for Lorelei, and the source of the strong magickal odor.

At the end of the row, the Labrador stopped, looking from left to right. The stink was strongest down the left-side corridor, disappearing into a shadowy area that he was certain he had never explored before.

"Any luck?" Kraus asked, coming to a stop beside him.

Gabriel peered down the corridor and started to growl. There were sudden flashes of bright light, followed by the moans of someone in obvious pain. Milton grew even more nervous, the mouse's repetitious track up and down Gabriel's back becoming more frantic.

The Lab turned left, barking three times for Kraus to follow, then he bounded down the corridor, not sure exactly what he was getting himself into but not really caring. If Lorelei needed him, then so be it.

It didn't matter what was waiting.

The magickal smell grew stronger as he ran full tilt toward

the searing flashes. It reminded him of the lightning and thunder he had been frightened of before Aaron had changed him, made him better.

The flashes lit the corridor, helping to direct him.

Gabriel barked once again, a loud, frantic sound to let Lorelei know he was coming.

Slowing down at the end of the long hallway, he cautiously peered around the corner into an alcove. It had been a very long time since he'd last peed out of fear—he'd probably still been only a pup—but what he saw then almost caused him to revert to the habits of his younger days.

Gabriel turned the corner, his hackles raised. Even Milton had stopped moving, the little mouse frozen by the disturbing sight.

Lorelei floated above a circular table upon which was an unwrapped scroll. Other books and pieces of parchment orbited around her as she hung in the air, held in the grip of something Gabriel could not see but could smell quite strongly.

There was a strange song inside Dusty's head, playing over and over again—the same song on a continuous loop. And even though he had never heard the haunting song before in his life, he knew that if he were to play it, he would usher in the End of Days.

The instrument was growing stronger again, insisting that he pay attention to its demands.

It was taking everything he had to fight it.

He had run as fast as he could to get away from the wreckage of the farmhouse, hoping that those who wanted him to obey the instrument had been destroyed.

But he knew better.

His entire body ached as if his every muscle had been beaten by a hammer, and the fact that it was cold and rainy did little to make him feel better.

The farmhouse had been in the middle of nowhere, at the end of a tiny road, surrounded by trees. Dusty had decided to leave the road, heading into the woods. He leaned against a tree to catch his breath, remembering the three figures and the dog that he'd seen while unconscious. Had they actually been there, or were they just another form of manipulation by the instrument?

The song played over and over again inside his mind, and Dusty found himself on the verge of humming the simple yet complex tune, stopping himself as he came close to the final notes. He didn't want to take any chances, not knowing what disasters merely humming the song might cause.

His body—and the instrument—protested his every step, but he needed to keep moving. Dusty pushed off from the tree, proceeding deeper into the woods, listening over the sound of the song inside his brain for any hint that he was being pursued.

The song ceased momentarily as he ran, and he became aware of strange rustling sounds. Believing them to be only small animals stirred by his presence, he didn't think of them as anything to be concerned about, but the instrument did not feel the same.

It warned him of an impending threat, trying to convince him that now was the time to make a stand.

Now was the time to call down the end.

Dusty fought the instrument. He stumbled over something in the dark, and fell hard to his knees, pitching forward onto his chest—the wind knocked from his lungs with the impact.

He lay there coughing, trying to catch his breath. The rustling grew louder in the patches of shadow around him.

Rolling over, Dusty began to stand, and was startled to see he had stumbled into a small cemetery. He rose to his feet amid a crop of gravestones. The instrument inside his coat pocket continued to warn him, and he thought he saw something slithering beneath the leaves on top of one of the graves.

Something other than the insistence of the instrument told him that maybe being in a cemetery wasn't the wisest thing, and he spied a path through the early morning light that he hoped would lead him out of the graveyard. He hurried his pace, but tripped and fell on his face.

"Damn it," he hissed, thinking he'd caught the toe of his boot on a protruding root. He rolled onto his side and reached down to pull his foot free, and then he was met with the most disturbing of sights.

A hand was sticking up from the dirt of a grave—a pale, withered hand that grasped the ankle of his boot with a powerful grip.

He remembered the slithering, eel-like things that liked to inhabit dead bodies. And here he was, in a used-car lot of dead bodies.

Dusty quickly reached down, attempting to pry the fingers from his boot, the thumb of the corpse's hand breaking away like a dry twig. He managed to get his foot free, but the ground around the hand started to buck and heave as something larger tried to force its way to the surface.

Scrambling to his feet, Dusty saw the dirt around other nearby graves begin to churn as well, and he started to run. But it was like running in a minefield, hands exploding up from the damp soil to try to seize him.

And all the while the instrument whispered a tune inside Dusty's head.

Up ahead on the path, Dusty saw a figure and was about to call out a warning, but the words caught in his throat like a piece of jagged glass as the tattered figure lurched from the shadows into the early morning light. It was a large man, more recently dead, his flesh deathly pale and loose but still holding on to his bones.

Dusty came to a stumbling halt, started to turn, and saw another corpse—a woman in a bright turquoise dress—coming up behind him, and there were still others behind her. All around him corpses in various stages of decomposition were rising up from their graves.

Dusty stuck his hand down into his coat pocket to grip the harmonica. The song became even louder in his mind, and he found himself growing dizzy as the instrument exerted its powerful influence.

He wanted to use it as a weapon to clear a path in order to get away, but he wasn't sure if he was strong enough to do only that . . . wasn't sure if he was strong enough to deny the instrument's desire.

The corpse of a little girl, her face withered and shrunken like that of a mummy, grabbed hold of his arm in a surprisingly strong grip.

"You . . . will . . . stay with . . . us," she said in an unlikely gravelly voice as she held him tightly.

Dusty was trying to pull his arm away when other corpses caught up to them, each of them taking hold of him. He tried to throw them off, but there were too many.

"You will . . . stay . . . with . . . us!" they all cried in their horrible voices.

Bony hands from beneath the dirt tugged at his ankles, holding him in place. There were so many of them now, and he couldn't use the instrument, even if he had wanted to.

The song blared louder and louder inside his mind, drowning out the corpses' awful chants. It was so loud and incessant that he felt his resolve slowly begin to crumble. He had to make it stop.

The corpses had hauled him off his feet, pinning him on the wet, muddy ground.

Suddenly there was a flash that illuminated the cemetery. Dusty knew who the corpses were holding him for, and he hoped that he was strong enough to face the angels, as well as the instrument.

He closed his eyes tightly, using all that he could muster to hold on to his will, to keep the instrument from taking control of his actions.

There came a series of sudden screeches, and the corpses' hold upon him lessoned. Dusty opened his eyes to see the zombies moving to attack a group advancing amongst the headstones.

The newcomers had wings, like the angels from the farmhouse, but each carried a weapon made of fire. The corpses didn't stand a chance, most of them exploding into flames as the weapons cut into them.

Dusty carefully got to his feet, ready to flee the cemetery, when a powerful voice called out.

"Dusty."

He turned slightly to see the guy from the scene inside his head. The attractive girl was with him as well, standing at his side, along with six others.

"I'm Aaron," the guy said, the shiny black wings upon his back gleaming in the light of the blazing sword at his side. "I'm here to take you to someplace safe."

CHAPTER EIGHTEEN

Lorelei could not wait any longer to try the powerful Archon spells to communicate with Heaven and ask the Creator for help.

She could sense that they were running out of time—that the world was running out of time. If she was going to do something, she had to do it right away.

Even though her body protested, so much weaker after locating the instrument, she managed to make it to the library, where the Archon writings she required were kept, separate from the rest. Scholar had explained that these particular writings were special, even to the Archons, for communication with the Almighty was not something to be taken lightly. One did not call to chat with God unless there was something incredibly important to say.

Lorelei believed that she had something to say, and so she

removed the scrolls from their special cabinet, probably for the first time in more than a millennium.

Just touching the ancient writings was an experience. Her hands tingled as if live voltage was running through them.

The spell was particularly grueling. The words were painful to speak, every syllable uttered like a tooth being pulled from her gums. A few times she wasn't sure if she'd be able to remain conscious, but then she thought about the repercussions of failure, for herself . . . the others . . . the world, and she managed to battle through. And the spell kicked in.

Magickal energies, the likes of which she had never before experienced, coursed through her body, like molten lava being pumped through every vein and artery, followed by five hundred thousand volts of electricity.

And then it really started to hurt.

Her mind was afire as flashes of the cosmos exploded before her eyes, and she caught glimpses of the most magnificent sight she had ever seen . . . a city . . . a city made from the golden rays of the sun . . . a city that sang a song so beautiful that she thought she might die.

But Heaven was not without its defenses. The forces of Heaven berated her arrogance. How dare she think that she could talk to God?

Lorelei felt herself picked up from the floor, preternatural energies leaking from her body to form a swirling maelstrom around her. Heavenly forces surged into her in an attempt to destroy her, but there was too much at stake.

She screamed as she was filled with the glory of Heaven, filled with a power not meant for one such as she, but she did not hide from it—she allowed the power to flow, using it to cry out for God's attention. Using it to beg for the lives of the Nephilim and the world they so desperately sought to protect. She begged the Creator to send someone to help them in their hour of need.

Did the Lord of Lords hear her pleas? She did not know, but as quickly as the heavenly energies were upon her, they were gone, and she found herself falling from the air—discarded—crashing down upon the tabletop, and rolling off to land in a heap on the floor.

She lay there, her body numb, fighting the inexorable pull of unconsciousness; then she sensed Gabriel's presence.

A cold nose moved across her face, followed by the lap of a warm tongue.

"Hey, you all right?" she heard him ask worriedly between licks.

She was too weak to answer, but she forced a limp hand up to gently pat the side of his face. The darkness began to recede, and she felt as though she might have lucked out again, this time with the help of a Labrador's love.

She felt a hand upon her brow, and she realized that Kraus was there as well. She wanted to tell him that she was all right, that she just needed a hundred years or so to rest, but he was already working his healer's magick upon her.

"Lie still," he told her gently, and she heard the sound of his medicine bag snapping open, and then the strong scent of medicinal herbs filled her nostrils as a cloth that made her feel cool in the most pleasant of ways was draped across her forehead.

Lorelei forced open her eyes and looked up into Gabriel's concerned gaze.

"Hey," she said, attempting to make herself sound stronger than she was.

"Hey, back," he grumbled. His head dipped down and he gave her another lick upon the cheek.

"How are you feeling?" Kraus asked her, holding her wrist and taking her pulse.

"Like crap," she managed.

"Can I ask what you were attempting to do?" Kraus questioned.

"I was calling for help," she replied. And then it hit her. She'd nearly killed herself but no one had answered her. Not God, not anyone else. "But I guess nobody was home," she added quietly.

Then, as if in response to her comment, a strange sound filled the library and the floor beneath her began to shake.

"What's that?" Lorelei asked, using what little strength she had left to push herself up into a sitting position.

The sound grew louder, and Gabriel was at full attention, growling and barking as the noise intensified. Milton burrowed beneath the Labrador's collar.

Then the roof of the library caved inward as something crashed through the ceiling to land on the floor in an explosion of fire, smoke, and dust. The sound, like a jet engine, was deafening.

The bookshelves surrounding the group toppled, creating a protective roof above their heads, saving them from the pieces of burning wood and rubble that were thrown into the air at the object's impact.

Kraus lay on the ground, coughing wildly in the choking dust. Lorelei managed to crawl beneath the canopy of shelves, toward Gabriel. The Labrador stood at the edge of an enormous jagged hole in the wood floor, peering down into the swirling smoke and darkness.

"There's something moving down there," the dog said.

Lorelei joined him at the edge, testing the floor with her weight before getting too close, but it held, and she was able to peer over the edge too.

Her first thoughts were that they were under attack, that the Powers angels that wanted to bring about the End of Days had somehow found their location.

But then she had the strangest of thoughts.

What if it wasn't an attack at all? What if her attempt to communicate with Heaven, with the Creator, had been successful, and He had answered her cries for help?

Gabriel began to bark as something stirred down in the pit.

She saw it too, and reached over to calm the dog, to let him know that maybe this was a good thing.

And then what had fallen from the sky roused the smoky air with its feathered wings, revealing its true identity. And Lorelei could not help but scream.

Dusty stared, head cocked to one side. It reminded Aaron of how Gabriel sometimes looked at him when the dog didn't quite understand something.

"I guess you're real," Dusty then said to Aaron, before his eyes rolled into the back of his head, and he slumped forward, falling to the cemetery ground.

Aaron knelt beside the boy. He could see that Dusty was struggling with something.

"You're going to be all right," Aaron reassured him. "Hang in there."

"You . . . you don't know what it's like," Dusty said through gritted teeth. "It wants . . . it wants to trigger . . . to trigger the end. . . ."

Dusty thrashed in Aaron's arms. Aaron pulled him closer in an attempt to lend him some of his strength. He wanted to tell the youth that *yes*, he did understand. He remembered the fear and turmoil he had experienced when his angelic nature had first started to manifest, how it, too, had wanted to take control, suppressing his human nature.

But Aaron had fought that untamed, divine spirit, bending it to *his* will, eventually melding the two halves of his dual nature into one magnificent being.

"Fight it, Dusty," Aaron urged, picking up the trembling youth. "You just need to show it who's boss."

Vilma's cry interrupted his thoughts. "Aaron, look out!"

Then Aaron was struck by a searing blast of divine energy that would have burned the flesh from his body had he not instinctively shielded himself within his wings.

Aaron let Dusty fall from his arms and spun in the direction of the attack, his fiery sword raised. He gasped as he saw four angels hovering above the cemetery. Their garments were tattered and burnt, their faces blistered, as though they might have been in some sort of battle recently.

These are the last of their malignant kind, Aaron thought. *These are the last of the Powers.*

"Give the boy here," the leader demanded. "I won't tell you twice, abomination."

Aaron couldn't help but laugh as he leaped into the air to attack. The last of their host, their leader gone, and still they thought they were the top dogs.

Lashing out with his sword of fire, the Powers' leader blocked Aaron's attack with a blade of his own; an explosion of searing embers filled the air as the swords connected.

"Is this how it's going to be, Nephilim?" the Powers' leader asked, pushing Aaron back with great force. "And here I was, content to let you and your loathsome kind die along with the rest of the world."

Aaron touched down upon the ground. Vilma guarded Dusty, her own sword of fire poised and ready if need be. The other Nephilim gathered around their leader, ready for whatever was to follow.

"The world isn't dying anytime soon, angel," Aaron said. "It's under our protection, as is this man." He pointed the end of his sword at Dusty, who trembled as if freezing, but Aaron knew otherwise. The youth was fighting to maintain control, fighting for the life of the world, and they were going to do everything they could to help him.

"Under your protection," the angel repeated with a sneer. He turned his head to glance briefly at his silent brothers. "The world was once under our protection," he said. "And it's still overrun with monsters and half-breed trash. No, it's better that we let it die."

Aaron took note of the thick gray clouds forming in the sky behind the angels. At first he had believed it to be a natural occurrence, but now he wasn't so sure.

"I want you to be ready to leave when I say," Aaron ordered in a voice low enough that only the Nephilim could hear.

The Nephilim looked at him, not sure how to react.

"Aaron, we're not going to—"

"You will leave when I say. Take Dusty with you. The fate

of the world depends on it," he explained, eyes on the darkening clouds that swirled in the sky above their heads.

"You heard 'im," Jeremy said. "When he says go, we go." A battle-ax of fire formed in his grasp with a hiss.

And that was when the sky opened up, raining down swollen, soaking drops of water—and something else all together.

Aaron had no idea what to call them. Gremlins, perhaps? Demons? Whatever they were, they came in the clouds, their bodies a shiny, rubbery black, about the size of a city pigeon, with bat-like wings. They fell with the rain, their large mouths open and rimmed with razor-sharp teeth.

"Go, now!" Aaron roared, springing off from the ground, swiping at the flying beasts as they swarmed around him.

"Do you see, Nephilim?" the Powers' leader cried over the sound of the torrential downpour. "Do you see how far we've fallen? We ally ourselves with what we most despise, but we do it for the good of all."

The demons flew about Aaron, many attaching themselves to his body and biting into his tender angelic flesh. Aaron fought the best he could, but as he killed more and more, three times as many took their place.

The Powers' leader droned on above him.

"Allow this world the mercy of a quick death, Nephilim."

"How about we help you on the way first?" Aaron said, flapping his wings all the harder and propelling himself at the

Powers' leader and his silent ilk, a growing flock of demonic pursuers following him on his course.

The Powers' leader roared his disapproval, but it didn't do him much good. At the last possible minute, Aaron dipped down, flying beneath the Powers as the demonic swarm continued straight on in their flight path, attacking the angels in a cloud of leathery wings, claws, and teeth.

Flying earthward, Aaron saw with disappointment—and anger—that the other Nephilim had not yet left.

"Go!" he screamed at them as he flew closer. "I'm not going to tell you again!"

He could see that they were dealing with the odd demons attacking from the sky, and the zombies that crawled up from the earth.

Vilma looked at Aaron defiantly, not wanting to leave him.

"You heard me, get out of here!" he roared.

There was a sudden explosion of searing heat from behind, and Aaron was thrown to the ground with the intensity of the blast. He landed atop a grave marker, the marble cross shattering as his body struck it.

He looked up into the sky. The Powers had ignited their bodies in divine fire, incinerating many of the flying demons that they had brought with them.

They were descending now, coming to claim their prize.

"If you love me, you'll go," Aaron said to Vilma, chancing a look at her. "Take Dusty and go . . . please."

He could see that it pained her, but she listened, running back to the trembling youth. Aaron watched as Vilma took Dusty into her arms and spread her wings.

He mouthed the words *I love you* as their eyes met. Then Vilma's wings closed around her, and she and Dusty were gone.

The other Nephilim hesitated, ready to fight by Aaron's side, but the world would need them.

"Go! Go! Go!" Aaron cried as fire rained down from the sky. He shielded himself with his wings, and ran across the cemetery, motioning for the others to get away. One by one he saw them go, and felt as though they still might have a chance to win the war.

Aaron was ready to face his foes again in flight when a ball of fire hurled him back.

"Where have they gone?" the Powers' leader demanded, touching down in a crouch, the other angels flanking him.

Aaron struggled to his feet, dazed by the intensity of the fire. The ground around him was burning as if doused in napalm. Thick clouds of choking black smoke obscured his vision.

He heard the sound before his saw it, the blade of fire slicing through the air toward him. Aaron managed to lift his own weapon just in time, preventing the razor-sharp instrument of divine retribution from severing his head from his body.

The Powers' leader appeared before him, one of his feathered wings lashing out with enough force to hurl Aaron backward into the side of a concrete mausoleum.

"You will take me to the carrier, or I will call down the monsters that hide upon this world and they will feast upon the innocent and guilty alike!" the angel roared.

"What will it matter?" Aaron wiped a trickle of blood from the corner of his mouth, ready to battle till the end. "If your intentions are to end the world."

The angel smiled and it was a disturbing sight, void of any humor.

"There is much to be said for a merciful death." The angel nodded. "And I would even bestow it upon the likes of you if—"

"Go to hell," Aaron snarled, charging at the angel.

It was then that the three other Powers attacked, swords of fire all pointed at the Nephilim. At first Aaron wasn't doing too badly, but the attacks were relentless, never allowing him even a moment to gather his wits.

He'd been driven back to a cemetery monument depicting a traditional angel: peaceful smile, adorned in flowing robes, wings and arms spread wide, accepting the inevitability of death and the glories of the afterlife. Aaron was ready to make his stand. He could feel the fatigue starting to overwhelm him, but still he fought.

Two of the Powers angels had taken to the sky once again, dropping a halo of divine fire around the monument, the intensity of the flames keeping him from running.

But he had no intention of running.

The leader strode through the flames unaffected, burning blade held at his side, the others followed at his heels. "To think that you killed my master, Verchiel," he said. "He must have wanted to die."

The leader attacked, his weapon crackling like the melting of glacial ice as it cut through the air. Aaron did all he could to avoid the relentless onslaught, but he knew that he was slowing down, and that it was only inevitable that the leader's blade would soon find him.

Suddenly a fissure opened in the earth, separating Aaron from the Powers. At first he wasn't sure what had happened. Then another winged form unexpectedly dropped down from the sky to stand at his side, a crackling battle-ax of divine energy clutched in his hands.

"Think it's time for you to get going," Jeremy said, eyes fixed on the advancing Powers.

"I thought I told you to leave," Aaron said tightly.

"And when have I ever really listened to what you had to say?" Jeremy asked with a wink, before turning his attentions to their foes. "Now go, the others need you more than they need me."

Aaron started to protest, but he saw that this was something Jeremy wanted to do . . . *needed* to do. This was his sacrifice for them, for the world, and Aaron had to accept that.

And he did as Jeremy told him, wrapping himself within the folds of his wings. Aaron's last vision of the graveyard was of the British Nephilim swinging his battle-ax, cutting a blazing swath through the air on his way to meet his enemies.

The blade of his ax buried itself deep within the chest of one of the Powers.

The angel screeched like an enormous bird of prey, clutching at the offending weapon as his body began to smolder and burn.

Jeremy yanked the blade free and spun to meet his next attacker. The remaining three angels held back, watching him with cold, merciless eyes.

"Oh, you are a wild one," their leader spoke.

Jeremy sneered, spinning the handle in his hands. The ax spat flecks of fire as it twirled. "I am that," he agreed. "Now, who wants to be next?"

"There is a fire in your eyes, Nephilim." The leader began to pace slowly, his burning sword held close to his side. "The fires of madness, I think."

Icy fingers clutched at Jeremy's heart at the angel's words.

"How many have I seen, just like you, over the centuries," the leader continued. "Clinging desperately to sanity as the angelic force inside eats it away."

"Shut your bloody mouth," Jeremy demanded. He could feel his wild, divine nature surge, fighting against his control.

The leader chuckled.

"It was an act of mercy, killing them," the angel said. "No

matter how desperately they fought to stay alive, the look in their eyes was always one of thanks when I stilled their beating hearts."

It was like trying to hold on to a leash with a ravening pit bull on the other end. Jeremy did his best, but the angelic nature got the better of him. The Nephilim spread his wings and lunged, flying through the air as he screamed out his bloodlust, swinging his blazing ax.

But the Powers' leader was faster, soaring above his attack and bringing his own blade down upon one of Jeremy's wings.

The boy cried out, falling to the ground and rolling to extinguish the smoldering gash. He was about to attack again when the skeletal remains pushed up from the ground, wrapping its withered arms around his neck. Jeremy drove the hilt of his battle-ax back into the face of the corpse, but others had come to join the fray. There were so many that they pinned his wings and held him to the ground, the fetid smell of their decay making him gag.

His heavenly nature was insane with rage, but there was nothing that he . . . or it . . . could do. The corpses held him fast, no matter how hard he struggled.

The Powers' leader approached, looming above him as he lay entwined in the arms of the living dead.

"There," the Powers' leader said. "Now we can talk."

Jeremy growled like a wild animal, struggling to break the corpses' grip but to no avail.

"Where did the other Nephilim go? Where did they take my prize?"

"Go to hell," Jeremy sneered.

The angel looked around him. Parts of the cemetery were still aflame, and animated corpses stood around waiting for orders. Some of the black-skinned demon things clung to the trees.

"Too late," the angel said, before turning his attention back to Jeremy. "I'll only ask one more time."

Jeremy remained silent. He knew that Lorelei's magickal barriers would protect the school from any unwanted attention. They would never find it, even if they tried.

"Good," Jeremy said with a mischievous grin. "I was getting tired of hearing your voice."

The leader's stare was laser-beam sharp, and Jeremy tensed for what was to come. The angel looked around and raised a delicate hand, motioning for one of the walking corpses to amble closer. The body of the middle-aged man was fresher, probably in the ground for no more than a month and showing only minimal patches of rot.

"I need to know where the Nephilim have taken the carrier and the instrument," the angel told the corpse.

The animated body listened intently.

"I want you to get that information for me," the leader continued.

The corpse looked from the angel to Jeremy.

"Maybe if you ask me nice," Jeremy cracked.

"He will not tell me," the corpse gurgled wetly with a shake of his head.

"I didn't expect he would," the Powers' leader admitted, turning his malevolent gaze back to Jeremy. "I want you to go inside and take it."

Jeremy wasn't sure what that all meant, but he noticed that the corpse actually appeared flustered.

"He still lives," the zombie began to explain. "There will be conflict."

"Then it's a fight I hope you will win," the Powers' leader said with finality. "Get me that information, or I would hate to be one of your species."

The corpse hesitated, looking around at his rotting brethren.

Jeremy strained against the corpses' grip, but they held him fast. He watched as the middle-aged corpse lumbered toward where he lay. Looming over him, the dead man slowly opened his mouth with an awful creaking sound as the jaw unhinged. Jeremy's heart raced as a black eel-like thing surged up from the back of the corpse's throat, slithering into his mouth, then dropped onto the Nephilim's chest.

They were all watching now, the corpses as well as the angels.

"What is it going to do?" Jeremy asked, struggling against his captors as the eel slithered across his chest and up onto his chin.

The Nephilim thrashed his head from side to side. An idea

of the fate that was likely to befall him filled him with equal parts terror and disgust.

Decaying hands grabbed at his chin and lips, prying open his mouth as the eel patiently waited.

"Open wide," Jeremy heard the Powers' leader say, and he felt thousands of tiny, furry legs dancing upon his tongue.

CHAPTER NINETEEN

INTERLUDE

The angel lay at the bottom of a deep, dark hole. His naked body burned with the fires of punishment, cleansing flames meant to scour away the sins he had committed in the name of his Creator. Everything that he was had been stripped away by the Lord of Lords. Down to the molecular level, every cell of his being had been dissected and reassembled.

The Almighty had wished to understand where He had gone wrong with His creation, but the mystery had eluded Him. From what He could surmise, there had been no error in the design, no flaw that had led to the angel's perpetration of such horrendous acts. Nothing had been amiss.

The Lord had reassembled His creation and had returned him to life, asking, *"Why did you offend me? Why did you commit such atrocities in my name?"*

And the creation had gazed lovingly at Him, with only truth in his eyes, and spoke: *"Everything that I did, I did for you."*

The Creator of All was angered by this, enraged by the knowledge that such sins—such atrocities—were committed in His most holy name. But instead of destroying the offending creation in His fury, the Almighty wrapped the angel in the divine flames of purity and cast him down from the heavens to the earth.

For was He not a kind and merciful God?

The angel, having fallen, now stirred, slowly rising to stretch his muscles and wings, which he had feared would never feel the winds beneath them again.

And he turned his gaze up, to look upon the faces of those peering down upon him.

A woman cried out, obviously overcome by the mere sight of him.

And Verchiel could not help but agree, for he had always been a most awesome vision to behold.

Aaron threw open his wings as he stumbled forward, gasping to capture his breath.

Vilma was waiting, a sickly looking Dusty by her side. The other Nephilim were gathered around them and greeted Aaron with expressions of concern.

"Where's Jeremy?" Vilma asked.

Aaron turned, hoping to see the familiar shimmer as Jeremy appeared behind him.

But it didn't come.

"He told me to come back," Aaron explained, a wave of guilt suddenly coming over him. He looked at Vilma. "He said that I was needed here more than him."

Vilma's eyes grew moist. "It doesn't mean he's dead . . . right?" she asked.

"Right," Aaron agreed, looking over his shoulder again, hoping the teen would appear. But still there was nothing.

He stepped closer to Vilma and placed a comforting arm around her shoulders. He wanted to tell her that Jeremy would be fine, but he had seen what the boy was going up against—alone—and he didn't have the heart to say that Jeremy might not have survived.

Aaron felt his regret growing, and he was considering going back when—

"I want to thank you," Dusty spoke up. He was shivering, as if racked with fever.

"How are you feeling?" Aaron asked him.

Dusty's hand had been in his pocket, and he removed it to reveal a harmonica.

Aaron found himself stepping back and away from the seemingly harmless object, pure instinct setting off alarms of danger. "Is that it?" he asked.

"Yeah," Dusty answered. "It's quiet now. As soon as we got

away from them—the angels—and those dead guys . . ."

Aaron came in for a closer look. He laughed but with little humor.

"What's funny?" Vilma asked.

"It's a harmonica," Aaron said. "The instrument to call down the End of Days is a *harmonica*. Am I the only one who sees humor in that?"

"I don't see humor in any of this," the Nephilim Melissa said, folding her arms tightly about herself. "I'm not sure if I'll ever see humor in anything again."

Aaron didn't know what to say, but he watched as Cameron walked over and took her hand in his. That was what they had to do. They were all in this together and would need to help one another through the difficult times.

"It used to be a horn."

Aaron looked to Dusty. "Excuse me?"

"This," Dusty said, holding up the harmonica. "It was a horn before I got it. I guess it takes the form of the instrument that you're most familiar with," he suggested. "Does that sound right?"

"It sounds as sane as anything else I've heard these days," Vilma said, staring expectantly out across the campus, checking for their missing comrade.

Aaron was furious with himself for leaving Jeremy.

"Whatever the shape, it's dangerous and we need to figure out a way to keep you—and it—from falling into the hands of the Powers," Aaron said.

"We should probably bring him to Lucifer," Vilma said.

Aaron watched the expression on Dusty's face, knowing exactly what it would be.

"Did you say Lucifer?"

"It's a long story, but yeah. It's *who* you think, only he's not *what* you think, if that makes sense."

Dusty smiled weakly. "About as much as anything else I've heard these days," he said, echoing Vilma.

Aaron was about to suggest they head over to the administration building to find Lucifer when they all heard a loud, familiar sound. It was the sound of a reality being slowly torn in half. It was the sound of Nephilim appearing as they traveled within their wings from here to there.

The Nephilim turned toward the sound, and Jeremy appeared in a crouch, still wrapped in his brown-and-white-flecked wings. Aaron could not help but glance at Vilma. She looked so relieved now.

He was being stupid. He knew it. Aaron quickly pushed his feelings away. There were more important things to think about right then, one of them being Jeremy's safe return to the school.

"You made it," Vilma said, moving toward Jeremy.

Aaron grabbed her arm, stopping her. Something wasn't right. He could feel it in the air around them. The angelic sigils that adorned his flesh in times of battle began to rise to the surface. That wasn't a good sign.

Then three others appeared beside Jeremy: the Powers angels in all their horrific glory.

Jeremy stood awkwardly, his face a sickly shade of white.

"I'm sorry," he said as the ax of fire came to life in his hands, and he sprang to attack the Nephilim.

The Morningstar was paralyzed with indecision.

It was all so much bigger and more complex than even he could have imagined. Certainly he had been aware that shadowy forces existed, but he had never imagined the extent of their menace.

The child's laughter distracted him from his troubling thoughts, and he turned to see him reclining upon a great throne of ice.

"What is it?" Lucifer asked.

"I'm just happy," the child said, bare feet kicking against the throne as they dangled. "Everything is moving along exactly as I anticipated."

The temperature within the chamber became startlingly colder, and the smoother sections of the great ice walls frosted over with a crackling sound.

Lucifer tensed, unsure of what was happening. Images began to appear on the opaque surfaces of the ice, as if on a movie screen. At first Lucifer didn't know what he was seeing, then recognized an image of earth shown from a great distance as it hung in the blackness of space.

"What is this?" he started to ask, looking toward the child.

"Patience," said the child, feet kicking faster, as if watching his favorite television show.

The perspective changed, and Lucifer realized the cold bleakness he was seeing was the moon.

Lucifer glanced over to the child again.

"Watch," the child commanded, as if anticipating his questions.

They were approaching a crater now, one of the larger ones visible upon the barren surface, and their point of view then traveled up and over the rocky lip and down into the darkness.

"We have to go quite deep," the child said, his voice an excited whisper.

"For what?" Lucifer asked, his curiosity piqued.

"To find him," the child said.

"To find whom?"

"The angel," the child said with a sense of wonder. "The angel that will help make all my dreams come true."

Something gradually began to appear on the black ice wall. As it took form, Lucifer began to realize the extent of the child's plans.

"The Abomination of Desolation," he whispered.

"A harsh name," the child said. "But appropriate, I guess. I like to call him by the name given to him by God."

A view of a sleeping giant took form. Like a fetus suspended in the womb, the angel hung there, enormous wings furled upon its back, its body clad in ornate armor covered in the sigils of ending. God's hand had put those markings upon the angel and its bodily armament, in case there ever came a time when the earth needed to end.

"Wormwood," said the child, in awe of what was projected before them.

This angel was a last resort for a world suddenly plagued with evil.

And now it was about to be manipulated by the very being it was created to destroy.

"I don't understand," Lucifer said, staring at the image of the slumbering angel. "I gather you've been behind the remaining Powers' attempts to locate the instrument and inspire its use."

The child was now sitting cross-legged upon his ice throne, listening with anticipation.

"You're doing quite well," he said, urging Lucifer to continue.

"But I don't understand the gain," Lucifer confided. "Why would you awaken something that could potentially destroy you and your family, and all their horrible creations, not to mention the earth itself? It doesn't make sense."

"You're right on so many levels," the child said, now standing on the throne, moving excitedly from foot to foot. "Yes, oh yes, the Desolation Angel could most assuredly destroy me, my family, all its creations, and the world. I most certainly agree."

Lucifer glared at the child, annoyed that he still couldn't see the big picture. "Then why would you wish to wake it up?"

"Because it *can* destroy us," the child said, stifling a giggle.

Lucifer felt his anger spike. He hadn't experienced fury this intense in centuries, and his Light Giver blazed to life as if he were holding a ray of the sun.

"I grow tired of your games," Lucifer snarled. "Tell me why you'd wish to awaken the angel."

"To prepare the world for my coming." Despite the intensity of the sword's glow, the child looked at him, defying the light, the darkness in the child's gaze seeming to absorb the blade's radiance.

"By destroying it?" Lucifer questioned. "If Wormwood is allowed to fulfill its purpose, then—"

"He will be stopped way before that," the child interrupted.

"Stopped?"

The child nodded, a sly smile upon his young face. "Killed after severing the world's connection to God and Heaven, but before the deathblow can be delivered."

Lucifer could not believe what he was hearing.

"Somebody is going to kill the Abomination of Desolation?" he asked incredulously.

The child hopped down from the ice throne and approached him.

"A group of somebodies, actually," he said.

Lucifer was still perplexed. Who could possibly have the power to kill God's angel born with the sole purpose of—

And then the Morningstar came to understand.

The child stood before the wall of ice where the body of the Devil was frozen, staring through the glacial wall at the scarlet-skinned beast enshrined within.

"The Nephilim are far more powerful than even you believe," the child spoke. "And your son . . ." The child turned from the frozen Devil to look at Lucifer.

"He is the most powerful of them all."

Lucifer could no longer contain his fury. With a roar, he lashed out, swinging the Light Giver at the child. Lucifer knew he would likely do little damage to the child's phantom form, but this was purely an act of rage.

The child vanished as the blade struck the wall of ice with incredible force, a flash of searing white illuminating the chamber.

"Why so upset?" the child's disembodied voice asked, echoing through the chamber. "If you're going to serve me—"

"I'd never serve the likes of you," Lucifer snarled, thrusting out his burning sword, igniting the pockets of shadow as he searched for the child.

"That makes me sad," the child said.

The voice seemed to be coming from everywhere, but Lucifer continued to search.

"Where are you?" the Morningstar demanded. "Show yourself."

"I want to assure you," the child's voice spoke, "that this isn't what I wanted at all."

There was a loud cracking sound, followed by a rapid succession of pops and snaps.

Lucifer whirled around and saw jagged cracks forming in the section of the wall that contained the body of the Devil.

The enormous blood-colored beast exploded from its cold confines. Clawed hands reached down to take hold of the Morningstar in an impossible grip.

"We could have been so special together," the child spoke, now wearing the body of the Devil. "Such a waste."

CHAPTER TWENTY

Geburah remembered the words of his leader.

At the time, the Nephilim scourge had reached its zenith. The great Verchiel had gathered the Powers within the frozen remains of the ark, located deep within a dormant volcano atop the mountain Ararat.

The Powers' leader had believed the ark of the holy man Noah to be the perfect place to reveal his plans for purging the world of evil. It was symbolic. The Creator had sent a great flood to wash away the world's sins, and now Verchiel would attempt to cleanse the planet of the growing Nephilim threat.

Aboard the vessel of petrified wood, partially buried in tons of snow and ice, they had been roused by their leader's words, but then the angel Verchiel had grown strangely stoic, and had begun to speak of another plan . . . the final solution if they were to fail.

That was when Geburah, and five others of the Powers host, had been singled out. They were to leave their brethren, to live amongst the humans and take note of the amassing evils. If all went according to plan, this evil would be wiped away when the greater Nephilim threat was no more, but if Verchiel should fail . . .

Geburah shook himself from his recollection, hovering in the air above the Nephilim's hiding place. Now was the time to complete his master's wishes, now was the time to expunge all the evil that had malignantly grown upon a world once blessed by God.

Now was the time to bring it all to a close.

The hairs on the back of his neck bristled, and the Powers' current leader sensed that he was in the presence of the profane. Geburah turned his gaze to the air behind him, watching with a slight unease as the sky became black with the arrival of the monsters that had allied themselves with the Powers.

Beasts of the air—gargoyles, imps, and demons—were driven from their hidey-holes with a promise that they would be allowed to live if they were to serve the Powers on this most sacred of missions. It was a lie to be certain, but a lie to achieve a greater good.

If all went according to plan, none of them would survive, the blessed or the accursed.

With the flapping of leathery wings at his back, Geburah turned his attentions to the earth below him. In the shadows he could see more horrific shapes moving, marching, stomping, burrowing, and slithering—others of the monstrous ilk that joined the Powers' cause in the hopes of having mercy bestowed upon them for their service.

In the time it took for Verchiel to try to achieve his sacred goals—and fail—the earth had become overrun with evil; beasts of every conceivable size and shape waited for an opportunity to claim the world for their own nefarious purpose.

It troubled the angel to be in the presence of things so foul, but it was all for the best. That is what he would tell himself, over and over again.

A mantra to the end of the world.

Evil had come to their home, emerging from the cover of shadows and dropping from the sky.

And the Nephilim rose to battle.

Each bore the power of a divine being inside of him, made all the stronger by the melding of a human nature as well.

They were the perfect blend of the heavenly and the earthly; two of the Creator's most prized creations merged to form something entirely new.

That was what they had been told—what had been explained—in order for them to understand what was happening to them.

They had all known they were different, believing they didn't belong.

They knew they were special but hadn't known how.

Aaron had brought them here, to this abandoned school, from the lives they had known outside, to teach them their purpose.

The world was a wonderful place filled with light, but from the light, shadows were created, and in those shadows there were things that did not belong.

The Nephilim soon learned that this was their purpose: to shed light upon the darkness and to destroy the things that waited there. This was what they were learning to do.

The Nephilim waited before the school building that had become their home. They had learned about their abilities, had learned to control the divine power that lived inside of them. Out in the world they had seen evil and had eliminated it. Some of their number had given their lives to the task, but those who had survived had grown bolder with each new mission, preparing them for this.

William let the angelic power flow, just like Aaron had taught him.

His sword of fire blazed a ferocious red as he waded into battle. His enemies were the beasts in the air, on the ground, and in the woods that surrounded the school. His entire focus was on two things: wiping the creatures from existence, and keeping himself alive.

Russell wanted to run away. He had faced monsters before on other missions, but never so many as now, and never all at once. He recognized some of the beasts advancing on them. He'd slain their kind before, but others he had never seen.

The first of his spears of divine fire hummed in his hands, waiting to be thrown at its target, and he had never wanted anything more than to race into the school and to hide someplace safe.

But he knew he wasn't going to do that, no matter how afraid he was. These were his friends.

And this was his job as a Nephilim.

The troll surged up from the ground directly in front of him, trying to stab a filthy knife between his ribs.

But Cameron was faster, evading the monster's thrust with a flap of his wings, bringing the burning blade of his rapier across his attacker's thick muscular neck.

No matter how many times he performed the act of killing, Cameron could not get used to it, and he felt as though a little piece of himself—of his humanity—went away with every death he delivered.

It was a kill-or-be-killed world that he lived in now, and he did not want to die, but Cameron had to wonder if any of who he actually was would be left, once all the killing had finally stopped.

Or would only the angelic survive?

Melissa caught sight of Samantha struggling with four bony, catlike demons. She had never really liked the girl. Sam had always seemed to think she was better than Melissa.

But seeing Sam grapple with so many monsters made Melissa angry. They may not have been the best of friends, but they *were* sister Nephilim.

In a burst of rage, Melissa pierced the eyes of the walking corpse she fought with her twin daggers of white-hot fire. Her immediate foe vanquished, she raced to Samantha's side.

Wings erupted from Melissa's back and she sailed through the air, connecting with one of the demonic cats and sinking the first of her knives into its cold, black heart.

"Thought you could use a hand," she said with a smile, placing her back against Samantha's.

"Thanks," Sam said.

"Don't mention it."

And they fought together, one no better than the other, the beginnings of a friendship forged in heavenly fires and the blood of combat.

Russell was dying; he could feel it. He was leaking copious amounts of blood from multiple bites, and he could feel himself beginning to grow weak. He'd always known he could die. Aaron and Lucifer had told him as much, but one never thinks it could happen to him.

His blood was drawing more of the beasts. They emerged from the shadows, risking daylight to get a piece of him, attacking and then scurrying for cover, watching and waiting for him to fall.

Russell looked to the others for help, but they all seemed to be locked in battles for their own lives. It was solely up to him, which is how it had been for most of his life. He never knew his family, and had lived in state care for as long as he could remember.

His first try at family was here, with the others of his own kind. It had been wonderful, but now it was coming to an end.

The spear of fire dropped from his grasp, fizzling away to nothing before it could even touch the ground.

Russell stood weaponless and watched his attackers grow brazen, stalking toward him, some already wearing his blood upon their lips.

And that just pissed him off.

His anger was extreme, and instead of a sword or an ax he imagined it as a ball of flame, growing larger and stronger inside of him. Barely able to stand, Russell painfully lifted his arm and gestured for his foes to come closer.

That seething ball of rage became larger, and larger still, and he wasn't sure how much longer he could hold on to it. But he managed, waiting until the monsters were just near enough.

And then Russell set it free.

Cameron heard a familiar scream just before the explosion of heavenly fire threw him to the ground. As he scrambled to get back on his feet, he saw that where he'd last seen Russell was now a blackened patch of smoldering earth.

Not wanting to think about what had just happened, he pushed it to the back of his mind, where he stored all of his horrible memories. There were monsters coming through the wafting smoke, things that slithered upon their bellies, others that crawled across the battle-scarred earth on multiple spidery limbs. He glanced quickly at his forearm—twelve burns, twelve kills, since he'd first spilled the troll's blood. It was time to add another.

A bat-like thing swooped down on him with a hiss, attempting to sink its fangs into the soft flesh of his throat. But Cameron reached out, grabbing the bristling fur of the nightmare flier and slamming its fragile body to the ground, driving a fiery dagger into its heart and extinguishing its life.

The bat-thing screamed briefly and then was still.

Cameron looked up to see other beasts now coming to challenge him. But first he placed the burning blade against his flesh.

Thirteen.

And he was sure there would be more.

Samantha saw the monsters converging on the man they'd saved at the cemetery.

Dusty.

He had been placed behind their line of defense, but in all the insanity that was going on, he appeared to have wandered out into the open. Sam knew that the young man was important and that she should do everything in her power to see that he was safe. He looked as though he was having a hard time staying conscious, swaying upon his feet as four trolls stalked him. The ugly beasts were almost there, and Sam didn't know if she would be fast enough to get to him in time, so she imagined a weapon that could reach Dusty faster.

A bow blazed to life, followed by an arrow of orange flame.

"Sweet," Samantha said, placing the arrow against the bowstring of fire. She didn't have time for a practice shot, and hoped her aim was true.

Squinting through one eye, she drew back and let the arrow fly. She could hear it hissing as it flew through the air, finding its target in the center of one of the trolls' foreheads, igniting the monster's entire skull as if it were the head of a torch.

Sam walked steadily toward the monsters that had now turned their attentions to her. One flaming arrow after the next found its target, turning the attackers into piles of barbecued troll.

Dusty stood there staring, mouth agape.

Samantha smiled. The boy was cute, and she found herself ashamed to be thinking of such trivial things in the heat of battle. Getting her head back in the game, she considered where she might take Dusty to keep him from harm, and was extending a hand to escort him away when a spear tip entered her back, exiting through her chest.

She tried to turn, to take out the troll warrior, but she

could no longer move. Her bow and arrow of divine fire disappeared in a flash. And she fell to the ground, consumed by death.

The instrument screamed. Dusty's hand burrowed into the pocket of his jacket, wrapping around the blazing-hot harmonica, and drew it out into the cool New England air.

He'd watched one of the angels who was trying to protect him go down. And now the monsters were coming for him again.

Dusty wanted to run, but the dizziness was too much. It was the instrument's fault, he could sense it. The device created to signal the end of the world was trying its best to influence his decision, but he had to be strong. He had to prove who was boss.

The monster who had struck down the angel pulled its rusty, bloodstained spear from the angel's back, and licked the blade with a tongue that looked like a giant garden slug. It laughed a low gurgling sound as it fixed Dusty with beady eyes and pointed to the angels that hovered above the school grounds.

"They want you alive," the monster spoke. "If we deliver you unharmed, we get to live."

Dusty slowly backed away from the advancing creatures. The instrument was pleading with him. But he wouldn't listen. It wasn't time. He would not play the song.

One of the monsters charged at Dusty from the side, throwing a heavy woven net over him with a roar. Dusty tried to evade it, but the net still managed to snag him, the heavy material dragging him down to the grass. His attackers roared their approval, loping across the ground, each of them grabbing an end of the net to make sure that Dusty couldn't wiggle free.

Even though he was so weak he could barely keep it together, Dusty tried to fight back. He kicked at the loathsome creatures when they attempted to restrain him. This just made them laugh all the harder as they pulled the net tighter to restrict his movements.

Dusty didn't want this . . . didn't want to be anyone's prize. The instrument was still warm in his hand. Reluctantly, he brought the harmonica to his mouth.

Yes! Yes! Yes! It screamed inside Dusty's mind, believing that its wishes were about to come true, but Dusty used all his remaining strength to correct it.

"No, not for that," he strained, bending his mouth toward the hand that held the instrument. His lips wrapped around the warmth of the metal, and he puffed briefly into the harmonica.

The noise was brief, deafening, and devastating; it obliterated the net in which he was confined, and turned the monsters that had captured him into a fine black spray, which decorated the landscape.

Dusty lay upon the ground, listening to the sounds of the battles going on around him, fighting to stay conscious . . . fighting to maintain control, the song of desolation echoing painfully—insistently—inside his brain. Briefly he shut his eyes, only to feel the instrument grow stronger, trying to force its will deeper. Dusty shook free from its clawing grasp, opening his eyes to gaze up into the smiling face of an angel.

An angel he'd tried to kill earlier with the instrument.

An angel desperate to hear the song of the world's doom that was playing incessantly inside Dusty's mind.

There was an explosion of sparks as Aaron's sword met Jeremy's battle-ax. Aaron beat the air with his wings, propelling himself backward, and away from the young Nephilim, now suddenly his enemy. He had no idea what had happened to the youth, but it seemed that he was internally fighting something that, despite his efforts, was winning the battle.

Jeremy surged ahead in the air above the school with a roar. His wings flapped frantically as he came at Aaron full throttle, ax ready to hack his enemy to pieces.

Aaron changed course, flying up and over in an aerial acrobatic maneuver that made it seem as though he'd flown off, but actually dropped him behind his foe. Lashing out at Jeremy, the son of the Morningstar brought his sword of fire across one of the boy's wings, causing him to spin out of control and plummet toward the ground.

From above, Aaron watched Jeremy catch himself, touching down with barely a stumble. There was madness in the boy's eyes as he again prepared to take to the skies.

"Jeremy," Vilma called out.

Aaron watched as the boy stopped and turned toward the young woman.

Vilma was drawing nearer to him, a far more delicate sword of fire in hand, but held low to her body in a less threatening gesture.

"You need to get ahold of yourself," she instructed. "What's wrong? Tell us so we can help you."

Aaron dropped to the ground beside his girlfriend.

Jeremy's skin was flushed a bright red and sweat dripped from his face in rivulets.

"I . . . I can't fight," he said through gritted teeth. "It's strong . . . very strong . . . it wants to own . . . me."

"What does, Jeremy?" Aaron asked. "Tell us and—"

But Jeremy was gone again, whatever it was inside him exerting full control.

Then the boy threw his ax at them, the spinning weapon throwing swirls of fire as it hurtled toward them.

Aaron leaped to one side as the ax whizzed past. Vilma barely evaded the blade as well, and it struck the ground behind them in a fiery explosion.

But it was all a distraction. Jeremy charged at them, twin swords of scorching white fire in his hands. He came at Aaron first, swinging the weapons wildly. Aaron tried to back away, but his attacker was too fast. The hungry blades took nasty bites from his shoulder and wing.

Suddenly Vilma was there, her own powerful wings spread as she tackled their opponent in midflight. She flew with him across an expanse of lawn, slamming him fiercely against one of the school buildings. Glass shattered and pieces of brick wall crumbled as Jeremy struck.

Leaping back, Vilma again summoned her more feminine blade.

"Please fight this," Aaron heard her say as the Nephilim struggled to shake off the effects. "Remember what we talked about, how you told me that you never wanted to lose control? Don't do it now."

Aaron didn't know what the two had shared during their time away from the school, but it seemed to be having some kind of an effect. Jeremy had dropped to his knees. His entire body was smoldering now, small burn holes forming in his clothes as parts of his body became superheated. Aaron guessed that whatever was inside of Jeremy was attempting to override any control and tap into the power of the angelic essence within him.

"Oh God!" Jeremy cried out. His body was glowing with the intensity of the heat of his flesh. His wings looked as though they were made of fire, their flapping movements tossing tongues of flame as they fanned the air.

Aaron ran to Vilma, attempting to pull her away. If this continued, Jeremy's angelic essence was likely to explode, destroying its human host as Russell's had.

"We have to help him," Vilma said, struggling in Aaron's grip.

"There's nothing we can do," he told her, holding her tightly.

Jeremy continued to scream, sinking his fingers into the soft soil, sending streaks of hungry fire out across the ground.

Aaron leaped from one of the tracks of fire, Vilma clutched in his arms. The ground ignited, violently hurling the two of them back. Aaron rose, checking to be sure that Vilma was all right, and found that she was only stunned.

Jeremy's angelic essence was out of control, and Aaron knew that there was only one thing to do.

He had to put it down before it could do any more damage.

Aaron summoned his sword once more and ran toward the boy who was once his comrade. He didn't want to do this, but he had no choice.

It was an act of mercy.

Snakes of fire leaped from Jeremy's fingertips, and Aaron jumped through the air, slashing at the writhing tendrils, absorbing them the best he could with his own weaponry. Finally close enough to his foe, Aaron lashed out, the pommel of his sword connecting with Jeremy's twisted face and knocking him backward.

Lording above him, Aaron saw his target and knew what needed to be done. Eyes fixed upon Jeremy's exposed neck, Aaron brought up his sword to start its fateful descent.

"Stop!" barked a familiar voice that caused Aaron to hesitate.

He turned toward Gabriel, and slowly lowered his blade. There was a look in the dog's eyes, something that Aaron had seen growing there for quite some time, since the dog had been touched by the power of the Nephilim. Aaron had always known there was something special about the Labrador, even before he'd brought him back from the brink of death. And he was now about to find out how special he actually was.

Gabriel could smell the boy's pain.

The dog had left Lorelei and Kraus in the library to find Aaron, and fill him in on what had happened—on *who* had happened—when Jeremy's pain had cried out to him.

First things first, thought the dog in the midst of chaos.

He'd found Aaron about to do the unthinkable and was glad he was able to stop him. Now it was up to him.

There was angel fire everywhere, as whatever was causing Jeremy's pain attempted to exert control. Gabriel knew he had to be careful. That fire could hurt him badly.

He could sense Aaron close by, ready to strike if necessary.

Gabriel approached Jeremy, brown eyes scrutinizing the Nephilim. With his special vision, he could see the boy's pain, a dark mist hovering about his head.

Gabriel chanced a quick glance at his master, to let him know that everything was going to be fine.

And then the dog remembered what had appeared inside the library, and wasn't quite so sure. But that was a worry for another time. First Gabriel had to save Jeremy.

He was close enough to speak to the boy now.

"Jeremy," Gabriel barked for his attention.

The boy lifted his head, tears steaming from his flushed face in the cool air.

"Get away," Jeremy said, the pain in his voice obvious. "Don't know how much longer I can hold it back."

The boy's clothes were gone, burned away by the intense heat radiating from his body. There were tiny blisters developing upon his flesh, and Gabriel knew he had to act quickly.

The dog inched closer. Gabriel could feel the power of Jeremy's heat, but did not back away.

"Put your hand on my head," Gabriel instructed.

"Can't," Jeremy protested. "Won't hurt you . . . please . . ."

"Do it!" Gabriel barked, dropping down upon his elbows and baring his yellowy-white teeth. The dog could feel the boy growing weaker, the thing inside him causing the pain to strengthen.

Jeremy began to lift a smoldering hand but quickly put it down again.

"Make him go away!" Jeremy begged of Aaron and Vilma.

"Gabriel," Aaron called out cautiously.

The Lab could hear the concern in his master's voice. He loved Aaron more than anything, and would die for him and his cause. But Jeremy was part of that cause, and Gabriel must help him.

"Put your hand on my head!" Gabriel demanded again, moving closer to Jeremy. The heat was powerful, and he could smell the acrid stink of his own fur as it started to burn, but there was no turning back now.

Gabriel turned his gaze to the boy and saw that his eyes had gone nearly white, whatever it was inside exerting nearly full control.

The thing inside saw Gabriel, and made Jeremy smile.

It was a horrible smile, more like a snarl. It made Jeremy reach for him.

The dog yipped in pain. The burning was like nothing he had ever felt before. He gathered his focus, drawing the pain away from the possessed Nephilim, like poison from an infected wound, and giving Jeremy his strength to fight back. It was intense, but Gabriel held his ground.

He felt his body begin to tremble. All that suffering . . . all that darkness. Gabriel pulled upon it, like one of the games he played with Aaron, Gabriel pulling on one end of a rope, Aaron tugging at the other. . . .

Jeremy screamed, his body blazing brightly before the flames that had covered it were extinguished in a whoosh of air. The boy fell forward onto his stomach, his naked form racked with powerful chills as he twitched upon the grass.

Gabriel sat weakly upon his haunches as his own body dispelled the pain back into the air, where it could do no more harm.

Jeremy began to cough and retch, and something long and worm-like slithered from his mouth onto the grass.

Gabriel shot to his feet, eyes locked upon the serpentine shape, and pinned the creature with his paw. The foul thing shrieked. The dog bent down, grabbed the horrible creature in his jaws, and pulled, tearing the monstrous worm in two and silencing its nightmarish squall.

He gave the remains of the worm in his mouth a violent shake before letting them fly, watching as part of them landed in a patch of sunshine and began to disintegrate.

Jeremy moaned, slipping further into unconsciousness. Gabriel sniffed his body and found no trace of the thing that had been trying to control him.

Aaron and Vilma were suddenly at his side, praising him as they patted his head and rubbed that special spot near his tail. For a moment Gabriel basked happily in the attention, wagging his tail and licking their faces.

Then he remembered what awaited them in the science building.

"There's something I need to tell you," Gabriel said, feeling suddenly weak from his exertion and lying down on the cool grass.

"I think it's going to have to wait," Aaron said, he and

Vilma looking off toward the front of the school. "The others need our help."

"But, Aaron," Gabriel protested.

The dog was about to tell him what had happened, what Lorelei had brought back to the world, when a sound filled the air. It was a horrible noise that hurt his sensitive canine ears, and he began to howl. It was a tune the likes of which he had never heard before, and never wanted to hear again. It sounded like the end of the world.

CHAPTER TWENTY-ONE

The Devil hurled Lucifer to the floor, ice shrapnel spraying the air with the ferocity of the impact. Circles of color expanded before Lucifer Morningstar's eyes as he fought to remain conscious. Using the powerful muscles in his back, he flexed his wings, pushing himself up, the Light Giver blazing in his grasp.

Lucifer was about to confront the red-skinned demon again when a sound permeated the icy chamber. Lucifer hesitated as the noise shook the cavern—and his very self—to the core. Though he had never heard its like before, Lucifer recognized the sound, and knew that he was too late.

The Devil roared, his laughter mixing with the lingering apocalyptic sound.

"It's happening," the Devil said with excitement. "Just as I planned."

Lucifer spread his wings, preparing to flee the chamber. *Perhaps there's something I can do to—*

A massive cloven hoof dropped down upon his armored form, crushing him against the frozen cavern floor.

"You're going nowhere," the Devil informed him. "There would be little you could do anyway. Why don't you just watch it all unfold with me, and perhaps reconsider what I have offered you."

Using all his strength, the Morningstar pushed the offending hoof away and slid out from beneath it. Then he swung the Light Giver, the blade biting into the Devil's fur-covered ankle.

Rearing back with a scream, the Devil lost his balance, his massive form falling backward against another frost-covered wall. New images of the sleeping Abomination of Desolation flashed upon the shattering ice. Lucifer could not take his eyes from the sight, even as he took flight to attack the Devil.

The Devil was ready for him, muscular, leathered wings exploding from his back, swatting the fallen angel aside as if he were an annoying insect.

Lucifer struck another wall, his eyes again riveted to the fragmented images. The Angel of Destruction's eyes opened, shining brightly like twin moons hanging in the velvet black of a night sky.

"No," Lucifer hissed, climbing to his feet. He tried to wrap himself within the feathered confines of his wings, to picture the school that had become his home, but the voice of the Devil prevented him from focusing, and escaping.

Lucifer spun around to see the Devil bearing down on him. He slashed out with his sword of fire, severing the tips of two of the giant's fingers.

The Devil roared, clutching the wrist of his damaged hand, but then he began to laugh, and the lava-like blood bubbling from the stumps began to grow into new fingers.

"Why do you fight me?" the Devil asked, lashing out with a perfectly healed hand.

The blow was like being caught in the thrall of a hurricane, hurling Lucifer from the chamber and down the lengthy corridor. He bounced, before crashing to roll upon the ground. Grunting in pain, he pushed himself to his feet.

He was back in the corridor that held the child's—the Devil's—siblings.

"Just imagine, you could be the evil they always imagined you to be," the Devil cajoled. "Pledge your obedience and a new kingdom awaits you."

"I'll fight you until my dying breath," Lucifer gasped, as the Devil bent to enter the corridor.

There was a sudden rumbling sound, followed by earsplitting snaps as the ice containing the other monsters broke open.

And the monsters within awakened.

"You'll be fighting more than me," the Devil said with a

malicious twinkle in his yellow eyes. "And my brothers and sisters are far less merciful than I am."

The cold blackness of the void was all that it had ever known.

Until now. The Abomination of Desolation opened wide its eyes and knew what it had to do.

It turned its gaze to the crater opening above its head, seeing its destination far in the distance. Floating in zero gravity, the angel spread wide its wings. Slowly at first, it flapped its powerful wings—twin sails forged from the metal of Heaven's foundry.

It was all new to the angel. This was its first waking since it had been fabricated by the Creator, and it delighted in this sense of purpose.

Up from the belly of the moon it propelled itself, the power of divinity allowing it to fly within the vacuum of space.

The Abomination of Desolation surged up from the crater to glide above the lunar landscape. Its eyes scanned the surface, void of life, and it was mildly amused. The earth would soon be like this one.

The Abomination turned its attentions from the surface of the moon to the stars and planets above.

The call of the instrument lingered in the cold, summoning Wormwood to perform its duty assigned by God.

Like a beckoning finger, the instrument summoned the Abomination, and the Angel of Destruction flew through the darkness at nearly incalculable speeds.

Its destination grew larger in its vision—the planet that would die at its hands.

It was the worst sound Vilma could ever have imagined. It was a sound like babies crying so desperately that they couldn't catch their breath, brakes screeching for what felt like days before the inevitable thump of metal striking flesh, a telephone ringing in the dead of night and the knowledge that devastating news waited on the other end. It was all of these and more, mixed together to create a cacophony all the more horrible: the death knell for the planet and all that lived upon it.

Vilma, Aaron, and Gabriel ran back to the front of the school and saw the Powers' leader standing beside the beleaguered Dusty, the tool of destruction against his lips as he played.

The way the boy's eyes fluttered and rolled, Vilma could see that he was no longer in control, having succumbed to the demands of the instrument.

"We have to make him stop!" Vilma screamed over the song.

"Wouldn't matter," Aaron said with a sad shake of his head. "Can't you feel it? It's already begun."

"Don't talk like that," Vilma snapped at him. "There has to be something we can do to make this right."

She was in a panic; the harmonica's song placed the most horrible of images in her mind. Vilma saw flashes of her aunt . . . her cousins. They were dead . . . and the world outside their home was dead as well.

The whole world was dead. . . .

"No!" Vilma cried as she squeezed her eyes shut. "No, not yet. There has to be something we—"

The wind suddenly picked up; leaves, dust, and loose debris were tossed around by the powerful shift in air. It became darker, as if a storm was brewing, and in a way, it was.

Vilma looked up to see thick black clouds whizzing past, and something else . . . something that grew larger in the sky above them . . . something that was descending.

Gabriel started to bark and whine, and Vilma knelt beside the dog, placing her arm around him, not only to comfort him but to take some comfort for herself.

"It's all right," she told him, her eyes fixed to the growing shape.

"No," Aaron said then, looking to the heavens. "No, it's not."

The shape had become more defined, and all the more familiar. It was an angel. Huge in stature, it wore armor that glinted in the weak rays of sun that peeked through the shifting miasma of storm clouds. Even its wings were armored, each individual feather sheathed in metal.

Vilma felt herself begin to unravel. She felt herself regressing to the scared little girl she had been after the loss of her mother, after coming to the States to live with her aunt and uncle. She didn't want to be like that again. Scared. Helpless. And looking at Aaron, she saw a glimmer of that in him.

"What do you mean, no?" Vilma said to him. "You're sup-posedly the Chosen One. . . . Do something."

Aaron looked flustered, his mouth opening and closing as he struggled with what to say.

The giant angel was beautiful—but also terrifying.

Is this what the end of the world looks like? she wondered.

It was at least twenty feet tall, but it touched down upon the school grounds without a sound.

Vilma noticed then how incredibly quiet it had become, real-izing that the song being played on the instrument had stopped.

"Aaron," Vilma said, her voice a pleading whisper.

"I know," Aaron whispered back. "I'm the Chosen, I should do something . . . but what?"

That's a good question, Vilma thought, her eyes riveted to the harbinger to the end of the world.

Geburah looked upon the Abomination with joy.

The behemoth of Heaven stood perfectly still, its metal wings slowly furling with a sharp clacking sound. Wormwood appeared to be assessing the situation.

Geburah knew it would not be long before the angel dis-cerned what needed to be done.

The Powers' leader looked out over the grounds. Worm-wood's mighty presence had brought a stop to the battle. Nephilim, monsters, and angels all stood in wonder of its for-midable sight.

Geburah spread his wings, leaping into the air to welcome the Abomination of Desolation. The others of his host followed his lead and they soared toward it. It was time for them to welcome Wormwood, exalt it for what it was about to do in the name of God, Heaven, and in the memory of their former leader, Verchiel.

As the angels approached, the Abomination took on a more defensive posture, areas once smooth and molded to its musculature became sharp and bristled with spines of metal.

He believes us threats, Geburah realized with surprise.

He slowed his ascent as arcs of crackling blue-white energy erupted from the barbs—divine energy—and it sought out each of Geburah's followers, burning them black as they were struck. Their bodies fell heavily to the ground and exploded into clouds of ash.

The Powers' leader managed to summon a sword of fire in an effort to deflect the angel's energy. But Wormwood's strength was mighty, and it obliterated Geburah's weapon with ease, boiling the flesh from his bones.

The Powers' leader dropped to the ground amongst his dead brethren, choking on their powdered remains.

Why? he wanted to ask the Emissary of Ending. *Why did you attack us when we, too, are instruments of the Creator?* But Geburah's vocal cords had been seared, and speech was impossible.

All he could do was lie there, staring at the awesome sight of the angel, a spectator as Wormwood prepared to bring this disease-infested planet to an end.

Dusty gradually awakened, as if emerging from a feverish dream, his body racked with bone-shaking chills.

He dropped to his knees, no longer able to keep himself upright, his vision coming alive to the chaos before him.

Drawing in a trembling gasp, Dusty looked upon the giant that loomed above him. Its armored body prickled with lethal-looking spines, blue lightning arcing from tip to razor-sharp tip. It bent its armored head and stared at Dusty. Its eyes shone like the headlights of an eighteen-wheeler, floating in the darkness peeking out from the helmet's visor.

It was then that Dusty realized he could no longer hear the instrument. The heavenly tool had been silenced.

He took his hand away from his mouth and looked at it. The heated metal had melted his flesh around the harmonica. It didn't hurt, but he knew that it was only a matter of time before it did.

The giant extended one of its huge arms, opening its hand above him. A strange humming then filled the quiet air.

See, I knew it was only a matter of time, Dusty thought as he felt the first knives of pain in his damaged palm.

He looked down to see that the instrument was gradually losing its shape, no longer resembling a harmonica but a living, liquid metal. It slithered out from between his fingers forming a spinning silver orb that hung momentarily in the air before surging up into the giant angel's waiting hand.

There was a blinding flash. Dusty averted his gaze, explosions of color blossoming before his eyes as he gradually turned his attentions back to the armored giant.

The instrument was transforming—becoming something else entirely. It was no longer a horn, or a harmonica, or a metal sphere. Dusty watched as the instrument transformed into an enormous sword.

The weapon of a giant.

The angel held the metal blade out before him as if admiring the enormous weapon. The metal spines that protruded from his body came to life once more. Bolts of mystical energy leaped to strike at the blade, and it glowed with an eerie, pulsing light.

Aaron could feel it to the depths of his being. It was time to act.

"Aaron?" Gabriel asked suddenly, turning his trusting gaze to his master as if he could sense a change in his mood.

Aaron didn't answer the dog, or respond to the plaintive look in his girlfriend's eyes. He didn't want to see the disappointment there.

He let his angelic nature flow through his body, the combined power of some of Heaven's greatest warriors. He felt his skin begin to tingle, the sigils of the angels that had served Lucifer, and had fallen in battle during the Great War, rising to adorn his flesh.

Aaron let his nature decide on the weapon he would use; images of an entire angelic armory rushed through his brain until he fell upon a decision.

The sword was massive, taking shape like a solar flare shooting up from the surface of the sun.

Aaron loosened his wings, freeing his black-feathered appendages of flight.

Vilma called forth her own weapon, readying herself to stand by his side in combat. And by the look upon Gabriel's face, the dog was ready to fight with him as well.

"No," Aaron said to them, already on the move. "I'm going to need for you to hold back, in case I . . ."

He didn't finish the sentence, not wanting to concern them, though he guessed they were already way beyond that. The world was about to end, he could feel it in his bones . . . at the tips of his wings. There was a part of him that just wanted to give in, to drop to his knees and accept what was about to happen.

Thy will be done.

But that was complete and utter bullshit, and he was about to tell this angel . . . to *show* this Wormwood . . . that very thing.

Aaron leaped into the air, blazing sword of war clutched

to his side. Flying over the battlefield, he saw the nightmare of twisted bodies of things that a year ago he would never have believed existed, and the faces of those who had looked upon him as their leader.

Wormwood sensed his approach, turning to meet its attacker. Aaron flew at his armored enemy, lashing out with his weapon and a battle cry. His plan was a simple one . . . a savage one, but it was all he had. Destroy Wormwood and halt the end of the world; it was the best he could come up with on the fly.

His fiery blade skidded off the shoulder of the Abomination, severing one of its person-size spikes. The angel reacted with an echoing roar, bringing its own sword of divine power around and nearly slicing Aaron in two.

Aaron barely evaded the giant blade, dropping beneath the pass and flying toward Wormwood's covered face. Aaron quickly scanned for the targets before him: the throat, the eyes, places where if he struck—and struck savagely—he might kill his enormous foe.

But the Angel of Destruction would have none of that.

Again, the spines that adorned the armored angel came to life, humming with unbridled power. Aaron became trapped between two arcing discharges, and he felt himself immediately powerless. He fell to the ground like a rock, in pain like he had never experienced before.

Struggling to remain conscious, he fought to stand,

retrieving his sword from the ground. As he was about to turn his attention back to the Abomination, Aaron was momentarily distracted by the sound of laughter.

The Powers' leader lay with the corpses, his body severely burnt, his flesh nearly charred from his bones, but still he lived.

"Lay the sword down, boy," the leader spoke in a strained whisper. "It is too late for you . . . for the world. . . . It is here now, accept your failure. . . . It is over. . . ."

That small piece of Aaron, that thread of angelic nature conditioned to accept the will of God no matter how awful, almost asserted control. . . .

Almost.

Aaron flapped his wings again, preparing to take flight into battle, but Wormwood's actions froze him cold.

The giant angel turned its helmeted head to the heavens and emitted a mournful cry, as if bemoaning what it was about to do.

Before Aaron could act, before the thought could even register, the Angel of Desolation took the point of his great and terrible sword and drove it into the ground with one savage thrust.

And the earth cried out, for its end was at hand.

The earth was on its own now.

Like a limb poisoned with infection, the world was cut

off—severed from the influence of Heaven, from the reach of the Lord God.

Everything that lived and breathed upon the earth could feel the change. They could not necessarily say exactly what had occurred, but they knew in their souls that the connection was no longer present.

A sadness and a desperation rippled out through the world, and the things that had lived in the darkness of shadow grew confident, for they knew that God was no longer present.

And the world, and every living thing upon it, belonged to those that slithered, crawled, flew, and stalked.

They could emerge to claim what had long been denied them, for the light of Heaven no longer shone upon the world.

Darkness was triumphant.

CHAPTER TWENTY-TWO

Aaron didn't know what to do.

Wormwood stood there, clutching the hilt of the sword in its armored hands, as energy pulsed down into the earth. The monstrous things that had accompanied the remaining Powers—the trolls, demons, imps, and gargoyles—writhed upon the ground, the divine force emanating from the Abomination of Desolation's sword killing their evil kind, as it began to kill the world.

Aaron felt eyes upon him, and he turned to see William, Melissa, and Cameron, their faces bloody and slack from battle. They looked to him for guidance, but this time he had nothing to give them.

They had failed . . . failed on so many levels.

All Aaron could do was watch as the world was gradually put down for the count.

"Is that it?" called a voice from somewhere nearby.

Aaron turned, along with the others, searching for the source.

Then they saw him coming up from the science building, wings gradually flexing, burning sword in hand.

"Is that all you have, Nephilim?"

Aaron felt as though he might be sick. *First the end of world—and now this.*

"After the fight you gave me, this is how the struggle continues?"

Vilma stepped up beside Aaron, and he glanced at her quickly to see that her eyes were fixed on the approaching figure.

"Aaron," she said as though using all the air inside her lungs. "It can't be him." She squeezed his arm so tightly that her fingernails were on the verge of breaking the skin.

He didn't know how to answer, wondering if it was some sort of hallucination caused by the Angel of Destruction as it brought about the End of Days.

"Maybe it was mere luck that you defeated me," the figure said as he came closer.

"It is him," Gabriel spoke up. *"I've been trying to tell you."*

Aaron looked to the dog. "Gabriel, this isn't exactly a good time for games. What have you been trying to tell me?"

The figure stopped, tilting his head ever so slightly as he studied them.

"Look at yourselves," he said. "No wonder the world is on the brink."

"Gabriel," Aaron urged, two steps away from thinking he'd gone insane.

"Lorelei thinks she did it," Gabriel explained. *"She called Heaven for help and—"*

"And this is how Heaven answered?" Vilma asked in horror.

"She asked for help, and this is what fell from the sky," the dog responded.

Aaron squinted his eyes, taking in the horrific sight before him. The Powers' previous leader, Verchiel, stood there in front of them looking perfectly healthy and quite untouched by God's wrath, just as he had the day he'd murdered Aaron's foster parents.

"God had nothing to do with this," Aaron snarled, lunging at his foe with a roar.

Verchiel reacted to the attack, stepping back, but ready to fight.

"Now *there's* the Nephilim that defeated me in combat, and sent me back to face the wrath of the Creator," Verchiel said, blocking multiple strikes of Aaron's sword.

Vilma had joined the fray, no doubt recalling Verchiel's torturing as he attempted to destroy Aaron and keep him from his destiny.

"It's too bad all this rage and fury couldn't be put toward something a bit more useful," Verchiel went on, continuing to parry their assaults. "Like stopping Wormwood from ending the world?"

Verchiel cut a swath of fire in the ground, creating a wall that separated him from Aaron and Vilma.

Aaron stepped back, and was readying his next wave of assaults when it struck him: Verchiel had been fighting defensively. The Powers' former leader had not attacked Aaron and Vilma at all.

Vilma was preparing to spring at Verchiel when Aaron reached out to take hold of her arm. She looked at him with fury in her eyes.

"What are you doing?" she asked. "If we both attack, we can kill him."

"We . . . we can't kill him."

Vilma looked as though she'd been stabbed, her startled gaze returning momentarily to Verchiel, who stood behind the line of fire with his sword poised.

Aaron wrestled with the concept that Verchiel had been sent to help.

"Are we done?" Verchiel asked.

Vilma spun at him with a snarl, jumping through the barrier of fire, swinging her sword toward the angel's neck.

Aaron moved with the speed of thought, halting the blade, although he would have liked to see it land.

"Back off," Aaron warned Vilma, saddened that he had to speak to her in such a way, but there wasn't a choice.

With an angry glare, she lowered her weapon and stepped away.

Aaron turned to Verchiel, mere inches from the angel's face.

"Why are you here?" he demanded.

"Perhaps this is my punishment," Verchiel suggested, his stare never wavering. "Or perhaps I'm the only hope this world has of surviving after what you've done."

"We've done nothing."

"Exactly," Verchiel said, and roughly pushed past him through the dwindling line of fire, their shoulders striking, causing Aaron to stumble. "But now is the time to change that."

Aaron and Verchiel looked toward Wormwood. The giant angel knelt upon one knee. Its hands glowed with arcane energies that pulsed from the blade into the earth.

"Hopefully it's not too late," Verchiel continued.

"What do you intend to do?" Aaron asked, feeling ashamed, but hoping that the vile angel had something, because he was all out of answers.

Verchiel looked at him, eyes black and filled with anger.

"I intend to save this miserable ball of mud from total annihilation," the angel said, followed by a disturbing smile. "What are *your* intentions?"

A monster of nightmare had shoved him inside its mouth.

Lucifer struggled in its awesome maw, jagged teeth biting

down upon his armor in an attempt to crush him and masticate his form into more manageable bite-size pieces for digestion.

But the Son of the Morning was nobody's . . . or no thing's . . . easy snack.

Getting his feet beneath him atop a slime-covered tongue, Lucifer stood to his full size in the monster's mouth, jabbing the Light Giver up through the roof of the great beast's mouth.

The monster cried out its pain, clawed appendages attempting to dislodge the growing annoyance from its maw.

Lucifer had had just about enough of this particular fiend, radiating a blast of intense divine fire up through the hilt of his weapon and into the creature's skull with spectacular results.

The monster screamed pathetically one final time before its head exploded, coating the underground chamber with whatever organ of thought existed within its malformed skull.

The Morningstar did not stop there. Still covered in the gore of the vanquished, he flew about the chamber in search of the next foe to obliterate. A creature resembling a giant armored snake coiled upon the icy floor, preparing to strike. Lucifer did not give it the opportunity, diving at the reptilian nightmare and swinging his great sword of fire through the thick muscle of the monster's neck, separating its arrow-shaped head from its segmented body.

The ancient behemoths screeched and roared their disapproval over the deaths of their brethren, but their rage only fueled Lucifer's own.

Lucifer saw the Devil standing back, watching with rapt fascination as his family attacked. But the great red-skinned demon did not come to their aid. It was almost as if he intended for Lucifer to cull their number.

Multiple tentacles exploded up from the shattered sections of ice, wrapping their muscular limbs around Lucifer's body, attempting to drag him down beneath the frozen floor.

Lucifer would not have it.

Calling upon the divine fire that coursed through him, the Morningstar increased the temperature of his body, his armored form starting to throw off an incredible, blistering heat. The monster that held him emitted a horrible moan as it fought to hold on to Lucifer, but its slimy green flesh began to sizzle, blister, and then burn. It could keep him no more.

The Morningstar rose, wings spread, his radiant form causing the ice walls to begin to melt. But that did not slow the relentless assaults upon him. When one of the ancient monstrosities perished, three more shambled forward to try to claim his life.

Lucifer gave it everything he had. He could feel the world dying, and he knew that was exactly what the Devil was hoping for.

Lucifer had to escape this chamber of horrors and get back to the school. Otherwise his students would unknowingly do irreparable harm.

Tapping into the berserker fury that had served him well

when fighting God and the hosts of Heaven, Lucifer dug deep within himself, summoning a part of his personality that he had long buried, and had once hoped was dead.

This was the side of him that had thrown Heaven into turmoil, and branded him as God's adversary.

Lucifer did not welcome its freedom, but releasing it was necessary if he was to survive.

Lucifer Morningstar became a thing of unbridled rage. All rational thought was gone, and now only the fight remained. The only thing that mattered was to vanquish all that stood in his way. It was no easy feat to slay the legion of ancient entities that swarmed against him, and their attacks grew more savage as their numbers began to dwindle.

Armor dented, and ripped away in places, the Morningstar continued to fight. His brain was filled with the images of all those he had slain. It was their deaths . . . their cries for mercy . . . that fueled him. He was unstoppable. One after the other, the creatures fell. Blood stained the floors of the ice cave in a kaleidoscope of gore.

Though his body protested, the Morningstar fought on until he could barely remain upon his feet. The last of the beasts, a black-shelled thing, more insect than animal, came at him, scurrying across the blood puddle. Lucifer lashed out with his sword, swinging at the giant bug's pincers as they snatched at him. The blade cut away the tops of the insect's claws, but he did not see the tail, like that of a scorpion, extended over the monster's back, plunging its hooked barb into the exposed flesh of the Morningstar's side.

Lucifer raged, his wings lifting him into the air with a scream reminiscent of the most fearsome birds of prey. He descended upon the insect's back, plunging the Light Giver, whose shine had dulled to murky gray, through the beast's shell, pinning its dying body to the cold floor.

Falling from the insect's back, Lucifer examined the bleeding wound in his side. He could feel poison starting to course through his frame but managed to halt its progress by tapping deeper into the fiery wrath that had turned him against his Creator so very long ago. The insect's venom traveled no further, diluted by another even more deadly poison: the poison of arrogance and envy.

Lucifer's body trembled with the recollection of how he waged a war against the One Who created him. Again he made an effort to suppress that offensive, monstrous side.

Then he sensed the awesome presence behind him.

Allowing the rage that defined the adversary to continue to exist for just a moment more, Lucifer spun to see the Devil rushing at him.

There was no hesitation as the Son of the Morning launched himself, missile-like, at his enemy, driving his still fiery blade into the chest of the blood-colored Devil.

Lucifer's powerful wings strained as he put all he could behind his sword, pushing it deeper and deeper into the heart of his foe. It surprised him that the Devil did not attempt to escape. Instead it extended its muscular arms around the Morningstar, drawing him close in a nearly loving embrace.

The Devil continued to hold him as Lucifer struggled in his grasp. It brought its large mouth of many teeth closer to his ear. Lucifer expected to feel the bite of the beast, yellow teeth chomping down on the flesh of his throat, but he felt the Devil's breath upon his neck, and heard the words spoken ever so softly.

"Thank you."

And before Lucifer could question what the Devil's thanks meant, the underground chamber began to quake in the throes of too much violence and death, and caved in upon them. The space filled with tons of ice and snow, and the corpses of things better left entombed and undiscovered.

The Abomination of Desolation had placed a sphere of divine protection about its kneeling form.

Aaron watched with cautious eyes as Verchiel flew out in front of them, heading toward the barrier of destructive energies that surrounded the giant angel at a breakneck pace.

Above the din of their flapping wings, Aaron called out for him to be careful, but it appeared as though the Powers' former leader had not heard, or at least had chosen to ignore his warnings.

Verchiel struck the wall of energy with a flash, his angelic form seeming to catch fire as he was violently thrown to the ground, rolling around in the dirt to extinguish the voracious flames.

Aaron, Vilma, and the other surviving Nephilim all stopped before the barrier, flying around the humming sphere of energy searching for a way to penetrate it.

Aaron's hair stood on end the closer he got to the bubble. Pulling back his sword arm, Aaron struck the shield, and the energy discharge repelled him.

Seeing that the blow did little, Vilma halted her assault.

"How can we stop this thing if we can't get at it?" she asked, hovering beside Aaron.

"There has to be a weak spot," he said.

William struck at the barrier from another angle, but to similar effects. The boy was thrown to the ground with a flash.

Aaron heard the sound of struggle and looked down to see Verchiel crawling unsteadily to his feet, wings flapping away the dust and dirt that covered them.

"And if there isn't one, we'll make one," Verchiel said, approaching the energy shield. He extended his hand as close as he could without touching it. "The barrier is of divine origins," he stated. Then, turning his cold gaze to Aaron, he said, "As am I and as are you and your friends."

His words seemed tainted with poison. Aaron knew it must have been difficult for Verchiel to admit something like that. It went against everything he'd once believed.

Aaron flew down to stand beside the angel.

"What are you suggesting?" he asked. It killed him to be asking anything of this monster, but the fate of the world was at stake, and time was of the essence.

Verchiel walked around the crackling sphere of power, peering in at the giant angel wreaking its havoc on the world.

"A collective strike," the former Powers commander stated. "We should combine our efforts, striking the barrier with all our might in one devastating blow." He fixed his stare on Aaron. "We just might be able to get inside, and once we're in . . . that's another story entirely."

Aaron believed it plausible, and at the moment it was the only plan they had. He gestured to the remaining Nephilim to join them, and they obliged, flying down to land before the barrier.

He could feel their suspicion of the former Powers angel but hoped to rally them as a single force to breach the Abomination's shield.

"Bring forth your weapons," Aaron instructed.

And one by one their weapons of heavenly fire sprang to life in their hands.

"And on the count of three, we strike the barrier together," he told them.

The Nephilim seemed to understand what he was asking of them, their eyes betraying their fear. Aaron would have been afraid too if he'd had the chance to stop and really think about their situation.

Aaron called Verchiel over to them.

"Together," Aaron stressed loudly, gripping the hilt of his sword in both hands. "One."

The Nephilim and Verchiel stood ready with their weapons. "Two."

Aaron gazed through the barrier at the divine giant, an angel of the Lord created to terminate all life upon the planet. It made him wonder about the kind of God that had been responsible for *his* creation, and the creation of all the Nephilim.

The idea of what would happen if they failed danced at the corner of his thoughts; what would happen to Vilma? To Gabriel, Lorelei, and the others . . . and what of Lucifer?

"Three."

He pushed aside the potential for failure, thinking only about what they were about to do, and once past the barrier, what they would do to defeat the angel Wormwood.

Aaron saw it all as if in a dream. Everyone moving in slow motion as one, their weapons cutting through the air on a course toward the energy shield. All of them hitting the near invisible barrier at once. With devastating effect.

The explosion of light drove them back as the barrier fell, but Aaron knew that they must surge ahead, attacking en masse if they were going to stop the angel from completing its mission.

They charged the space.

The Abomination of Desolation watched their approach, hands still clutching the giant sword's hilt.

Aaron felt in his gut that they had to separate the angel from its sword. He knew that destructive energies were being directed into the earth through the weapon's great length.

But before they attacked, Aaron wanted to try something else.

"Wormwood," he called out. "We are the protectors of this world, and we humbly ask you to cease your actions against it."

The angel's armored head turned as Aaron soared past, its giant, glowing eyes tracking the Nephilim.

"You were summoned prematurely," Aaron continued. "It is not yet time for this world to die."

For a moment Aaron believed that his pleas might have been heard.

The angel removed its armored hands from the hilt of the murderous sword, and turned its silent gaze toward those on the ground before him.

The situation suddenly felt very wrong to Aaron.

"Watch it!" he cried out in warning, just as the angel sent out devastating blasts of divine energy from the tips of its fingers.

The power was like a living thing, viper-like and infinitely more deadly. Five tendrils of heavenly energy lashed out at those who the angel believed were its enemies.

The Nephilim scrambled to escape.

Aaron watched in horror as one of Cameron's wings became enwrapped in a fiery tendril. The boy cried out in pain as his wing was consumed, leaving only a burnt nub.

Aaron flew down to help, but new tentacles of fire pursued him.

Vilma grabbed the injured Cameron, attempting to help him fly away, but she wasn't fast enough. Another tentacle of writhing fire followed her.

Evading his own pursuer, Aaron leaped into the air, flying with all the speed he could muster to try to intercept the impending attack against his teammates. Swinging his sword, he cut the twisting appendage of flame in two, the blade of his heavenly weapon absorbing the angel's hungry fire like a dry sponge.

He watched in horror as the fire expanded, morphing into a giant hand to snatch the pair from the air.

There was nothing he could do.

Then Verchiel appeared, pushing Vilma and the injured Cameron from the fire's path, taking the brunt of the flame's embrace.

The former leader of the Powers fell from the sky ablaze, landing at the angel Wormwood's feet.

This seemed to distract the giant. It tilted its gaze to the still-burning angel, and reached to pick Verchiel from the ground.

Kneeling beside Vilma, and a nearly unconscious Cameron, Aaron watched in wonder as the Abomination turned its attention to the holy entity it held in its hand.

*   *   *

Verchiel could feel an invading presence inside his mind.

The Angel of Destruction reached out to him psychically, probing the smoldering creature of Heaven in its hand. It did not understand why the divine creatures who served the Lord God were attacking it, and sought answers.

Verchiel experienced its immense presence, and that, coupled with the intensity of the pain he was experiencing as a result of being burned, made him wish that the fire had done its job and killed him.

Wormwood brought him closer, probing deeper, peeling back the folds of his mind in its attempts to find the answers it sought. It learned of the Nephilim, and how Verchiel had led the Powers in a wave to wipe them from existence, and how he had failed and been sent back to Heaven to face the wrath of God.

And it learned how desperately Verchiel wanted to be forgiven, and how he would do anything—even attempt to kill an instrument of the very God he sought absolution from—in order to get it.

Verchiel gathered his thoughts, painfully creating his awesome sword, and surged up from Wormwood's palm, thrusting the fiery blade through the opening in the visor of its helmet, and into one of its glowing eyes.

The Abomination of Desolation cried out its pain, hands shooting up to claw at its injured face.

Verchiel spiraled down to the earth, his body and wings

badly marred from Wormwood's assault. The others looked at him with shock and awe as he landed upon the ground.

"Kill it," he proclaimed, barely able to keep his head up. "Kill it, while we still have the chance."

CHAPTER TWENTY-THREE

Aaron watched for a moment as the angel called Wormwood stumbled about the lawn of the school, blindly roaring its disapproval in a deafening voice. Then he led the surviving Nephilim toward their injured prey.

He did not need to tell them how important this attack was. They were as aware as he was that if they did not stop this angel, they would all die. The world would end, and that would be that.

Verchiel had provided them with an opportunity they could not squander. For Aaron doubted they would have another.

Jeremy heard his mother calling to him. It sounded as if her voice was coming from very far away, from down some long, lonesome stone corridor.

"I need your help, luv."

He wasn't quite sure where he was at that moment: some-place dark and cool—hiding from the pain. At first Jeremy tried to ignore her pleas, snuggling deeper into the darkness. But he could still hear her. She simply called for him all the louder.

"You must come for me."

He knew that pain was waiting for him if he chose to answer her call. But what kind of a bloke would ignore the cries of his mum?

Jeremy rose toward consciousness, swimming through the inky blackness on his way back to a world of hurt. The closer he got, the more he remembered. The Powers angels and the *thing* that had crawled into his mouth and wrapped itself around his brain stem, taking over his body.

And he remembered trying to kill his friends and almost succeeding. If it hadn't been for the dog . . . for Gabriel . . . he might just have.

Jeremy opened his eyes with a moan, every inch of his body screaming for attention. It felt as though he'd been scoured with a wire brush and then dipped in brine.

Pleasant, it was not.

There was a struggle going on at the front of the school, and Jeremy strained to get to his feet, compelled to join his friends.

But his mother had other ideas.

She continued to plead with him. He looked around to see if she was someplace nearby but realized the sound of her voice was coming from inside his own head.

This is a new trick, he thought, struggling to maintain his balance as he continued to be racked with pain.

"Please, Jeremy," she begged.

He could hear the panic in her voice.

"You must come now, before they come for him."

There was an explosion at the front of the school, and the sound of screaming. Jeremy squeezed his eyes closed. Concentrating with all his might, he brought forth his battle-ax of fire. He was about to join the fray when his mother called again, diverting his attention.

"I can't do it alone, son. If they take him, there won't be any chance of fixing this mess we've gotten ourselves into."

"Who, Mum?" Jeremy asked the voice inside his head. "Who will they take?"

There was a pause, and the sounds of violence filled the air around him, and then she spoke again.

"The child," she answered. *"We must save the child."*

Jeremy had no idea who his mother was talking about, or how she was able to communicate with him, but he felt her urgency and was suddenly overcome with the need to do exactly as she asked.

The battle raged on at the front of the school, but it was no longer his concern. Jeremy had to get to his mother.

Painfully, he spread his wings and wrapped himself in the comfort of their feathered embrace. He thought of the hospital room where he'd last seen his mother, and prayed that he wouldn't be too late.

For the sake of the child.

For the sake of the world.

For the sake of Heaven.

Vilma soared toward the roaring giant. She knew she should be terrified, but she also knew that fear would only work against her. Being scared would only be an obstacle, something that would prevent her from doing what needed to be done.

The enraged angel loomed closer, and closer still. She thought of her aunt and uncle . . . her cousins . . . and all the other people whom she'd loved in her relatively short life. What she was about to do, she did for them, but she also did it for herself.

Vilma wasn't yet ready to die; there was far too much she still wanted to do with her life, and for these things to happen she had to try to kill the angel that was attempting to take her future, the future of the world, and the futures of everyone she loved.

And she wasn't about to let that happen.

The Abomination swiped at her. She felt the immensity of its hand as it moved through the air, and she managed to evade it. She summoned a spear of fire to her hands.

Energy leaked out from the wound beneath Wormwood's helmet, reminding her of the way that blood hung in the water, often attracting predators.

She'd never looked at herself in that way before, but as she flew through the discharge on her way toward the angel's face, she believed that it was right.

Vilma drew back her arm and, using all the strength she had left, let the spear fly. The projectile managed its way through the opening in the helmet's visor, finding its target of angelic flesh.

Melissa didn't want to die, which was why she fought.

She believed that was probably why the others did as well. This was it; if they failed, game over. The world was done, and they died.

It was hard enough finding out that she was a Nephilim, but having the safety of the world on her shoulders as well was a huge responsibility, and one that she never in a million years imagined that she would have, but here it was. It was as big as life, as big as the thing before them that they were attempting to stop . . . *to kill.*

Melissa had summoned the biggest sword she could envision, and swung it repeatedly at the ankle of the angelic Abomination, hoping to do some sort of damage, hoping to help save the world that she and her friends were now responsible for.

Melissa had never before wanted to hurt anything so badly.

She focused everything she had on one specific spot on the Abomination's ankle, striking it repeatedly, over and over again, sending sparks of divine fire into the air with every violent blow.

And gradually, a dent in the angel's armor began to form, and then a jagged chink appeared.

William paused in flight, his wings beating the air as Vilma threw her spear.

"Yes!" he exclaimed excitedly as the flaming weapon penetrated the darkness behind the visor. He relished the cries of pain that came from the being that was intent on destroying their lives.

He flew in low beneath the angel's thrashing arms, aiming for a bend in the giant's armor at the knee. If they could make it fall, they might have an easier chance at defeating it. The broadsword he summoned was a monstrous thing, created for maiming and murder, and as he flew past Wormwood's knee, he swung out with all his strength, burying the burning blade in the opening just below the kneecap, where the armored shin brace began.

The angel lurched forward, the strike indeed having some effect upon the towering giant. William was ready to come around again, to take aim at the angel's other leg, when he was snatched from the air.

Wormwood held the struggling William in hand, gazing down at him as if he were an annoying insect.

He struggled in the giant's grasp, feeling the grip intensify—his bones starting to crack and his internal organs rupture. He tried to escape, using every ounce of strength he could muster, but it wasn't enough. For a moment he experienced the crushing weight of disappointment found in failing his friends, in failing his world, but he managed to overcome it all when he felt the Abomination painfully lurch to one side when it attempted to put weight on the leg he had damaged.

Yes, William was dying, but at least he had left his mark.

And as he felt his life begin to ebb, in a final act of defiance, he flipped the angelic monstrosity the middle finger.

Take that, you son of a . . .

Aaron watched in horror as Wormwood crushed William and tossed aside his limp body.

"Damn it," Aaron hissed, again taking flight, anger bubbling up inside of him—an anger that he could barely contain.

But he had to be cautious. This wasn't some simple creature of darkness they were facing, this was a weapon of God, and it could very easily end them.

Flying closer, Aaron noticed that the angel lurched to one side as it moved.

As if its leg had been injured.

And that was when he noticed the divine energy seeping from where William's broadsword had struck.

Maybe he didn't die in vain, Aaron thought.

He flew through the air with new purpose. He passed Vilma, who wielded her own special sword of fire.

"Distract it," Aaron called out as he whizzed past her.

And she did just that. He could hear her behind him, rallying the others to continue the attack.

Aaron was fixated upon Wormwood's knee, on the damaged section of armor, as he willed the equivalent of a medieval war hammer into his grasp.

"This is for William," he said as he swung the heavy combat hammer toward where William had already weakened Wormwood.

The hammer broke through the divine metal, crushing the angelic flesh and bone beneath, and the Abomination of Desolation cried out in surprise and agony, tipping to one side, its leg no longer able to support its massive weight.

The angel went down with a sound like thunder.

Aaron dove from the sky, ready to strike his foe again.

But Wormwood was ready for him. The giant shot out its gauntleted hand and hurled a ball of divine fire. Aaron spun out of its path, continuing on his course to the wounded angel.

He could see its injured eyes blazing from inside the heavy helmet as it readied to defend itself against his attack.

With a ferocious roar, Aaron brought forth a mighty sword and slammed it down upon the angel's helmet. A rush of heavenly power exploded from the fissure. Aaron acted instinctively, one of his wings coming across his body to shield him as he dropped toward the ground.

Just before he struck the earth, he opened his wings wide to capture the wind and break his fall.

Wormwood loomed above him, the helmet that once protected his head broken into pieces.

Aaron gazed upon the true face of his enemy, and it stopped him dead in his tracks. It was a face not hardened and monstrous but calm and peaceful. A face sculpted by the hand of God.

Its eyes touched his soul, and Aaron lowered his weapon. The angel's expression told him not to be afraid of what was to come.

Wormwood turned its gaze to the others that flew above its head like angry gnats, and their acts of violence upon it ceased at once.

They returned to the ground to stand with their leader.

In its gaze, Aaron found meaning in the act the angel was trying to perform. The world had become diseased, the evil growing upon it poised to spread out into the universe itself, to the kingdom of Heaven.

It had to be stopped. For the greater good, it had to be stopped.

Aaron looked to Vilma. There were tears in her eyes.

"We have to let this happen," Aaron said to her.

She nodded in acceptance.

The weapons they held were extinguished; they would perpetrate violence against the angelic entity no longer. They understood what Wormwood had come to do, and why the world needed to end.

Aaron watched as the giant began to crawl, hauling its armored form across the expanse of lawn, moving toward the body of the great sword that still protruded from the ground.

They were all watching Wormwood. The guilt they felt for hurting such a wonderful creature with a divine purpose made them want to bow their heads in shame, but they could not take their eyes from the amazing creature.

The sound of a dog's incessant barking shattered the peaceful calm, and Aaron turned to look toward the Labrador retriever.

"Quiet," he ordered the animal, slowly remembering that his name was Gabriel.

"Aaron, what are you doing?" the dog asked. *"Why aren't you trying to stop it?"*

Aaron turned from the dog to look at the angel, who had almost reached the sword. He didn't answer, knowing how difficult it would be for the animal to understand the immensity of Wormwood's mission.

"Aaron!" the dog barked, accompanied by a throaty growl as he surged forward to bite at the boy's leg.

Aaron cried out in pain and anger, a blade of fire coming to life in his hand, a blade that he now raised and prepared to bring down upon the offending animal.

Gabriel cowered, ears flat against his blocky skull.

"Aaron, what is wrong with you?" the dog asked with a sad whine.

And for a moment Aaron pondered that question as well.

What is wrong with me?

Aaron finally understood the validity of Wormwood's mission, but why did that understanding suddenly feel so very wrong?

Gabriel jumped up on him, licking at his neck and face, even though Aaron still held the sword raised above his head.

And realization dawned on Aaron. Looking upon the face of the Abomination had clouded their minds, bending the Nephilim to the giant's will.

Wormwood had reached the sword.

The angel's hand moved through the air, its armored fingers extending to grip the giant sword's hilt once more, and to finish what it had begun.

Aaron knew that as soon as those fingers closed upon the weapon, it would be done. He could feel it at his very core.

This was the end of the world, and he had managed to get himself a front row seat.

In the wink of an eye, the other Nephilim awoke to the reality of their situation . . . to the world's situation.

"Oh my God," Vilma said, her eyes fixed on Wormwood.

Aaron heard the gasps and sobs of sorrow from the others

as they all came to the same horrible realization: they had failed the world they were supposed to protect.

Then suddenly there came a bloodcurdling scream as something flew through the air above their heads. With wings blackened and charred, Verchiel rocketed across the sky, his sword glowing as if it had been plunged into the heart of the sun.

The former leader of the Powers descended as the Abomination's fingers began to close upon the hilt of its weapon. With a blow so swift that the act was seen as only a blur, Verchiel brought his blade down, severing the armored hand of the Angel of Destruction from its wrist.

Wormwood reared back, the life stuff of angels streaming from the stump of its wrist. It gazed in shock at the sight of its hand momentarily twitching, before going still on the ground.

Verchiel did not stop there. Wings pounding furiously, he leaped into the air, hovering before the face of the giant. Verchiel's burning blade descended once more, this time burying itself deep within Wormwood's skull, and bifurcating the angel's face.

From the open skull of the angelic entity that had been summoned to destroy the world, there came an explosion of fire and light, followed by an eerie silence.

The Nephilim looked at the sight before them. Verchiel was kneeling upon the ground, his body smoldering. Much of his hair and the first layer of flesh had been burned away. His armor was filthy with char and soot.

"Must I do everything?" he snapped as he forced himself to stand.

The body of the Abomination of Desolation lay still upon its side, decomposing swiftly in the sun. It would be no time at all before there was nothing left of the apocalyptic giant. But its sword was still in the ground, still radiating a sense of menace.

Verchiel looked as though he might fall over at any moment. "I need time to heal," he said, marching across the lawn turned battlefield.

As he passed a body lying in the grass, it lifted its blackened head.

"What . . . have . . . you done?" Geburah asked.

Aaron watched as Verchiel stopped. The charred form grabbed hold of Verchiel's ankle with its blackened skeletal hand.

"This . . . this was yours . . . this was your plan. . . ."

"Times have changed, Geburah," Verchiel responded. "This was not the answer."

Geburah turned his disfigured features up to his former leader.

"Traitor!" he cried, extending a bony finger to point at Verchiel. "Traitor to the cause of the heavenly host Powers. Traitor to—"

Verchiel's movement was swift, his sword silencing the accusing angel by separating his head from his body.

Aaron was shocked.

"We're done here," Verchiel said, not looking at any of them as he passed.

But Aaron disagreed.

Standing there at the dawn of a new day, he could feel that things were different now.

They were far from done.

In fact, he sensed that this was only the beginning.

CHAPTER TWENTY-FOUR

A Few Days Later

*D*amn it.

She had failed again.

The newest attempt at finding him had given her only a deep, cold nothing.

Lorelei tried for more, digging deeper, searching, stretching the spell as far as she was able. . . .

But Lucifer was nowhere to be found; it was as if he had somehow left the earth.

The Nephilim magick user opened her eyes with a gasp, returning from the freezing void to her weakened body.

"You okay?" Aaron asked, kneeling beside the old wheelchair where she sat.

She was still clutching the metal urn in her lap, where she had burned the ingredients of her Archon spell, including that of a black feather from one of Lucifer's wings. The thick, strange-smelling smoke still wafted up from the bowl to gently stroke her face, forming an undulating ring of gray about her head.

"I'm fine," she lied. Since communicating with Heaven, she'd never felt worse. Lorelei could barely stand on her own, which was why she needed the wheelchair.

Milton perched on her shoulder, close to her ear. It seemed as if the little mouse had adopted her since Lucifer had gone missing. She felt his whiskers tickle her neck, and reached up to rub the soft fur on Milton's tiny head.

"You don't have to keep doing this," Aaron told her. He took the smoking urn from her lap and placed it on one of the lab tables.

From beside her chair, Kraus reached down to grasp her wrist and check her pulse. "Her heart is racing," the healer said. "She's overdoing it."

Aaron seemed upset, but these days when didn't he? Things were bad, and getting worse. Staying alive wasn't going to be easy in the days to come.

"I don't want you doing any more magick until you're feeling stronger," he instructed her.

Lorelei leaned her head back against the chair.

"Yes, sir," she said, eyes closed, hands in her lap. "I'm sorry, I still can't find him."

A dark cloud passed over Aaron's face.

"Where is he?" Aaron asked beneath his breath. "When we need him the most, he drops off the face of the earth."

Milton squeaked his concern from Lorelei's shoulder. He missed his friend. . . . They all missed their friend.

"It feels like that," Lorelei said. "When I search the ether, all I come across is a bottomless, freezing nothing. No trace of him at all."

"But where could he have gone?" Aaron asked, thinking aloud.

Lorelei could see how much this was bothering the boy, almost as much as it was bothering her. They needed the Morningstar if they were going to survive what was coming . . . if the world was going to survive what was coming.

"There might be something I overlooked in the Archon writings," she suggested. "Let me go to the library and—"

"No," Aaron snapped. "No, no, and no again," he stated flatly. "You're going to rest, and you're going to get better. We agreed. This was the last spell that you were going to perform for quite some time. Remember? We made a deal."

Lorelei sighed—recalling that she had indeed agreed to stop—before she started to argue.

"But I think there might be a spell that would allow me to search further . . . into another plane of existence even."

Aaron's stare was penetrating, his dark eyes reaching deep into her soul.

"I can't lose anybody else," he said to her. "I need you. . . . *We* need you. Please, no more. It's going to kill you if you keep on with this."

Lorelei knew when to quit, leaning her head back once more.

"Fine, I'll rest," she said. "But as soon as I'm feeling better . . ."

"Finally," Kraus said. "Something sensible from her mouth."

The sound of hard toenails clicking across the floor made Lorelei turn the wheelchair toward the open doorway and Gabriel.

"There's my beautiful boy," she said as the dog came over to her, tail wagging.

"Feeling better?" the Labrador asked, standing up with his paws on her legs to lick her withered face.

"I was until you crushed me, you horse," she moaned jokingly, pushing the dog from her lap.

"Sorry," Gabriel said, sitting down and leaning against the wheelchair so she could scratch behind his velvety soft ears. The dog closed his eyes and groaned with pleasure.

Aaron thanked her again, telling her to get some rest, and left with Gabriel, leaving her and Kraus alone.

"Do you want me to take you to your room so you can lie down?" he asked, taking hold of the chair's handles, ready to wheel her there.

"No," she said flatly. "I want you to take me to the library."

Milton squeaked close to her ear, cautioning her. But mice were always cautious.

"Lorelei," Kraus began. "You heard Aaron. He doesn't—"

"Yeah, I heard him," Lorelei interrupted. "He told me to rest, but I'm not that tired right now."

She took hold of the chair's wheels and started to wheel herself toward the doorway.

"Maybe a little light reading before bed will put me in the mood."

The time for caution had long since passed.

Leaving the science building, Aaron noticed that the sun had already started to set, and it was only a little bit after two in the afternoon.

This was how it had been since the instrument brought the Abomination to the world. Even though the angel did not succeed, darkness came earlier now.

Gabriel stopped, lifting his snout in the air. *"It's earlier than yesterday,"* the dog grumbled about the dusk. *"Not by much, but still earlier."*

Aaron looked up into the sky and wondered if there would come a time when there would be only darkness, but he already knew the answer. He was going to try to fix that with the others of his ilk. It was only one of the many things they would have to repair to restore some semblance of normalcy to the world. Aaron wasn't sure he knew what normal was anymore.

Crossing the school grounds, Aaron came across Vilma and the others. His heart did a little flip when he saw her, as it always did, and as she turned to look in his direction, he wondered if her heart did the same.

She seemed different since Jeremy had gone missing. They'd searched for him as well, with about as much luck. Even though Vilma told him that she was fine, Aaron sensed that something was off.

Was he being paranoid? Perhaps even a little jealous? Yeah, there was that, but Aaron could see a change in her. And like the world now, she seemed a little bit darker each day.

"Hey," she said, leaving the others to continue practicing with their weapons.

Melissa held a sword of fire in each hand, doing some impressive combat moves, while Cameron sparred with some imaginary enemy. The boy seemed as good as new, even his damaged wing was growing back, something that they had been unaware that Nephilim could do.

Aaron liked that they were getting better at tapping into the full potential of their angelic natures. They were going to need it if they were to survive what was coming.

"Have you talked to him yet?" Vilma asked, moving into his line of vision.

"That's where we're going," Gabriel barked.

Aaron had been putting it off, hoping that his father would return from wherever it was that he'd gone, but . . .

"I still don't trust him," Aaron said.

"We've talked about this, Aaron," she said. Vilma stepped

a little bit closer, reaching out to touch his arm. "We need guidance, and since Lucifer is missing . . ."

"I think he'll be back," Aaron said quickly. "Maybe we should just give it a little more time."

"I don't know if the world has more time," she said. "Have you seen the news?"

He had. Creatures were emerging from the shadows to stake their claim on the changing world—a world not equipped to deal with threats of a supernatural nature.

"So much has happened in such a short period—the threat has become so much bigger," Aaron said, looking at her. "I'm doing the best I can."

"I never said you weren't. It's just like you said, so much has happened. But if we're going to beat this, we need some-body with experience."

Aaron laughed sarcastically. "Aren't we in this mess because of him?" he asked. "Isn't it because he and his Powers buddies were too busy killing us—killing the Nephilim—that these things were allowed to survive?"

He turned his face from her.

"Doesn't sound like the kind of experience we need."

Vilma crossed her arms, and Aaron knew she was getting frustrated.

"That was his job before the whole obsession with wiping out the children of fallen angels. Maybe he's forgotten that, but even if he can remember just a little, it'll be a help to us."

"Ya think?" Aaron asked, chancing a look at her.

Yeah, she is frustrated, on the way to being pissed.

"We need help, Aaron," Vilma said flatly. "We lost more than half our original number dealing with Wormwood, and even before that we were stretched pretty thin."

"She's right, Aaron," Gabriel grumbled, looking up at his friend with dark, penetrating eyes.

"Of course she's right," Aaron replied, reaching down to ruffle the Lab's ears. "She's always right." There wasn't a hint of condescension in his voice. He agreed with Vilma. "But in this case, I just don't *like* that she's right."

"I don't like it either," Vilma said, moving up closer.

It was bad enough that Aaron had fought alongside the Powers angel to defeat Wormwood, but for him to be a part of their daily life? It made his skin crawl.

"I feel like I'm betraying them," Aaron said. "Everyone he and his thugs killed, my parents, Stevie . . ."

Vilma ran her hand along his arm.

Aaron shook his head as if trying to loosen some sort of secret meaning as to why this was happening.

"I don't get it," he said, growing angry again. "Why would God do this? Maybe He does hate us. . . . Maybe we are monsters in His eyes, like the Powers believed."

Melissa and Cameron stopped their training as Aaron's voice grew louder, and were watching him.

"I don't think that's the case at all," Vilma said forcefully, upset by his angry words. "I think what we're dealing with here is a lot bigger than we realize, and a whole lot more complicated."

"If you say that His ways are mysterious, I'm gonna laugh in your face."

"Well, they are," she argued. "He's God. I doubt He thinks like you or I do."

"You know what I think?" Aaron asked, then launched into answering his own question. "I think He's a jerk to put us through this . . . to put the world through this."

"What makes you think He has a choice?" Vilma asked Aaron. "How do you not know that this isn't how He plans to fix everything?"

Aaron could feel himself becoming even more pissed off, and decided maybe he should quit while he was ahead and just talk to Verchiel.

They stood there for what seemed like a very long time before Vilma broke the silence.

"You know, you're very sexy when you're tormented," she said, seemingly trying to suppress a smile.

Aaron didn't want her to see him smile, fighting—unsuccessfully—to remain angry, so he turned away before she could see.

Vilma came up behind him, wrapping her arms around his waist.

"Whether it knows it or not, the world is depending on

us," she said to him in a whisper. She rested her chin upon his shoulder. "I know it's hard for you to have him around. . . . It's hard for all of us, but it doesn't seem as though he's going anywhere, so we might as well utilize what he has to offer."

Aaron sighed as she squeezed him tighter, resigning himself to the task at hand.

"Are you going to do this or not?" Gabriel then asked, obviously tired of hanging around, and of their displays of affection.

"Yeah," Aaron said, mentally preparing himself. "Is he still in the chapel?"

"Last I checked," Vilma said, releasing him from her embrace. "He's been there since the battle with Wormwood."

Gabriel had gotten up, starting to walk in the direction of the chapel.

"Coming?" the dog asked, turning to look at him.

He hesitated momentarily before willing his legs to move.

"Good luck," Vilma called after him.

Aaron waved over his shoulder as he caught up with Gabriel, the two of them walking side by side as he thought how he'd rather be fighting trolls, or Corpse Riders, or even angels of destruction.

On their way to speak with Verchiel.

Dustin Handy stood before the Abomination of Desolation's giant, protruding sword blade, which had become a monument to the battle that been fought there.

He was nearly blind now, able to see only shadows and the outlines of shapes. He imagined that it wouldn't be long until this, too, had left him.

But here, before the sword, Dusty could see differently. He guessed that it had something to do with his connection to the instrument. After all, it had become Wormwood's sword. He'd believed that the instrument had abandoned him after he'd called the Abomination of Desolation, but that didn't seem to be the case at all.

The sword had started to call to him.

At first he'd believed that it was nothing, just his remaining senses growing more acute now that his sight was leaving him. But then the strange voice began to call to him. Even though he was practically blind, he was able to follow the summons, leaving his new room in the dormitory and exiting the building into the cool fall morning.

It didn't take him long to realize what had drawn him from his bed. He couldn't see it, but he knew he was standing before the sword. The closer he got to it, the louder it spoke.

The sword wanted him to touch it, and for a moment he hesitated, remembering the last time he'd touched the instrument, and what it had cost his newfound friends and the world.

But the instrument needed him, and in some sad, twisted way, he needed it, as well.

Dusty placed his hand upon the body of the blade, and even though he was nearly blind, he saw.

He saw.

The blade showed him the evil in the world, where it was, and where it would strike.

Dusty hadn't yet told them, Aaron and the others, what he saw when he touched the sword, only that it might help them with their efforts. It was all still a little confusing for him. The instrument was eager to show him other things too. He believed the blade was attempting to show him the future, trying to show him what was in store for a world cut off from the attentions of Heaven.

Dusty had always believed that the future was malleable, that nothing was predetermined, that the time ahead could always be changed. After seeing what the sword had shown him, he wanted to believe that now more than ever.

For his sake, and the sake of them all.

The bond with Heaven had been severed, and the silence was deafening.

Verchiel knelt upon the altar of the chapel, gazing up at a section of wall where a cross had once hung. It now showed only as an outline on the dirty white wall.

Normally, this was where his kind could feel that connection to the Creator and the Kingdom of Light the strongest, but now there was only a void.

The former place of worship had been reduced to an empty vessel, and the former Powers leader could not help but relate.

Even before Wormwood had been called, Verchiel's connection to the Lord of Lords had been strained. It had been quite some time since he'd last heard his Creator's voice, and even if He had been trying to communicate, would Verchiel have heard Him? Would he have listened?

In retrospect, Verchiel had been blinded by his hate for them—the accursed Nephilim—and that hate had driven him further and further from the love of his Heavenly Father. But he had not been able to see it. His hate had made him deaf. His hate had also made him blind.

Verchiel continued to kneel, and pray for answers. Answers that did not come—would not come, for the world was now alone.

There was an anger that still existed inside of him, a fury that yearned to be released upon those that offended him. It took everything he had not to turn this rage upon the Nephilim.

But have I learned nothing?

This was what he asked of himself when the murderous urges arose.

No matter how abandoned he felt, the Creator had sent him back to a world where his offenses were nearly innumerable.

The Nephilim's Chosen had defeated him in combat, sending him back to Heaven to face the Almighty's judgment, to suffer for his sins, and this is where he now found himself. Was it punishment? Penance? Perhaps a mélange of both?

Verchiel was desperate, searching for answers that did not

come from the stain of a cross high upon a chapel wall.

What do you wish of me?

There was suddenly a shift in the air. A cool breeze within the structure caused some dry leaves to skitter across the warped wooden floor, and ruffled the feathers of his wings.

A sign of some kind?

Perhaps.

The angel heard the sound of the heavy wooden door slam closed behind him, and Verchiel slowly turned his head to see that he was no longer alone.

Aaron pulled open the heavy chapel door and stepped inside the gloomy space. He held the door to let Gabriel follow, before letting it close with an echoing boom behind them.

It took his eyes a moment to adjust to the semidarkened conditions, but he saw Verchiel up ahead, kneeling at the end of the center aisle leading up to the altar.

"I'm going to wait right here," Gabriel said, lying down upon the dusty floor.

Aaron started down the aisle, every footfall echoing in the space that had once been a place of worship but had been deconsecrated when the Catholic school and orphanage were abandoned.

He kept his eyes upon the angel's back as he knelt, ramrod straight, his large wings closed tightly upon his back. There was no chance that Verchiel didn't know he was there, but the angel remained silent.

Aaron stopped, not wanting to get too close, just in case. He had a hard time even thinking of Verchiel as an angel—a creature of Heaven. Because of what Verchiel had done to him, his family, and his friends, there wasn't a chance that he could still be considered divine.

He thought that he'd seen the last of him, but here he was again to plague him.

Or maybe it was something more complex, as Vilma had suggested.

They were all in a terrible place. The Abomination of Desolation had done some serious damage, damage that could see the world falling into dark times if somebody with the proper skills didn't stop the decline. The Nephilim's numbers had been decimated, and Lucifer was among the missing. As it stood, there wasn't much they could hope to do against the rising tide of evil.

Or was there?

Aaron stared at the angel, his gaze burning a hole into his back. He hated the thought of this, but maybe . . . *maybe* . . . this was how it was supposed to be.

Tired of waiting to be acknowledged, Aaron cleared his throat.

The angel remained silent, and Aaron began to wonder if the former Powers leader was asleep. Aaron moved closer, noting the black, paint-chip-like pieces of skin and burnt feathers that littered the floor, shed as Verchiel slowly healed from the extensive injuries he'd received while fighting the angelic giant.

"Verchiel," Aaron said, his voice echoing about the chapel.

At the last reverberation of his voice, there came a flurry of movement, as if the very shadows around him had been stirred, and Aaron was temporarily blinded by a flash of celestial fire. When he regained his sight, he found himself looking down the length of a burning sword.

"You disturb me at your own risk," the angel said with a ferocious snarl.

Aaron could feel the heat of the blade upon his face, as well as the intensifying heat of his own anger. He knew he should tamp down his rage, but this was just too much for him to bear.

Aaron called upon that which made him Nephilim. Wings of ebony black sprouted from his back, punishing the air with a single beat and carrying him back and away from his enemy's blade, as his own weapon of fire ignited in his grip.

"You draw a weapon on me at yours," Aaron said.

"*Aaron,*" Gabriel barked from the back of the chapel. "*This isn't what we talked about.*"

"I know, Gabe," Aaron said, his sword still pointing at Verchiel. "I'm sure we'll get to it eventually."

Verchiel glared at him, eyes blazing with an inner fire fueled by hatred. "I asked not to be disturbed."

"I'm afraid you don't have that luxury anymore," Aaron

said. "Besides, you've been in here for three days. It's time to come out and face the world you've left us."

"*I've* left you?" Verchiel asked with a tilt of his head. "This is a far darker place than I recall leaving it."

"No thanks to you," Aaron told him. "If it wasn't for your soldiers stirring the shadows, I'm sure we—"

"Spare me," Verchiel interrupted. "What happened to this place would have happened eventually." He lowered his sword, dropping it to his side. "My soldiers just sped up the process a bit."

Aaron repeated the gesture, but one better, wishing his weapon away in a crackling flash. "And here we are," he said, flexing the muscles in his back, drawing his wings beneath his clothes and skin.

"And here we are," Verchiel repeated, his own weapon disappearing in a whoosh and flash.

They stood there like that for quite some time, each daring the other to take the encounter to the next level.

Wanting to be away from the angel as soon as possible, Aaron decided to give in.

"I have no idea why you're here," he began.

"That makes two of us," Verchiel responded.

"But you have to be here for something."

Verchiel cocked his head bird-like to one side, as Aaron continued.

"The world . . . God's world . . . is in a very bad place

right now, and that's something that I intend to fix."

Verchiel smirked.

"You're going to fix it, Nephilim?" Verchiel asked. "And how, may I ask, do you intend to do that?"

"Don't know," Aaron said. "But I plan to find out."

"Do you now?" Verchiel hissed.

"I'm the Chosen One," Aaron said. "Written about in angelic prophecy . . . that has to count for something."

The Powers' leader shook his head ever so slowly.

"The audacity of your kind," he said. "You actually believe that you're something special. That there is something that you and yours can do to reconnect this world to Heaven."

"If there's a way, I'll find it," Aaron said. "And then I'll do just that."

Verchiel returned to the altar to kneel. "Leave me," he said. "You make me despise myself even more than I already do for failing to destroy you and all your kind."

Aaron stood there for a moment, trying to decide what he should do next. If he listened to the angry voice inside his head, he would storm off, leaving the angel alone in his misery. But Aaron was feeling above all that now that he'd had his say.

"I have no idea why the Creator sent you back here," Aaron said. "But what if this *is* the reason?"

He paused, waiting for some kind of reaction that did not come.

"What if you've been sent back to help us?"

Verchiel continued to ignore the Nephilim.

"What if this is your penance?" Aaron suggested. "To help us keep the world safe, while trying to find a way to reconnect with Heaven and God."

He waited again, but still the angel did not respond.

"Think about it," Aaron said, turning away from Verchiel to walk down the aisle and meet up with Gabriel.

"C'mon, boy," Aaron said to the Labrador. "We should leave him to his misery."

Aaron's hand had just closed upon the door handle when there came a voice.

"You do realize that we're likely to fail miserably," Verchiel called out.

Aaron looked back down the aisle. Verchiel still knelt there, his back to him.

"We'll never know unless we try," Aaron said.

Verchiel had no response.

Aaron pushed open the door, heading out into the premature darkness.

Into the End of Days.

EPILOGUE

The yetis moved across the merciless Siberian tundra, their white fur adorned in the blood of the Inuit tribe they had recently slaughtered.

More beast than man, the hairy monsters loped along the snow-covered landscape, no longer caring if their kind was seen. For centuries they had hidden from the eyes of civilization, but no longer.

A new age was beginning, and they would hide no more.

The tribal leader raised a clawed hand to the moaning winds, stopping their number.

His name was N'Karr, and it was he who had first heard the call of their master, the one who had brought about these special times for their monstrous kind.

A voice had spoken to him in a language birthed in shadow and not heard for multiple millennia. It urged him and his like to emerge into the light, dragging the darkness behind them like a cloak for all the world to see.

"*Come to me,*" the voice had called. "*Come to me and let nothing block your progress.*"

And N'Karr and his yeti tribe crawled from their hiding places deep beneath glacial ice, answering the summons of their Dark Lord. These abominable snowmen did exactly what had been asked of them, even as they had come across the Inuit village. For an instant it had been difficult for N'Karr and his folk. Normally they had shunned the human encampments, choosing to remain invisible.

"*But now it is different,*" cooed the voice of their master. "*Now is the time to bring fear to humanity.*"

And this time the yetis did not turn away from discovery. They entered the Inuit camp without shame, killing with abandon.

Their fur stained with the blood of their prey.

Now N'Karr brought them to a stop, his keen senses picking up unusual scents in the frigid environment, scents that did not belong.

The yeti leader grunted for his legion to follow, and they scaled the jagged face of a mountainous formation of ice, the fierce Siberian winds threatening to tear them from their purchase.

N'Karr was the first to reach the top, squinting through the whipping snows to gaze down into a small valley. Below, mysterious shapes formed a circle around a particular section of frozen ground.

The yetis roared, spilling down the sides of the ice wall to confront those waiting there. Wanting to again experience the bloodlust of the Inuit camp, the yetis charged. Then N'Karr—speaking in the language of shadows—ordered his people to halt.

There wasn't a human among those that waited in the valley, monsters one and all. Monsters that had also answered the call of the Dark Master.

The yetis approached, sniffing the air rife with the scent of supernatural beasts.

N'Karr and his tribe joined the circle, no longer individual species of monster but one unified tribe, waiting for the arrival of the one that had liberated them.

The yeti's gaze was drawn to the center of their circle, but all he saw there was ancient ice and shifting snow. He grew impatient, as did the other members of his tribe. He was about to roar his displeasure when a sound from the sky above filled the air, and a great shadow appeared overhead.

Panic passed through the circle as they gazed up into the snow-filled sky. An enormous shape, like a flying lizard, pounded the air with leathern wings.

Dragon.

It glared down at them with glowing yellow eyes, and N'Karr was temporarily filled with terror, until sensing a kindred spirit in the great scaled and spine-covered beast.

The others sensed it too, all of them gazing up at the hovering dragon, waiting for it to act.

The dragon reared back its head, bending forward suddenly with its mouth agape, venom flowing from its mouth and igniting in a stream of orange flame that rushed to earth to engulf the center of their circle.

The heat was like nothing N'Karr had ever felt before, but he and his tribe, as well as the other beasts, did not break the circle.

They continued to stare at its center, waiting for their new Dark Lord to arrive.

The miles of ice and snow that he'd been trapped beneath gradually began to liquefy.

The dark child had been inexorably making his way to the surface, from far, far below, his progress halted by ancient ice, miles in thickness. But the ice did not stop him, it just slowed him down a bit.

This was very much like the time he had been waiting on the earth, putting plans in motion, some taking millennia to come to fruition.

But what was the passage of time to a being that had existed before the Creator brought forth the light? He had all the patience that was needed, and then some.

He thrashed beneath tons of snow as the intensity of the heat from above turned it to slush, climbing to the surface.

To a world that would soon belong to him.

The Dark One used the powerful wings of its shape to ascend all the faster. Everything had fallen into place as he had planned. Of course there had been some wrinkles here and there, but that was to be expected.

And sometimes these alternatives were pleasant surprises, ending up far better than what had been originally anticipated.

Like the body he now wore.

He'd always coveted it but never imagined that he would have the opportunity to take it as his own.

But the opportunity had presented itself. And the body was his.

The Dark One turned his new eyes to the boiling waters above his head, the light of the world above beckoning to him.

Beneath the scalding fluid, he spread his feathered wings of ebony, pushing through the water and propelling himself to the surface.

And to the adoration of those that awaited his ascension.

He exploded from the boiling water into the fires of a dragon's breath, allowing the searing heat to dry his armored body. And there he hovered, wings flapping in the air, for all to see. He spread his arms, allowing them to take in his formally divine appearance.

They were all in awe of him, this he could tell. Many of them had known the form he wore from days long past, when it had belonged to the Son of the Morning.

The Morningstar.

But now the body belonged to him, and Lucifer was no more.

"Bow before me," he proclaimed in a voice that rumbled like thunder.

"Bow your heads before Satan—the Darkstar—

"The Lord of Shadows."

THE END?

READ HOW AARON'S JOURNEY AND THE WAR BETWEEN HEAVEN AND HELL BEGAN.

THE FALLEN

FROM SIMON PULSE

PUBLISHED BY SIMON & SCHUSTER

ABOUT THE AUTHOR

THOMAS E. SNIEGOSKI is the author of more than two dozen novels for adults, teens, and children. His books for teens include *Legacy*, *Sleeper Code*, *Sleeper Agenda*, and *Force Majeure*, as well as the series The Brimstone Network.

As a comic book writer, Sniegoski's work includes *Stupid, Stupid Rat-Tails*, a prequel miniseries to the international hit *Bone*. Sniegoski collaborated with *Bone* creator Jeff Smith on the project, making him the only writer Smith has ever asked to work on those characters.

Sniegoski was born and raised in Massachusetts, where he still lives with his wife, LeeAnne, and their French bulldog, Kirby. Visit him on the Web at www.sniegoski.com.

Don't miss Kelly Keaton's

DARKNESS
BECOMES
HER

Beneath every beauty, evil stirs.

UNDER THE CAFETERIA TABLE, MY RIGHT KNEE BOUNCED LIKE A jackhammer possessed. Adrenaline snaked through my limbs, urging me to bolt, to hightail it out of Rocquemore House and never look back.

Deep breaths.

If I didn't get my act together and calm down, I'd start hyperventilating and embarrass the shit out of myself. Not a good thing, especially when I was sitting in an insane asylum with rooms to spare.

"Are you sure you want to do this, Miss Selkirk?"

"It's Ari. And, yes, Dr. Giroux." I gave the man seated across from me an encouraging nod. "I didn't come all this way to give up now. I want to know." What I wanted was to get this over with and do something, *anything*, with my hands, but instead I laid them flat on the tabletop. Very still. Very calm.

A reluctant breath blew through the doctor's thin, sun-cracked lips as he fixed me with an *I'm sorry, sweetheart, you asked for it* look. He opened the file in his hand, clearing his throat. "I wasn't working here at the time, but let's see. . . ." He flipped through a few pages. "After your mother gave you up to social services, she spent the remainder of her life here at Rocquemore." His fingers fidgeted with the file. "Self-admitted," he went on. "Was here six months and eighteen days. Committed suicide on the eve of her twenty-first birthday."

An inhale lodged in my throat.

Oh hell. I hadn't expected *that*.

The news left my mind numb. It completely shredded the mental list of questions I'd practiced and prepared for.

Over the years, I'd thought of every possible reason why my mother had given me up. I even explored the idea that she might've passed away sometime during the last thirteen years. But suicide? *Yeah, dumbass, you didn't think of that one.* A long string of curses flew through my mind, and I wanted to bang my forehead against the table—maybe it would help drive home the news.

I'd been given to the state of Louisiana just after my fourth birthday, and six months later, my mother was dead. All those years thinking of her, wondering what she looked like, what she was doing, wondering if she thought of the little girl she left behind, when all this time she was six feet under and not *doing* or *thinking* a goddamn thing.

My chest expanded with a scream I couldn't voice. I stared hard at my hands, my short fingernails like shiny black beetles against the white composite surface of the table. I resisted the urge to curl them under and dig into the laminate, to feel the skin pull away from the nails, to feel something other than the grief squeezing and burning my chest.

"Okay," I said, regrouping. "So, what exactly was wrong with her?" The question was like tar on my tongue and made my face hot. I removed my hands and placed them under the table on my thighs, rubbing my sweaty palms against my jeans.

"Schizophrenia. Delusions—well, *delusion*."

"Just one?"

He opened the file and pretended to scan the page. The guy seemed nervous as hell to tell me, and I couldn't blame him. Who'd want to tell a teenage girl that her mom was so whacked-out that she'd killed herself?

Pink dots bloomed on his cheeks. "Says here"—his throat worked with a hard swallow—"it was snakes . . . claimed snakes were trying to poke through her head, that she could feel them growing and moving under her scalp. On several occasions, she scratched her head bloody. Tried to dig them out with a butter knife stolen from the cafeteria. Nothing the doctors did or gave her could convince her it was all in her mind."

The image coiled around my spine and sent a shiver straight to the back of my neck. I *hated* snakes.

Dr. Giroux closed the file, hurrying to offer whatever comfort he could. "It's important to remember, back then a lot of folks went through post-traumatic stress. . . . You were too young to remember, but—"

"I remember some." How could I forget? Fleeing with hundreds of thousands of people as two Category Four hurricanes, one after another, destroyed New Orleans and the entire southern half of the state. No one was prepared. And no one went back. Even now, thirteen years later, no one in their right mind ventured past The Rim.

Dr. Giroux gave me a sad smile. "Then I don't need to tell you why your mother came here."

"No."

"There were so many cases," he went on sadly, eyes unfocused, and I wondered if he was even talking to me now. "Psychosis, fear of drowning, watching loved ones die. And the snakes, the snakes that were pushed out of the swamps and inland with the floodwaters . . . Your mother probably experienced some horrible real-life event that led to her delusion."

Images of the hurricanes and their aftermath clicked through my mind like a slide projector, images I hardly thought of anymore. I shot to my feet, needing air, needing to get the hell out of this creepy place surrounded by swamps, moss, and gnarly, weeping trees. I wanted to shake my body like a maniac, to throw off the images crawling all over my skin. But instead, I forced myself to remain still, drew in a deep breath, and then tugged the end of my black T-shirt down, clearing my throat. "Thank you, Dr. Giroux, for speaking with me so late. I should probably get going."

I pivoted slowly and made for the door, not knowing where I was going or what I'd do next, only knowing that in order to leave I had to put one foot in front of the other.

"Don't you want her things?" Dr. Giroux asked. My foot paused midstride. "Technically they're yours now." My stomach did a sickening wave as I turned. "I believe there's a box in the storage room. I'll go get it. Please"—he gestured to the bench—"it'll just take a second."

Bench. Sit. *Good idea.* I slumped on the edge of the bench, rested my elbows on my knees, and turned in my toes, staring at the V between my feet until Dr. Giroux hurried back with a faded brown shoe box.

I expected it to be heavier and was surprised, and a little disappointed, by its lightness. "Thanks. Oh, one more thing . . . Was my mother buried around here?"

"No. She was buried in Greece."

I did a double take. "Like small-town-in-America Greece, or . . . ?"

Dr. Giroux smiled, shoved his hands into his pockets, and rocked back on his heels. "Nope. The real thing. Some family came and claimed the body. Like I said, I wasn't working here at the time, but perhaps you could track information through the coroner's office; who signed for her, that sort of thing."

Family.

That word was so alien, so unreal, that I wasn't even sure I'd heard him right. Family. Hope stirred in the center of my chest, light and airy and ready to break into a Disney song complete with adorable bluebirds and singing squirrels.

No. It's too soon for that. One thing at a time.

I glanced down at the box, putting a lid on the hope—I'd been let down too many times to give in to the feeling—wondering what other shocking news I'd uncover tonight.

"Take care, Miss Selkirk."

I paused for a second, watching the doctor head for a group of patients sitting near the bay window, before leaving through the tall double doors. Every step out of the rundown mansion/mental hospital to the car parked out front took me further into the past. My mother's horrible ordeal. My life as a ward of the state. Daughter of an unwed teenage mother who'd killed herself.

Fucking great. Just great.

The soles of my boots crunched across the gravel, echoing over the constant song of crickets and katydids, the occasional splash of water, and the call of bullfrogs. It might be winter to the rest of the country, but January in the deep South was still warm and humid. I gripped the box tighter, trying to see beyond the moss-draped live oaks and cypress trees and into the deepest, darkest shadows of the swampy lake. But a wall of blackness prevented me, a wall that—I blinked—seemed to waver.

But it was just tears rising to the surface.

I could barely breathe. I never expected this . . . *hurt*. I never expected to actually learn what had happened to her. After a quick swipe at the wet corners of my eyes, I set the box on the passenger seat of the car and then drove down the lonely winding road to Covington, Louisiana, and back to something resembling civilization.

Covington hovered on The Rim, the boundary between the land of the forsaken and the rest of the country; a border town with a Holiday Inn Express.

The box stayed on the hotel bed while I kicked off my boots, shrugged out of my old jeans, and jerked the tee over my head. I'd taken a shower that morning, but after my trip to the hospital, I needed to wash off the cloud of depression and the thick film of southern humidity that clung to my skin.

In the bathroom, I turned on the shower and began untying

the thin black ribbon around my neck, making sure not to let my favorite amulet—a platinum crescent moon—slip off the end. The crescent moon has always been my favorite sight in the sky, especially on a clear cold night when it's surrounded by twinkling stars. I love it so much, I had a tiny black crescent tattooed below the corner of my right eye, on the highest rise of my cheekbone— my early high school graduation present to myself. The tattoo reminded me of where I came from, my birthplace. The Crescent City. New Orleans.

But those were old names. Now it was known as New 2, a grand, decaying, lost city that refused to be swept away with the tide. A privately owned city and a beacon, a sanctuary for misfits and things that went bump in the night, or so they said.

Standing in front of the long hotel mirror in my black bra and panties, I leaned closer to my reflection and touched the small black moon, thinking of the mother I'd never really known, the mother who *could've* had the same teal-colored eyes as the ones staring back at me in the mirror, or the same hair. . . .

I sighed, straightened, and reached behind my head to unwind the tight bun at the nape of my neck.

Unnatural. Bizarre. Fucked up.

I'd used all those words and more to describe the thick coil that unwound and fell behind my shoulders, the ends brushing the small of my back. Parted in the middle. All one length. So light in color, it looked silver in the moonlight. My hair. The bane of my existence. Full. Glossy. And so straight it looked like it had taken an army of hairdressers wielding hot irons to get it that way. But it was all natural.

No. Unnatural.

Another tired exhale escaped my lips. I gave up trying a long time ago.

When I'd first realized—back when I was about seven or so—that my hair attracted the *wrong* sort of attention from some of the foster men and boys in my life, I tried everything to get rid of it. Cut it. Dyed it. Shaved it. I'd even lifted hydrochloric acid from the science lab in seventh grade, filled the sink, and then dunked my hair into the solution. It burned my hair into oblivion, but a few days later it was back to the same length, the same color, the same everything. Just like always.

So I hid it the best I could; buns, braids, hats. And I wore enough black, had accumulated enough attitude throughout my teenage years that most guys respected my no's when I said them. And if they didn't, well, I'd learned how to deal with that, too. My current foster parents, Bruce and Casey Sanderson, were both bail bondsmen, which meant they put up the bail money so defendants could avoid jail time until their court appearance. And if the person didn't show for their appointment with the judge, we hunted them down and brought them back to jurisdiction so we weren't stuck footing the bill. Thanks to Bruce and Casey, I could operate six different firearms, drop a two-hundred-pound asshole to the floor in three seconds, and cuff a perp with one hand tied behind my back.

And they called it "family time."

My hazy reflection smiled back at me. The Sandersons were pretty decent, decent enough to let a seventeen-year-old borrow their car and go in search of her past. Casey had been a foster kid too, so she understood my need to know. She knew I had to do this alone. I wished I'd gotten placed with them from the beginning. A snort blew through my nose. Yeah, and if wishes were dollars, I'd be Bill Gates.

Steam filled the bathroom. I knew what I was doing. Avoiding. Classic Ari MO. If I didn't take a shower, I wouldn't get out, put on my pj's, and then open the damn box. "Just get it over with, you big wuss." I stripped off the last of my clothes.

Thirty minutes later, after my fingertips were wrinkled and the air was so saturated with steam it was hard to breathe, I dried off and dressed in my favorite pair of old plaid boxers and a thin cotton tank. Once my wet hair was twisted back into a knot and a pair of fuzzy socks pulled on my forever-cold feet, I sat cross-legged in the middle of the king-size bed.

The box just sat there. In front of me.

My eyes squinted. Goose bumps sprouted on my arms and thighs. My blood pressure rose—I knew it by the way my chest tightened into a painful, anxious knot.

Stop being such a baby!

It was just a dumb box. Just my past.

I settled myself and lifted the lid, pulling the box closer and peering inside to find a few letters and a couple of small jewelry boxes.

Not enough in there to contain an entire life story. No doubt I'd have more questions from this than answers—that's usually how my search went. Already disheartened, I reached inside and grabbed the plain white envelope on top of the pile, flipping it over to see my name scrawled in blue ink.

Aristanae.

My breath left me in an astonished rush. *Holy hell.* My mother had written to me.

It took a moment for it to sink in. I trailed my thumb over the flowing cursive letters with shaky fingers and then opened the envelope and unfolded the single sheet of notebook paper.

My dearest, beautiful Ari,

If you are reading this now, then I know you have found me. I had hoped and prayed that you wouldn't. I am sorry for leaving you, and that sounds so inadequate, I know, but there was no other way. Soon you will understand why, and I'm sorry for that, too. But for now, assuming you were given this box by those at Rocquemore, you must run. Stay away from New Orleans, and away from those who can identify you. How I wish I could save you. My heart aches, knowing you will face what I have faced. I love you so much, Ari. And I am sorry. For everything.

I'm not crazy. Trust me. Please, baby girl, just RUN.

Momma

Spooked, I jumped off the bed and dropped the letter as though it burned. "What the hell?"

Fear made my heart pound like thunder and the fine hairs on my skin lift as though electrified. I went to the window and peeked through the blinds to look one floor down at my car in the back lot. Nothing unusual. I rubbed my hands down my arms and then paced, biting my left pinkie nail.

I stared at the open letter again, with the small cursive script. *I'm not crazy. Trust me. Please, baby girl.*

Baby girl. Baby girl.

I had only a handful of fuzzy memories left, but those words . . . I could almost hear my mother speaking those words. Soft. Loving. A smile in her voice. It was a real memory, I realized, not one of the thousand I'd made up over the years. An ache squeezed my heart, and the dull pain of an oncoming headache began behind my left eye.

All these years . . . It wasn't fair!

A rush of adrenaline pushed against my rib cage and raced down my arm, but instead of screaming and punching the wall like I wanted to, I bit my bottom lip hard and made a tight fist.

No. Forget it.

It was pointless to go down the Life's Not Fair road. Been there before. Lesson learned. That kind of hurt served no purpose.

With a groan, I threw the letter back into the box, shoved the lid on, and then got dressed. Once my things were secured in my backpack, I grabbed the box. My mother hadn't spoken to me in thirteen years and this letter from the grave was telling me to run, to get to safety. Whatever was going on, I felt to the marrow of my bones that something wasn't right. Maybe I was just spooked and paranoid after what I'd learned from Dr. Giroux.

And maybe, I thought, as my suspicious mind kicked into high gear, my mother hadn't committed suicide after all.